four
thousand
friends

four thousand friends

Najum Qureshi

FEROZSONS (Pvt.) LTD.
LAHORE - RAWALPINDI - KARACHI

ISBN 978-969-0-02504-3

First published 2014 in Pakistan by
Ferozsons (Pvt.) Ltd.
60, Shahrah-e-Quaid-e-Azam, Lahore, Pakistan
277, Peshawar Road, Rawalpindi
Mehran Heights, Main Clifton Road, Karachi

Qureshi, Najum

Four Thousand Friends

Published by
Zaheer Salam, Managing Director,
Ferozsons (Pvt.) Ltd.,
60, Shahrah-e-Quaid-e-Azam,
Lahore-54000, Pakistan

Printed in Pakistan at
Ferozsons (Pvt.) Ltd., (Printing Div.) Lahore.

email: support@ferozsons.com.pk
www.ferozsons.com.pk

To My Mother

Gone, days of crowded solitude;
Now others' hearts know my heart's case.
Iqbal, Gabriel's wing
Translation by VG Kiernan

PROLOGUE

I n fewer than twenty four hours, I had become a Crown witness in a major terrorist activity, and had buried in the cold earth the wisest person I had ever known.

I stood by the grave for several hours. I gazed upwards. The sun had taken refuge behind the ever-darkening clouds. Shapes were forming in my troubled mind, contrasting with the swirling clouds. Everyone who had attended his funeral had already left the cemetery. I decided to walk back too. I looked over my shoulder and saw the policeman who was guarding me, follow. It began to drizzle gently, but inside me a violent storm of emotions was churning. Small raindrops slowly trailed down my face, simulating the tears that I was struggling to hold back.

I was finding it difficult to come to terms with the life-changing events that were happening at such a fast pace, and in such a short time. It was immensely painful to accept that I would never be able to meet Mr Nazir ever again, never be able to converse with him or hear his views. He never told me that he was, but I had no doubt in my mind; he was one of the four thousand friends of God in this world. Mr Nazir's voice echoed in my mind, "The gravitational pull remains functional because of these people: the soft caress of a summer breeze, the serenity of moonlight; the changing seasons; vegetation springing from barren soil. The life exists on this planet only because of the presence of these four thousand people." Some living people are a burden on this earth and some people carry the weight of this world, not only during their lives but even after their death.

I came out of Marble Arch tube station, and slowly walked towards the Edgware Road. The usual London hustle-bustle of a city evening: shoppers carrying bags and walking briskly towards bus stops and tube stations. I was deeply immersed in my own thoughts and so heard little of the inconsequential chatter going around me. A clock, outside a corner shop, struck six times like Big Ben. I didn't realise that I was coming back home after nine hours.

Edgware Road was alive with people who had come there to smoke in the shisha bars, before having their evening meals at the restaurants. The shisha bars were inviting customers with low stools, cushioned high back chairs and patio heaters. The scent of fruit tobacco was in the air. A group of youths were competing with each other to exhale the most shisha smoke. Curly, white smoke emanating from their mouths, floated like plucks of raw wool in the background of bluish shadows of the evening.

As I entered the house, I threw my keys on the console and continued to walk through the hallway. The house was quiet as usual. Mum was probably in her room, and my grandmother whom we called 'Bari Ammi' rarely came out of her room.

I heard indistinct noises coming from the TV: the news channel. Police foiling the terrorist attack of contaminating MP's food with E Coli was running as breaking news. The police had raided the terrorists' homes early that morning, and detained all the perpetrators. I immediately recognised the senior policeman who was swaggering outside New Scotland Yard, how he and his team of ingenious detectives had thwarted the terrorist plot. Only three people had known the real truth: me, the policeman and the third person who now rested six feet under the ground in a grave which was covered with rose petals.

Mum emerged from her room, her face was glazed with worry and her eyes looked red as if she had been crying. 'Ali, where have you been?' she said angrily. 'The neighbour's son got back from the cemetery ages ago. Your mobile was constantly going onto voice mail. You're eighteen, about to start medical school. You are no more a kid, you need to show some responsibility. I was getting bad thoughts about you.............. God forbid something happened to you.'

'I'm sorry, really sorry. I got delayed. My phone's battery died. I didn't take notice of the time.' I didn't feel like talking, but still had to make an effort to talk to her in order to reassure her.

Mum seemed to have regained her composure and said, 'I'm very sorry for your loss. Mr Nazir was indeed a very nice person. You became friends in no time.' Mum put her arm over my shoulder, looked into my eyes and said, 'How come he was buried so quickly? He only passed away yesterday.'

'He asked to be buried as soon as was conveniently possible. He mentioned this to the hospital staff as his last wish. He also consented to a form that no attempt to resuscitate him should be made. He knew that he wasn't going to live. He knew so many things that an ordinary person wouldn't know.' My voice deepened with the grief.

Mum put both her arms around me, hugged me and kissed my forehead.

'You look exhausted, I'll get you something to eat.'

'No Mum, I won't be able to eat anything right now. I'll just take some rest. I feel shattered.'

'OK. You go upstairs and get some rest. I'll go and pick your dad up from the airport. He's arriving in four hours. And listen, do see your Bari Ammi when you wake up. Her dreams are back. She had a good night's sleep last night. It's been a while. She's so happy, she's looking like a new woman now.' Then she recalled, 'Oh yeah, George also rang from Scotland. He cried like a baby when he heard the news that Mr Nazir had passed away. He regretted that he could not come to the funeral.' Mum conveyed everything to me like an efficient secretary.

'And, yes,' Mum said, 'there was a phone call from a girl, Sophie. Who is she?'

'Did she leave any message?' I felt my eyes light up as I asked her, ignoring her question.

'No, she didn't,' she replied.

My hopes were dashed. 'Sophie took me to the hospital the other night,' I told Mum. Perhaps she wanted to be sure that I deleted her phone number, I thought to myself.

I slowly climbed the stairs to my bedroom, closed the curtains and flung myself onto the bed. After the rain, freshness pierced the room; a solitary, diffracted ray of sunlight came through the curtain like a dagger, illuminating the dancing particles of dust in the corner. From somewhere nearby floated a faint noise of children playing carelessly on the road: in the room itself there was no sound except ticking of the clock. As I lay back on the bed and crossed my hands under my head, I could hear the beating of my heart. I stared up the ceiling. Today I had broken a basic rule of our household: you shouldn't hide anything from your mum. Yet some things in life need to remain hidden from your mother, at least for some time.

Long before, I had obtained A-star grades in my academic qualifications, my friends and relatives said that I had the looks of a "smashing nerd", and it's a fact that I wanted to learn about life and human nature. I trawled through Dad's collection of books as a child. But the events of the last twenty four hours had taught me more than any university could. Even before finishing my teenage years, I had learned more about life than I'd bargained for. I'd also been considered as 'indecisive' by my peers, but my passage from indecisiveness to decisiveness had led to three of my acquaintances being detained in police custody. It was not an easy decision, not easy by any stretch of the imagination. I could feel tears flowing down the side of my face. I was no longer afraid of dying or living with the prospect of getting killed by Omar's hit men. What agonised me most was plunging my friend into a prison. Every decision leads to a choice and every choice has its consequences. Some consequences one has to accept for the rest of one's life. I wiped my eyes with the palm of my hand and tried to think of something else.

I was pleasantly surprised at the sudden re-emergence of Bari Ammi's dreams and felt very happy for her. I wanted to go and congratulate her, but felt very tired, almost as if I'd run two marathons back-to-back. The thoughts of Mr Nazir wafted through my mind, and tears began to flood my eyes again.

I don't know when the emotional and mental exhaustion tipped me over to deep sleep.

CHAPTER 1

It was a warm summer evening, almost 10 o'clock. The sun was still visible on the horizon, shooting a deep orange glow throughout the sky.

I went upstairs to meet Bari Ammi. Although she was mainly confined to her room she always wanted to know what was happening in the house especially who was coming or going. Bari Ammi was 73 years of age.

'I'm home,' I said as I entered her room.

A pleasant smile spread over her face. She had concentric wrinkles around her mouth, which would deepen during eating and smiling. I liked her steel-grey hair which was neatly woven in a single plait, hanging on her back.

'Come close to me,' she said. 'Did you have a good day?'

'Yeah, I'm awfully hungry. I wish I had picked up some McDonald's on the way.'

'Why have you not had food yet? Where is your dad? He has not been to see me today.' There was annoyance hidden behind her questions.

'He's on call and was stuck in the hospital, but is on his way home now.'

'Okay, okay, please go and eat, it's getting late.' She held my head in both her hands, which were as bony as a skeleton's and planted a moist kiss on my forehead.

'See ya, good night.'

'Good night, my jan,' I could see oceans of affection in her eyes.

This has been dad's habit of visiting his mother every evening since she suffered a stroke. She was unable to see fully for some days and gradually her vision came back but a new symptom emerged: she stopped dreaming. I did not think this lack of dreams was a problem, but Bari Ammi made a really big fuss of this loss. She continuously whinged to dad that she no longer felt fresh after her sleep. She had various consultations with Dad's neurologist colleagues at the hospital, and numerous MRIs of her brain showed no problem.

* * * * * * *

Mum was very wary of spreading the smell of spices to the rest of the house and always cooked with the kitchen doors shut and the extractor fan on. Despite Mum's best efforts to contain its rich odour within the kitchen, I could smell dinner nearly ready in the living room.

I wanted to show mum my new mobile.

'Mum, it's wonderful, isn't it?' I asked her.

'How much is the monthly rent?' she asked back rather harshly without even looking at me.

'45 quid a month and it's got a way better camera than yours.' I took a couple of close-up pictures of Mum to please her and she made no effort to smile at me.

'You know, your dad only tops up his mobile for a tenner and that lasts him for more than six months. You don't earn money or understand that "earning" is a painful thing.'

'I will one day,' I said softly. 'So what's cooking tonight?'

Mum replied rather angrily now, 'You will find out soon enough.'

I thought it is better to flee the kitchen now and wait for 'soon enough' in the TV room.

I heard the noise of a key moving in the front door and I knew that Dad was home. I kept on flicking the TV channels. It was about the time for BBC's 10 o'clock news and I knew Dad would be coming to see the news as well. The door of the TV room opened suddenly as if it had been kicked open and I could not believe what my eyes were seeing. A person who was wearing a black face mask, revealing only his eyes had his handgun pointing towards Dad's head. Dad entered the room with both hands up in the air. The burglar was dressed all in black. A wave of fear swept across my body, my heart was beating violently and I felt tightness in my chest.

He pushed dad with the muzzle of his gun towards me and said, 'If you want your life, give me all the money and jewellery you have, or I'll kill you, kill you all. I need all your money and gold, no messing about.'

'We'll give you whatever you want but please do not hurt us.' Dad said politely.

I was very impressed with his composed manner. I could hear

my heart beating and felt my hands shaking.

Dad put his hand into his back pocket and brought out his wallet and handed over the cash to the burglar saying. 'We don't keep much cash at home.'

The burglar snatched the money from dad's hand and said, 'I need all the gold you have.' I know you Asians are loaded with gold! Come on, quick, give it to me or you'll all bedead…right here.'

I could hear the burglar's voice was trembling. He appeared a rather chubby person. His T-shirt was stretched over his protuberant tummy, his armpits were wet and appeared darker. I thought that if he was alone, both I and dad could easily overpower him. Perhaps, Dad sensed my thoughts and said, 'I am sorry, we don't keep jewellery at home. It is in the bank security safe but you can take our mobiles or laptops or whatever you want.'

'What's going on here?' Mum entered the room without realising that we were being burgled. Her eyes widened with fear when she saw us both in front of the burglar. The burglar pointed with his gun to Mum to move with us. He was sweating profusely, now the temples of his face mask were also appearing wet.

He looked at the ear-ring mum was wearing and said to Dad. 'You liar, you said you don't have any jewellery. What the fuck is she wearing? Take 'em off and hand 'em over to me.'

I felt sad when I saw Mum hurriedly taking her ear-rings off and throwing them on the floor. She also pulled her gold necklace off and threw it at the burglar and said, 'Take all this and now go away and leave my family alone.'

The burglar picked up the jewellery and stuffed it in the front pocket of his trouser. The chain of Mum's necklace was hanging loosely outside and he said. 'You are a good girl. Now give me all the gold you have got in your cupboard. Come on, quickly, or I'll kill you, kill you.'

'We don't keep jewellery at home, it's in the bank.'

'No, no, you're all lying, give me all of it or get killed!' he shouted loudly. 'Come on, tell me where you keep all the gold, and don't you lie to me. Who else is in?'

'My mother,' Dad answered politely. 'Please do not bother her. She is old and not very well. We're not lying. We don't have any jewellery here at home.'

'You'll soon find some for me.' The burglar said pointing his gun at Dad. 'Take me to the old lady. I am sure she had some gold for me.'

'Please, do not put my mother through this. She is a heart patient and may not take this,' Dad said.

But the burglar pushed Dad aside and ordered us to lead him upstairs to Bari Ammi's room.

'I can't let you do this,' Dad said in an angry tone and blocked his way to the stairs. 'You'll kill her just by your presence.'

'Then cut the crap and give me all the gold you have, mother fucker.'

The burglar shouted loudly. He was now breathing heavily. He looked jittery and was moving up and down the room like a lion in a cage. Suddenly, he took a deep breath, clenched his fist over his chest and fell like a stone on the floor. We were all taken aback with this new development. Dad was the first to leap forward. I could see the grip of the burglar's fist loosening on his handgun. He was lying motionless on the floor.

I heard Dad saying. 'Looks like he is having a heart attack.'

Dad peeled off his face mask, gently slid the gun out of his hand and said loudly, 'Hello, how are you?' He moved him by holding his shoulder. The burglar made no sound or any motion.

I felt a small knot of anxiety in my stomach as his lips dulled to dusky blue. Dad felt his neck pulse, leaned his face over his, very close to him as if he was trying to hear something, his eyes observing his chest and said, 'Ali, ring 999 and tell them: adult, middle aged, man had a cardiac arrest. Tell them our house number and post code.' Dad turned towards Mum and said, 'Rose, you ring the police'.

Dad started CPR. His hair was bobbing up and down with each thrust on the burglar's chest.

'Let him die, dirty rascal, evil scum,' Mum said with tears, fear and hatred on her face.

'No, he is a human, call 999 now,' Dad shouted at the top of his voice. Mum hurried out of the room.

I stabilised the burglar's head in my hands. He was white, probably in his fifties. His face was unshaven, white roots of his dyed, greasy scalp hair were enough to tell his life story. He smelt of a nauseating cocktail of odours of alcohol, tobacco and sweat. A streak of saliva was dribbling from the corner of his mouth. I could see his yellow teeth with black fillings. Inside, I was very worried: what if he died in our house or even worse if any of his accomplices barged into the house to kill us?

'Take over from me, I'm getting tired,' Dad said. Beads of sweat had appeared on his forehead. 'Two thrusts every second, make sure chest compressions are at least 5-6 centimetres deep.'

I started chest compressions. I had never thought doing resuscitation could be so tiresome. I felt my shoulders aching and was soon getting out of breath. Dad was kneeling down on the floor as if he was offering a prayer; he was closely supervising me doing the procedure and at the same time was observing the robber.

'He is coming back,' Dad said excitedly. 'Well done, Ali, you have done a great job, better than me.' I could see a smile, a sense of achievement on his face. Mum hugged me and tears overflowed from her eyes. I knew these tears were of gratitude and not of grief.

The burglar made a grunting sound and moved his left leg as if he was trying to get up. Dad quickly wiped dribbling saliva from his face with a tissue, opened his mouth to look inside and turned him onto his left side.

'This is the recovery position,' he said. 'It will prevent any inhalation of his spit.' Clearly, he didn't wish to miss any teaching opportunity. The robber was now making groaning sounds. His eyes were still shut.

The wailing sirens of an ambulance began to sound closely and blue light lit the room. Mum quickly went outside and guided in two paramedics who hurried towards the robber.

'He needs an ECG and if a myocardial infarction is confirmed he will need urgent angiography and stenting,' Dad said. 'I do not think his heart stopped beating for more than a couple of minutes. Carry on chaps.'

'No problem, boss, another life saved,' one of the paramedics - who probably knew Dad - said smiling.

'Just to let you know,' Dad said in a light mood, 'he came to burgle us all and we ended up doing CPR on him.'

'Lucky him, there is a God,' One paramedic said with a big smile on his face.

'But, Doc,' the paramedic said timidly, 'you will need to get your carpet washed, the bastard not only wet his trousers but also your carpet.' There were chuckles all round.

The robber was attached to a machine showing wavy lines

which was also making beeping sounds. He was placed on a stretcher to which he was strapped. His eyes were still shut, his face appeared glowing red and he was beginning to make snorting noises under his hazy oxygen face mask.

'Could you please let me know which ward he'll be going to? I'll visit him tomorrow,' Dad said to one of the paramedics.

'No probs. Will let you know.'

The sirens of a police car could be heard just outside our house. Mum steered two policemen into the front room. I was still trying to catch my breath after the CPR.

I could hear Dad narrating events to the policemen. 'As I turned the key into the front door, he quickly came out of the bushes in the front garden and pointed the gun at me.......'

'Well done, Doc. Once he is recovered he'll be quizzed. This is a unique robbery case where we don't have to take any fingerprints. We need to find out where he got the gun from, is he a part of some gang or working solo. We will call you to the station for statements etc. tomorrow,' said one of the policemen, who bent down and put the gun inside a clear plastic bag without touching it.

'We'll have to take the jewellery into our safekeeping. We 'll leave the money as it's less than £100 but for the jewellery you will have to prove evidence of your purchase as it was in his pocket. I am sorry but these are the procedures we have to follow. I am sure you will have the receipts for the purchase of these ear-rings and necklace.'

'No, we don't, we bought them a long time ago, one doesn't keep receipts for the rest of one's life,' Mum said. She still sounded a bit rattled.

'Don't worry, Mum, I have the evidence that the earring and necklace are yours,' I said calmly and loudly to impress everyone. 'I took close-up pictures of you on my mobile phone camera just before the burglary and there is a date and time on these pictures. I hope officer this evidence will do.'

'Certainly, sir,' one of the police officer's said, quickly scanning the photographs.

'We'll have a quick search of the back of your house and the area, just to make sure there isn't anybody else,' the police officer said.

'Dad, I'm glad we didn't have to do mouth-to-mouth on him. I would have never done that and I would have probably puked,' I said.

A loving smile appeared on Dad's face. 'Well, lungs and large blood vessels have enough oxygen to cope with a few minutes of cardiac arrest, provided you are maintaining a good circulation by chest compressions. If he had not come back that quickly, whether we liked or not we might have had to do it.'

Dad knew well that he was the hero of the evening. Mum hugged him and tears were flowing on her cheeks. I hugged both of them.

'Nobody bothers to tell me what happens in this house.' Bari Ammi slammed shut her room door to draw our attention and spoke grumpily, adjusting her hearing aids. As we turned around we saw her standing on the landing, holding the bannister. 'I could hear someone shouting. Is this a home or a fish market, have we forgotten the manners of how to speak at home?'

'No, we haven't forgotten any manners, I was just about to come to you upstairs and explain everything,' Dad said hurriedly.

'You better be quick,' she said and disappeared inside her room.

CHAPTER 2

Despite having diverse points of view about various things in life, both George and dad had been very close friends for as long as I could remember. On most Saturday evenings George would visit us. George was his surname. Many people including myself didn't know his first name and he never objected to be called that way. George worked as a consultant at the same hospital as Dad. He had a soft Scottish accent, had a great appetite for Asian food and unsurprisingly was heavily built. George was in his late fifties, had sparse hair on his head which gave him a wide forehead. His nose was slightly large for his face and turned upwards. He was wearing dark brown corduroys with braces, and a blue polo shirt, and as always, he wore the same old trainers.

George's grandfather was killed during the Second World War. He was very proud that his grandfather was a martyr, who gave his life for the sake of his country, for the betterment of coming generations. George was an idealist too. It's interesting that much is known about the inheritance of bodily traits from one's parents but there is little knowledge about the passage of views from one generation to the other.

George relished talking and would not allow any interruptions. I had no doubts; he liked the sound of his own voice. He had a point of view for almost anything and everything. I must admit, I never found his conversation boring.

Dad had told me that George's ward rounds in hospital were very popular among the trainees, where he not only taught management of medical conditions, but also verbal and non-verbal communication skills with patients and their relatives, which according to Dad were equally important in becoming a good doctor.

Dad had never objected, and in fact, encouraged me to join in with his friends' company. Dad would usually meet his friends in the study room, which was a small room on the right hand side as you entered our house. There was a study table, which was as slim as a console, a chair and a double-seated sofa in the room. Unlike Dad's other friends' study rooms, there was not a single book in ours. Dad used to receive an avalanche of medical journals every month, but he would either read or scan them, save the relevant papers onto his laptop and discard the rest. Dad always said that if you didn't have time to read a journal article now, then it was unlikely that you'd have time to read it in future either.

George was truly a warm-blooded person. He would often start a conversation with this opening sentence. 'It makes my blood boil!'

'As I was about to turn into your street, I nearly crashed into a car with a "Baby on board" message. It really riles me why people put "baby on board" stickers on the rear windows of their car? I am against this for two reasons. First, why on earth someone would like to advertise their fertility in open public by putting such messages, and second, are they trying to tell us to be careful as there is a baby in the car? This is ridiculous. Every life is precious. I would not ram into a car ahead simply because it had a granny on board.'

I was very impressed with George's ability to talk in 'bullet points', although I had a feeling that he used to make these points as he went along in his long discourses. He was a gifted talker, very articulate. He knew how to use hand gestures, how to dramatize his conversation by the pitch and volume of his voice. We all liked his company.

Sometimes, I thought that his views were very provocative, sometimes very convoluted, and difficult to understand. Last week, he said that everyone in this universe was on some sort of a quest for truth. I didn't understand what he meant by truth and he did not explain it either. He once dropped strings of cluster bombs when he made a statement that those who seek truth rather than follow the tradition of forefathers should change religion at least once in their lives. Then he described four categories of people in the way they react when they meet truth. He used the example to explain these categories like combustion oils varying from 'high octane' highly inflammable to very crude mineral oil, slow to be ignited. I asked him to explain to me his theory in simple terms. He laughed and said, 'Ali, when the time is ripe and right, you will understand it all. No explanation will be required. No simplicity of terms will be necessary. You will understand it fully and completely, just wait for the right moment.'

'Did you hear George,' Dad asked. 'That our Chief executive has bought a new car with the personalised number plate of "Boss no 1"!'

'You're joking. It's unbelievable! It's rude!' George's mouth opened with utter disbelief. 'I thought he was a decent person and a better manager than the ones we had in the past. I need to reconsider my thoughts about him.'

It was apparent from his face that he was thinking and talking. 'He must have spent a fortune to get that registration number. I could never understand why the hell people pay huge sums of money for personalised car registration number plates,' he paused for a moment, smirked contemptuously and said, 'it's vanity, narcissism and nothing else.'

'Could you clarify, George?' I was beginning to enjoy this conversation. 'Are you against paying huge sums of money or against personalised car registration numbers?'

'I am against both for three reasons.' George raised his hand, which was a gesture to warn us to be attentive to him.

'First, to pay an extortionate amount of money for a number plate is obscene. You know better than me, Taj. The money you spend on such a thing could feed a village in Africa for a whole year.'

'That's true.' Dad said solemnly.

'Second,' George said. 'Buying a plate number of Boss no 1 or Surgeon 1 does not automatically make you the best boss or the best surgeon, actually such number plates show a crying desire for the person to be known that way. Third, in this day and age everyone is so wary of revealing their identity but yet we see hundreds of cars driven around with the driver's name splashed over their car registration plates. This is nothing but vanity. We live in a celebrity culture. By getting their name on the back of their car, people pretend to act like celebrities but they aren't, they are living in a self-created world of deception.' George's face was glowing with excitement as he spoke.

'Let me tell you one more thing.' George said and both I and Dad knew that it would certainly be more than only one thing.

'The Government wants us all to get sucked into this celebrity culture of all sorts. It would be extremely naïve of you if you think that the government's support of sports is to promote the health and fitness of the general public. They do not. They do it to create a celebrity culture, to use it as a distraction, so that they can carry on making the right or wrong decisions in their offices while you are busy watching all these matches.'

'I think your point about celebrity culture sounds valid, but George, would you like to see the death of private number plates?' Dad said with a grin on his face. 'This is a multi-million pound business and some people will cry their eyes out on the death of number plates as they would do so on the death of their loved ones.'

'You may call me cynical but there are only three reasons why people cry after someone's death.' George continued his talk in his usual bullet point way of speech. 'First, pretending to weep over the loss of someone dear to us we really weep for ourselves, since we miss that person's good attitude, good opinion of us or deplore some curtailment of our wealth, pleasure or position. I regard this group of people as very simple and innocent.'

I could see a smile spreading over Dad's face upon hearing this.

'Taj, just don't laugh at me and let me finish first.' George raised his hand in the air and stopped dad from making any point.

'Second, this group of people I regard as less innocent as they aspire to the glory of a beautiful, immortal sorrow. These people pretend that time, the universal healer is not able to heal their wounds, and they persistently go on weeping, wailing and sighing; they are acting a mournful part and doing their best to make all their actions prove that their grief will only end with their lives. I saw a famous film actress, who falls in this category of people, in a TV interview, four years after the death of her husband. She was shedding tears as if her husband had passed away only a few minutes ago.' George paused to take a breath and continued again.

'The third group is of people who shed tears on anyone's death just to prove to other people that they are delicate and tender-hearted or even worse to avoid the disgrace of not weeping.'

There was a palpable silence in the room. Horizontal wrinkles deepened on George's forehead as if he was trying to think of another bullet point to carry on with his conversation. I was thinking how the heck he came up with such unique ideas. Did he get them by reading books or did they descend upon him from nowhere like finished products? I didn't know.

'Ali, do you agree with me about these varieties of wailing people?' I was not expecting George to ask me this question and immediately came out of my deep thoughts. 'Yeah, I totally agree, one hundred per cent, like always,' I said with a stutter.

Dad obviously looked impressed with George's three categories of wailing people and said with a smile on his face. 'There is yet another category of tears, George.'

'What type?' George, who thought he had stunned us all, was taken aback.

'Crocodile tears.' Dad said.

We all started laughing until we heard Mum shouting from the kitchen. 'Food is ready'.

George got up quickly from the sofa like a coiled spring and said. 'I can hear my guts wailing, here we come, food.' We all laughed again.

CHAPTER 3

Sajid was living in a university residence hall, which was quite conveniently located at a walking distance from our home.

I was in two minds: should I speak to Sajid about eating pork or should I just mind my own business? But who decides which business was whose? I thought, as I sauntered towards his residence hall. If everyone always minded their own business, would there be any change in this world? Perhaps not. It is also quite possible that Sajid did not realise that those were pork chops, it may have been an honest mistake or did he require a reminder regarding the subject of *halal*, *haram* food? I thought I should pickup this topic with Sajid.

Sajid was the son of one of our family friends. Sajid's dad had a corner newsagent shop in Bradford. Sajid was the youngest and the only child in the whole family to reach the university. He was doing a degree at London University in business administration. Sajid's dad was naturally quite proud that he had won the honours in the family of sending a child to university despite his meagre resources. Sajid was a hugely ambitious person. He promised to help his father after completing his degree. I couldn't forget his father's face, glowing with delight when Sajid said to him.

'I will turn your corner shop into a chain of superstores, *Abba Gi.*'

Sajid was probably a year older than me. He was tall, handsomely slim and was very sporty. An attribute of Sajid's personality which always made me envious was his apparent ability to make a decision. He was not attracted to the concept of doubt. I had not known Sajid long enough to know the consequence of his decisions but he would make his mind up pretty soon. These decisions were not decisions of life and death but the sort of decisions over which I would agonise for hours or days which ranged over trivial things like which colour trousers to buy, which brand of trainers, what present to give to Mum for her birthday, which mobile company to choose or important matters like what career: to become a doctor or a dentist or a journalist? But Sajid would decide all these matters in a split second. I couldn't do this.

As I climbed upstairs, I saw Sajid's class-mate coming down. He was wearing a flashy jogging suit and was waving his badminton racket.

'Is he there?' I asked him.

'Yup, in his room right now, see ya.'

'Cheers mate,' and I continued towards Sajid's room.

Sajid lived in a single dormitory and his room was always neatly kept. It had a study table with drawers and a chair and a single bed. A small fridge was tucked underneath a bookshelf. There was a wash basin in the corner of the room with a mirror on the wall. The mirror was of such a size in which he could only view his passport photograph sized image in it. A shelf below the mirror had Sajid's shaving cream and collection of deodorants and perfumes.

'Hi, Saj.' I said and entered his room at the same time.

'Marvellous to see you, where have you been hiding?' Sajid said cheerfully and emptied the chair of the books to make room for me to sit on. I think he was waiting for someone or about to go out as he was lying in bed, fully dressed and with shoes on.

'Just stayed at home. Not much.' I said. 'Seems you're gonna go out? I could come later.'

'No, no. I'm not going right now,' he said. 'You tell me, if you stayed at home, you must have read a lot of books and met loads of your dad's friends?' Sajid made a jocular remark.

'No, didn't read any book or meet anyone, pretty boring,' I answered with an artificial flavour of despondency.

'It was a good game of cricket last week,' I said. We had played a twenty overs match against our arch rival team. I took five wickets and Sajid hit four towering sixes in an over. We had a convincing victory. 'The poor bowler's face was turning paler and paler as you were hitting the sixes. Felt bad for him,' I said.

'Me too, but thoroughly enjoyed it. It was such good fun hitting the ball in the middle of the bat, clunk and the ball flew off the boundary.' Sajid said with a gesture of his hands as if he was holding a bat, 'the icing on the cake was the after the match celebrations. The food was so good. I never expected our tight-arse manager to spend any money on us. It was brill.'

'As a heavily paid inspector of the vegetarian society and also because of my unpaid job of your godparent here in London, could I ask you why you had pork chops when there was a vegetarian option for food at the cricket club do?' I asked Sajid in a made-up voice. 'An extremely respectable and reliable witness has seen you devouring pork meat, did you mistake them for lamb chops?'

Sajid looked surprised that I had brought up this topic.

'I am so sorry, My Lord, please don't send me to jail. I beg you to have mercy on me….. I was hungry, very hungry…….. I knew they were pork chops ……. but they looked absolutely divine, I couldn't resist. I just wanted to see how this meat tasted. You're allowed to eat pork if you're hungry, aren't you?' Sajid said light-heartedly.

I found his remark rather offensive and gently said. 'Sajid, you can't make use of a religious relaxation to justify your taste-bud curiosity. I'm sure you already knew that one is only allowed to have pork if one is close to death because of starvation.'

'I know this, I know this all,' Sajid said, sounding irritated. 'I've seen quite a few Arab boys from our university who would eat any sort of meat.'

'Sajid, someone else doing wrong does not make it right. I'm saying this to you only because look older and wiser than you and you've to listen to me.' I wanted to make our conversation a bit more pleasant. 'I'm just trying to tell you how I felt and what I feel is right. I certainly don't wish to offend or annoy you.'

'To eat and what not to eat and all this business of halal, haram are petty things. The thing, which matters most in life, is that you shouldn't harm others, you should be helpful, respectful to others. Benevolence, my dear, this is the important thing, the rest is just minor stuff, not worthy of consideration.'

'I'm not questioning the value of altruism and kindness but sometimes minor things do play a major role in life,' I said. 'Please don't laugh at what I'm about to say.'

I stopped for a moment and said. 'It may not make sense to you initially but if you try to understand it, it's an important, deep thought.'

'Go on, my little Socrates, I'm all ears.'

I looked into Sajid's eyes. He gave a stern expression in return. I could pick up early signs of disagreement, from this expression, with what I was about to say.

'Sajid, once, one of my dad's friends made a very philosophical comment for being extra careful about consuming halal food. He said that food eventually becomes a part of our body. Sometimes it becomes a red blood cell darting in our circulation carrying oxygen, sometimes a muscle fibre, or sometimes a molecule of glucose supplying energy to our brain. He said that we should try our best to have a "halal body" made up of having halal *tayyab* diet. Halal food facilitates us to do virtuous acts in the world, gives us positive thinking, whereas un-halal food makes us follow our wishes, our lust, which may lead us off track. Halal food not only means a food, which results from a certain ritual of slaughtering an animal, but also includes an earning by fair resources, without the contamination of fraud, theft, drug money or stealing. Such earning makes your food "un-halal", not suitable for consumption.'

'That is very un-scientific. I can't believe I've heard this silly, daft logic from you. Are you trying to tell me that a glucose molecule derived from pork or wine will have a different effect on your body than the one derived from the halal food?' Sajid said with a loud laugh from the back of his throat. 'Are you also trying to tell me that if a person after sweating and toiling all day and through his honest, hard earned money buys pork that it would still have an ill-effect on his brain cells and what not?'

'Yes, it will. I can't prove it now, no one can prove it but I feel this is true.' I said gingerly.

'You and your juvenile morality...' Sajid said.

'You can't trivialise an issue by just saying its juvenile. It's a very serious matter.' I interrupted him.

'Bollocks, absolutely fucked-up philosophy,' Sajid said.

I knew Sajid was peppering his argument and making it look heavy-weight by adding swear words.

'Trust me, Ali, you sound like an old soul, a really old and wrinkly soul. If you could prove your dad's friend's theory, you could not only win the Nobel Prize in biochemistry but also in medicine at the same time. Also a word of caution for my custodian, don't tell such theories to anyone else, you run a serious risk of getting a good bashing.'

I felt embarrassed at Sajid's remark and sensed my ears glowing and I said rather hastily.

'It's the biggest weakness of our time that we only believe what is scientifically proven, driven by evidence, full of fact sheets. There are a few things in life which go straight to your heart without having the seal of approval from a scientific body. Who knows in years to come someone could prove this theory?'

'Ali, sometimes you talk a load of rubbish, a shit load. I think you also need to stay away from your dad's friends. Do you really believe that all who eat un-halal foods only does all the evil and bad things? I know drunks cause a lot of mayhem on the streets over the weekends. Do you really believe that a halal eater does not commit any mischief in this world?' Sajid said peevishly.

I knew I had taken the argument too far with Sajid. 'You are absolutely right, a crime, an evil act can happen by any human being. I am simply making a point which you're quite entitled to disagree with that if you have respect for some higher authority in your life and obey His rules and regulations, it is more likely you will respect the views and rights of your fellow human beings.'

I felt out of breath for talking that long.

Sajid did not look convinced but he saluted me in ridicule and said, 'OK, Big Brother that was a mistake. No more pork chops but only on one condition.'

'What is that?'

'No more sermons for me.'

I had to make an effort to bring a smile to my face.

'Sorry, Bruv. I got to go now,' Sajid said by looking at his wristwatch. 'I'm so sorry not to have offered you any tea or coffee.'

'No worries, maybe next time.'

I decided to take a longer route home. I felt battered. I was thinking of myself as a failure as I was not able to convince Sajid. Was I imperious towards him? Was I trying to propagate a half-cooked idea? Why had I got such a strong desire that everyone should agree with me?

CHAPTER 4

Dad was getting ready to leave for the airport. He was going to do six weeks' charity work in Malawi. A team of doctors was also accompanying him. He was also taking with him an ultrasound scan machine which was lying redundant in his department to train doctors and paramedics in the diagnosis of congenital heart problems in new-born babies. He told me that an earlier diagnosis and referrals of such babies to the specialist units could save so many lives. It was also planned that they would run some adult resuscitation courses over there as well. Mum did not want him to go for that long but she also knew that she would not be able to convince him not to go.

Mum, as always, had packed Dad's suitcase. She knew exactly what he would need. All of us were fully convinced that she knew the art of the most efficient utilisation of space in a suitcase. Dad's suitcase was brown coloured, it was showing all the tell-tale signs of ageing and belonged to an era when there were no wheels or telescopic handles. Dad used to boast like a child in describing the high quality leather it was made with. The in convenience of actually carrying the suitcase could not deter him or make him replace it. Mum, quite rightly, thought that the only way he would buy a new suitcase would be if it was lost during travelling, but her earnest prayers for it to disappear during a journey did not yield the desired result. Dad did not wish to change his suitcase and said that it had character.

'Dad, you better check your bag,' I said. 'Mum has packed it'.

'No, I trust your mum,' Dad understood my jocular remark and said this with a smile.

'In that case you might either have to tell a lie at the airport that you packed your own luggage or go to prison.' I said teasingly.

'I would prefer to go to prison than to mistrust your mum,' Dad said in a made up voice.

'Oh, you two boys just behave,' Mum said, pointing her index finger at both of us. 'Taj, you make sure you take your anti-malarial tablets every day. I have put an alarm on your mobile to remind you.'

'I promise, I will.' Dad put his right hand on his chest and bent forward in a sign of obedience before Mum and this action brought a smile to our faces.

We were sitting in the living room and Mum was everywhere making last minute packing arrangements for Dad.

'Ali, I've a bit of a problem, one of my friends is arriving from Pakistan the day after tomorrow, and can I ask you to take care of him please?' Dad said in his usual gentle style of talking.

'Yeah, sure, do I know him?' I said.

'No, you've not met him,' Dad said. 'I might have mentioned him to you. He's really an extraordinary person, in a league of his own. I would have actually loved to look after him. He's not very well. He's coming to have some treatment here. He will be admitted to the Bromwell Hospital.'

'That's a private hospital,' I said.

'Yes, it is.'

'Will it be cold there in the evenings?' Mum asked dad from the top of the stairs. 'I haven't packed any sweaters for you. Do you want me to put in a sleeveless sweater just in case?'

'Well, temperature during the day time over there would be in the mid-forties and I doubt I would need any sweater there, no thanks,' Dad said.

'What's wrong with your friend, Dad?' I said.

'I'm not exactly sure but I think he has got some liver and kidney disease. I hope he gets better soon. I've known him for the past 30 years, since the time I came to the UK to sit the membership examination of the Royal College, and he was doing his masters in mathematics. We used to share a flat in East London at that time.'

Dad paused. His eyes were telling me that he was going back in time. A smile appeared on his face and he continued.

'I used to like Nazir for three reasons. Firstly, because he was extremely caring, kind and had a helpful attitude towards others. Secondly, for him being a super mathematician, and thirdly for his impeccable ability of direction sense. He would take us anywhere after having a cursory glance at the map, which was most impressive. Nazir used to joke that, like birds and bees, he can follow the electromagnetic waves of the earth, and I think he wasn't wrong.'

I smiled, listening to this from Dad and he continued.

'Unlike me, Nazir went back to Pakistan after completing his degree and began to teach maths in a school. I sort of lost touch with him after that, but I heard some reports that he was having some problems with his marital life. This was most surprising to me as I never expected this of him. I thought perhaps he was going through a rough patch and also, people do change.'

Dad stopped and looked at me and asked. 'Hope I am not boring you with these details?

'No, not at all. I'm listening, it's all very interesting!' I said.

'Taj, do you want to carry your safari hat?' Mum shouted again from upstairs.

'No thanks. If required, I'll buy one from there.' Dad turned his face towards the stairs and said this in a loud voice.

Dad looked at me, smiled affectionately and said. 'Then I heard that he was staying away from his home for days and weeks. He was spotted at the shrine of a Sufi, Ali Hejwari in Lahore. His mausoleum is located in the heart of the city. Ali Hejwari was commonly known as *Data Gung Baksh* which literally means 'one who bestowed wealth.' He played an important role in spreading Islam in the Indo-Pakistan region, about a thousand years ago. Ali Hejwari was a Sufi of the highest spiritual calibre. He guided thousands through the mystical way of life. Thousands of his devotees come every day to his mausoleum to pay homage to him. It is generally said that Ali Hejwari had a deep respect for all human beings, regardless of their religious beliefs or looks and anyone who visited him was provided with free meals and this happens even today but of course the food is cooked by his devotees in huge big pots called *Daigs*. Just to give you an idea of how big these Daigs are: you won't be visible from outside if you stand inside one of them.'

Dad stopped for a minute, he was choosing his words with deliberation and continued again.

'Death may be a powerful tearing force but not powerful

enough to interrupt the flow of certain deeds. On one side of the River Ravi, which is one of the widest and longest rivers in Pakistan, Ali Hejwari is buried. On the other side, the great, mighty Mogul emperor Jehangir's tomb is located. Only a handful of tourists visit Jehangir's tomb each day whereas thousands come to visit Ali Hejwari's grave. Ruling people is one thing and the rule of hearts is another. Every year his devotees celebrate the anniversary of the death of the great master,' Dad said.

'Very strange, they celebrate death.' I could not resist interrupting dad.

'Yes, it may sound odd but for a mystic, death means an eternal re-union with the creator. For a Sufi, the day he dies is really the day he lives. On that day, the courtyard of his shrine becomes open house for *Qawwali* musicians, who sit cross legged in two rows and sing Qawwalis which is the devotional music of Sufis. The whole atmosphere is enchanted, the air is thick with the heavy scent of roses and *Agar bati* smoke. Listeners moving their heads in circles, in a state of ecstasy.'

'This Hejwari dude,' I said, 'was he very rich? Was he actually giving money to the people?'

'No, no, don't be daft, it's not the worldly wealth we are talking here but it's the spiritual wealth which is meant here.' Dad laughed at my question.

'Is Ali Hejwari's mausoleum a university of some kind to teach mysticism?' I asked.

'No, it's not a university as such but is an unnamed, unregistered educational institution in this area for selected people. What are the selection criteria and who makes this selection is largely unknown, but there are people there who spot you or sometimes you are summoned there to be spotted. How it happens I don't know. It's very complicated.' Dad replied.

'But how is this person who is to be spotted summoned there, is it by telepathic means?'

'May be, I don't know, this is where it begins to get complicated.'

'How intriguing,' I said. 'Was Mr Nazir also summoned there....'? I stressed the word 'summoned' and mum came downstairs and interrupted.

'Taj, should I make you some sandwiches for the airport, in case your flight is late.'

'I don't think that would be necessary.' Dad said with a smile. 'I'll buy something at the airport if I need.'

Dad continued his conversation with me.

'I don't know and please don't ask him this question straightaway. What I know is that he is back with his family, still teaching maths. I have also heard that he holds some discussion forums at his home on a weekly basis, which I believe are very well attended by the public.'

'What does Mr Nazir discuss in these forums, mathematics?' I asked.

'Dunno, but I doubt it that people would flock around him to learn mathematics. You could ask him,' Dad said. 'An ambulance is going to pick him up at Heathrow. I'd really like you to meet him at the airport and accompany him to the hospital, but you've to be very careful with him. Sometimes he gets annoyed even over very small matters. He has a very sensitive personality.'

Mum who joined us in the room was also listening to all this conversation intently, her face was in the cups of her hands and she asked. 'Did he patch up things with his wife?'

'Yes, as far as I know,' Dad replied.

'Has he got any children?' Mum inquired again.

'Yeah, I did hear that he has a son. I think he is a physician in the States. I don't exactly know where he lives or works.'

'Very interesting,' Mum said. 'His son is a doctor in the States and he is coming over here for his treatment.'

'Yeah, I was also thinking about the same, but I didn't find it appropriate to go into the details with him. Maybe he's got more faith in British hospitals,' Dad said laughing.

'Maybe,' Mum said, 'it's our good luck that he has chosen to come here.'

I was fascinated to hear this introduction of Mr Nazir and really looked forward to meeting him. 'Don't worry Dad, I will take care of him,' I said.

'I'm sure you would,' Dad said.

'I have added roaming service to your mobile,' Mum said. 'I could drop you off at the airport.'

'Thanks for the roaming service,' Dad said. 'Hope I get mobile signals there otherwise I'll ring you from some landline. The charity has arranged a mini-bus to pick us all up from our residences to take us to Heathrow. I'll just nip upstairs to say goodbye to Bari Ammi. She was very worried to know that I was going away for six weeks,' he said and quickly climbed the stairs.

CHAPTER 5

Retrospectively thinking, Sajid's decision of giving me a spare set of keys to his hostel room did not prove to be a very sensible idea. He had given me the keys in case someday he lost his room keys or was locked outside. Also, sometimes I had to come to leave some food in his fridge when he was not in his room. This mistake had come to light one day.

As usual, Mum cooked some food for Sajid, as she would do quite often to provide him with some home cooked meals. Mum had a soft spot for Sajid in her heart. She always felt for Sajid, he was living away from his home here at university and she presumed that he must be missing out on home cooked meals. I may be wrong but I did not think Sajid was too fussed about living away from home or missing home meals. Mum asked me to deliver carefully packed boxes of food to Sajid which I could do on my way to my indoor cricket training sessions.

'Do I really have to deliver him this food today?' I asked Mum. 'I'm already late for my cricket. I'll drop it off tomorrow.'

'No, take it with you today. His room is on your way. It won't take you very long. Come on! Be a good boy.'

It was four o'clock in the afternoon and I was not expecting Sajid to be back from university. I briskly climbed up the stairs to his room, unlocked the door and as I went in, I saw and heard what I should never have - a mound of quilt was moving up and down and muffled grunting noises were coming out. The motion of the mound and noise stopped as I entered the room, I immediately closed the door and came out. I forgot to blink, unwilling to trust the evidence which my eyes had just seen. My heart was pounding. I left the food parcel just outside his door and began to walk hurriedly towards the staircase. Has he given his room key to someone else as well? I thought.

I heard Sajid calling me from behind, 'Ali, stop, and listen to me'.

'I got to go, getting late for my cricket training,' I said without looking at him.

Sajid ran towards me and held me by my shoulder. He was in his underpants and his shirt was still unbuttoned, showing his chest.

'Please listen to me.'

'Maybe later, I'm getting late. I'll come after the game.'

'No, no, you got to listen to me now, please, come with me.'

'Ok, quickly please, what do you want to say? If you're worried, be assured I won't mention this to anyone.'

'You caught me red handed today.' He had a crafty smile on his face.

'Sorry, I didn't know you were in.'

'It was good fun. I slept with her twin sister last week. I think she was better.' He said winking at me.

'Sorry, Sajid, I'm not remotely interested in your sexual conquests and I don't even give a damn whether you bring her, any other sister or her mum to your bed next time. I was not aware of this side of your personality.'

'Don't be sarcastic. Have fun, man, whichever way it comes.' Sajid looked at my face carefully and said. 'This should be our secret, a very well-guarded secret. And please don't have an attack of morality now. I know this is against our religion but all these girls chase me, so don't blame me. Blame them.'

'Oh yeah, you stud! All the women in the city are only after your body,' I said sarcastically. 'Don't worry, your secret will remain a secret, hidden in my heart. I promise no one will come to know about it.'

The door of Sajid's room swung open and a girl emerged. The back of my throat went totally dry, she was totally naked. I could not bear her nudity and unsurprisingly my gaze went to her feet and gradually worked upwards. She was a white, slim girl, with slender, long legs. A triangle of profuse, red curly pubic hair was very prominent. Her stomach was flat and she was wearing an ear-ring-like belly-button ring. She had gangly, tattoo covered thin arms that were placed on her hips, accentuating her breasts. Her thin neck supported her oval smooth, face. She had high arched pencil drawn eyebrows, deep brown eyes which appeared slightly smaller on her face. Her rounded nose had a prominent stud piercing, her flushed cheeks were smattered with freckles. Her red lips were pursed in a slight cynical smile. Her face was framed by fiery-red grown out perms that hung down to her shoulders.

The girl said to Sajid in a very angry tone. 'Come on, you finish it off for me now!' She had the predatory look of a carnivorous animal: about to strike.

Sajid said to the girl. 'Put on your clothes and push off.'

The girl looked at me and said. 'You fucking killjoy. If you don't wanna have fun, don't stop others having some.'

As she walked back to the room her bare body and curvatures looked even more prominent against the darkness of the room. I had nothing to say and in fact could not say anything but I immediately recognised this girl, she had been sitting on the ground next to the boundary line in the last cricket match. I failed to stop a boundary and nearly dropped a catch just because of her.

It was the final match of the super league. It was a perfect day for cricket with the sun shining brightly. A crowd of at least 300 supporters turned up to watch the final tussle. I had never played at that ground before but it looked very nice and well maintained with a pavilion and stands for the crowd. However, some spectators chose to sit on the ground near the boundary line. Our team batted first and were all out at the meagre score of 109 in 20 overs. Disappointingly, I got out for a duck on the very first ball I faced.

The opposing team could sense victory and celebrations had already begun in some parts of the watching crowd.

In the team briefing the captain said quite passionately that the only chance we had to win this game would be by excellent fielding and tight bowling. He said. 'Ali, you need to bowl wicket-to-wicket, just bowl good line and length, don't try to bowl fast, we can't afford any no-balls or wides.'

I was the opening fast bowler for the team. That day due to some reason, I was unable to find my bowling rhythm. I was thrashed for four boundaries during the first over of the match, neither the captain nor myself was happy with this disastrous bowling start. The supporters of the opposing team went ballistic with this excellent start for their team. The noise was deafening. I think it was due more to our captain's annoyance than a coincidence that I was asked to do fielding in the third man area – near the boundary. The batsman hit another powerful stroke sweetly from the middle of the bat – a perfect shot. The ball was racing towards the boundary. I ran fast to field the ball but before I could intercept it, this girl who emerged from Sajid's room was sitting among the front row and showed no hesitation in pulling her T shirt up to show her bare breasts: the ball crossed the boundary. The crowd cheered both the game of cricket and at the topless show. I felt very bad. I did not contribute any runs to my team's total; I gave away sixteen runs in my first over and now I failed to save a boundary which I should have done quite easily. I asked the captain if I could do fielding at long off, away from this distracting crowd especially away from this girl, and was moved to the new position.

The opposing team began to lose wickets. There were a couple of run outs due to misunderstandings between the batsmen and then their middle order batting suddenly collapsed unexpectedly. The match had suddenly become a real cliff-hanger.

It was the last ball of the match and three runs were required for the opposing team to win the match. Three possible outcomes of the match were: score three runs to win; two runs to equalise, we win the match by not allowing more than a run. The person facing the last ball was a well-known slogger of the ball. He looked around like a hawk to see gaps in the fielding area. The last ball was bowled and the batsman swung his bat with full might. The ball ballooned up in the air towards me. I could hear the bowler shouting. 'Catch it, catch it.' I kept my eyes on the ball, came underneath it and caught the ball, which popped out of my hands, but I quickly bent down and scooped it up, inches above the ground. The whole cricket ground erupted, we had won the match. I threw the ball upwards in sheer delight and the next moment I found a naked girl wrapping her arms around my neck, planting a massive kiss on my cheek.

She said, 'you have big hands, baby, I'd love them all over my body.'

I could feel her breasts tightly pressed against my chest and her deep breath all over my face. Before I could make any attempt to free myself from her, she ran away. She was the same girl who had earlier distracted me. The girl was chased by two grounds men; one of them was holding a white table cloth which he had hurriedly removed from the trophy table. I ran towards the bowler to congratulate him over his wicket, the whole team enjoyed the victory amplified by this streak show.

I know Sajid had played a match at the same ground three days ago, though, I was not aware of his post-match activities.

The girl came out of the room – this time fully dressed. She had a small back pack slung on her one shoulder and gave Sajid a very angry look. She said, 'fuck you.'

'Can't wait for that, see you soon sweetie,' Sajid said to the girl and looked at me. 'Let's go inside and have a chat.' I reluctantly followed Sajid.

There was a smell of stale breath and a kind of mashed potatoes in the room. I felt nauseated. A crumpled tissue was lying on the unmade bed. Sajid followed my gaze and quickly pulled a tissue from the box and wrapped the tissue lying on the bed in it and threw it into the basket and went straight to the wash basin to wash his hands.

'Ali, if you ever want to pull a bird, please feel free to bring her here,' Sajid said. 'I'll provide you with privacy and protection.' He stressed the word 'protection'. 'Our hostel has no restrictions on bringing in girls and in fact at night time this place resembles Bangkok.'

He was not ashamed or even faintly embarrassed.

'Thanks for the offer.' I said. The air in the room was suffocating me and my heart was still racing. 'Would you allow the same sexual freedom to your own sister?'

Sajid's face turned fiery-red like a pomegranate with anger. 'No, never. How dare you say this? If someone else had said this, I would have smashed his face. You know in our culture boys are different from girls.'

'Don't you think this is discrimination? There should be equivalence and a level playing field,' I said, ignoring his angry face. 'We look at men through a different lens and women with another?'

'Oh, you shut up, don't tell me this *Gora* philosophy of equality. You don't have a sister-that is why you are talking all this rubbish.'

'It's not about having a sister, it's about how we think, how we approach this issue so differently,' I said.

'Perhaps you should be going now.' Sajid said, looking really annoyed.

'Yeah, I better be going now, I'm getting late for the nets.'

Sajid still looked wounded with my earlier remark and said, 'you consider yourself a walking paragon of religion. I don't think you are a good Muslim either, I've never seen you saying *Namaz*, not even Friday prayers.'

This was a totally unexpected comment and I knew it was meant to incite me but I was not going to lose my cool that easily. 'Listen, Sajid. First of all, saying prayers or not is an exclusive matter between me and my God. Second, God is never going to question you about my prayers. Maybe one day God will give me *taufeeq* and I'll start offering my prayers, who knows?'

Sajid smirked, looked a bit embarrassed and said, 'I'm sorry but Ali, please don't tell this to anyone, please.'

'I won't, I promise.'

It echoed in me what Dad once said to me. 'The essence of all religious teaching is that you should not do anything which could be a source of embarrassment to you in future.'

I felt ashamed and guilty. I had also committed a misdemeanour by looking at a naked girl. I should not have raised my gaze or have looked away, I could have done that but why didn't I? Was this deliberate or was I satisfying some hidden innate curiosity? It was certainly a wrongdoing, a physical transgression may be bigger than a visual one but it is still a transgression.

It's a pressure cooker situation — open culture, quadraphonic blasts of pornography in the media, religious expectation of chastity before marriage, availability of chances to satisfy physiological urges and no wonder sometimes the cooker blows off, I thought as I walked to the cricket ground.

CHAPTER 6

I checked the flight arrival on my iPhone, and was surprised that it was on time, so far it had been my experience that all flights coming from Pakistan were delayed by at least two hours.

'Mum, I'm going to Heathrow to meet Mr Nazir. He's arriving in fifteen minutes.'

'Are you taking the car?' Mum inquired, as she walked down the stairs.

'No, I'm gonna catch the tube, and I'm hoping to have an ambulance ride with Mr Nazir on the way back to the hospital.' I said, 'I've always wondered what it'd be like to go in an ambulance.'

'Be very respectful towards him.'

'Are you trying to say I'm generally not?'

'No, you always are, but I'm just reminding you what your Dad said. He's a very sensitive person.'

'Yeah, yeah, yeah… I remember.'

It took me three-quarters of an hour to reach Heathrow. The flight had landed but no passengers had begun to come out. The waiting area at the airport was swarming with people, mainly Asian, who had come to pick up their friends and relatives. In Asian culture, the high respect of a guest or relative is shown by the number of people who come to receive them at the airport: the higher the number the more respected the guest – at least this is how it was portrayed. Perhaps, the other reason could be that Asians did not wish to miss out on any opportunity for an outing, even if it was to an airport.

The young girls who had come to the airport to meet their husbands or relatives looked animated with face make-up, henna dyed palms and dazzling new dresses, which they could have worn for their own or any other wedding. I found it amazing that Asian women liked to display their gold jewellery whenever they went out: heavy, multi-layered necklaces, bangles from wrists to elbows. It seemed that the men who accompanied these women cared less how they dressed. The majority of them wore *Shalwar Kamiz*, and talked to each other in loud voices. Urdu, English, Punjabi voices merged: I could overhear their conversation but could not understand. There was an ambience of celebration and of happiness. Everyone wanted to be near the metal railing, which marked the boundary of the waiting area and arrivals, so that they could catch a glimpse of the arrival of their loved ones, before anybody else. I thought there was an element of subtle competition in this. There were the usual hugs, kisses, tears and screams of re-union, all adding to the emotive atmosphere.

Soon the passengers began to arrive; they were pushing luggage trolleys with their stacked suitcases and carton boxes. In some cases, the passengers were completely hidden behind their towering luggage and it appeared as if the trolleys were being pushed by some invisible supernatural force.

Dead-eyed drivers, who looked bored to death, held placards with passenger and hotel names. I saw a paramedic holding a board on which it was written with a black marker, 'Mr Nazir - Bromwell Hospital'. The paramedic was wearing a high visibility jacket with green and yellow stripes. He was tall and broad like a rugby player; he was hugging the stick under his left arm on which the placard was attached. He was looking at the arriving passengers and carelessly consuming crisps, some of which did not make it to his mouth but fell on the floor.

'I've also come to meet Mr Nazir.' I said to the paramedic.

'Thank God, now I don't have to hold up this banner.' He brought the placard down and held it between his legs. 'Is he related to you?' he said with a smile.

'Nope, I've never met him. I don't know what he looks like, so you better keep holding that banner up mate.'

'Okay, okay, it's not a problem. Tell you what, we'll be here for a long time I suspect. Wheel chairs usually are fast-tracked through immigration but still they come out last and by the way my name is Rob.'

'Well, Rob,' I said. 'We'll have to wait and see…'

What would Mr Nazir look like? I imagined: a very frail, exhausted, ill-looking person wearing *Shalwar Kamiz*, being pushed in a wheelchair.

'What time do you finish today?' I asked Rob just for the sake of conversation.

'As soon as I drop Mr Nazir off at the hospital,' he said with a wide smile, exhibiting his yellow stained teeth.

'I'll go and check that book shop,' I said, pointing.

'That's fine. I'll give you a shout if he arrives early. I doubt if he will.'

The bookshop was full of people browsing. A teenage boy with long braided hair looked deeply engrossed in a motor racing magazine. A tall, middle-aged man, who had a fence of pens in the front breast pocket of his jacket, was hastily leafing through a magazine and at the same time looking around from the corners of his eyes. I suspected he was holding the magazine from an empty space on the top shelf. I walked to the 'fiction' part of the shop. There were quite a few books on a 'buy one get one free' basis on sale in the section. I smiled, as I remembered George once making a cynical comment in his usual cutting Scottish accent that the unique feature of such deals was that for the price of one, you ended up with two rubbish books. My thoughts were interrupted as I heard someone talking to me. I turned around and saw a lady who did not appear particularly old but was talking to herself whilst reading a newspaper. Later on I realised she was reading the horoscope to herself. Tabloids and broad sheet newspapers seemed to have lost their crispness after a day of idle browsing and looked second hand. I wondered who would like to purchase a newspaper at this time of the evening when all the news had gone stale and when a fresh newspaper was due in a couple of hours. As I came out of the shop I noted that all the customers who were standing in the queue to pay the cashier had either purchased a chocolate bar, a packet of crisps or a bottle of water. No one had bought a book or a newspaper.

I walked back to Rob who had seen me approaching him. 'They are coming thick and fast now. I hope we won't be long here.' He was still eating crisps.

A person who was wearing a steel grey three piece suit, red necktie and sensible shiny shoes looked around and then headed towards Rob. There were no signs of tiredness on his face. He was pulling on a medium-sized trolley suitcase.

'I am Nazir,' he said with a smile.

Rob and I looked at each other, surprised.

'Sorry, can I just confirm your name and the address where you are going to,' Rob said as if he had a stammer.

'Yes, sure,' Mr Nazir put his hand in his jacket's breast pocket and brought out a folded piece of paper which he handed over to Rob.

Rob carefully read the paper and said, 'that's absolutely fine. I've come to take you to the hospital and this gentleman is here to receive you as well.'

'*Assalam-o-elakum*, I am Dr Taj's son, Ali. Dad is out of the country and he asked me to meet you at the airport. I hope you had a good flight,' I said while shaking hands with him.

'Thank you very much; I am most delighted to meet you. I knew your Dad well before you were born, and yeah, the flight was OK.' It looked as if he always had a smile on his face.

Mr Nazir seemed to be in his early sixties. He was of medium height with a fair complexion.

'Would you be alright walking to the parking area? It's about 5 to 10 minutes' walk from here,' Rob asked Mr Nazir hesitantly, indirectly suggesting a wheelchair.

'No, I could easily walk for 10 minutes but not very fast,' Mr Nazir said with his usual smile.

'Would it be okay if I come with you to the hospital?' I asked Rob.

'No, not a problem, jus' jump in.'

'This is my office,' Rob said pleasantly as he opened the rear door of the ambulance.

The inside of the ambulance was like a hospital accident and emergency room. There were ECG monitors, defibrillators, oxygen cylinders, face masks and stashes of bandages. Every nook and cranny of the ambulance had been fully utilised. There was a stretcher and a bench which could easily accommodate a family of four.

Rob helped Mr Nazir to climb into the ambulance and fastened his seat belt.

'This is my first time inside an ambulance,' I said to Mr Nazir as I sat opposite him.

'Mine is not. It's becoming a usual mode of transport for me,' Mr Nazir said in a sombre voice. 'Thanks be to God it could have been worse.'

Mr Nazir's face was neither oval nor round. He had a wide forehead with deep horizontal wrinkles on it like birds flying in a painting. He had bushy, black eyebrows which were hanging over onto his eyelids. His eyes were clear, deep and penetrating and not only seemed to look at you but seemed to know your thoughts.

'The weather has been really nice here recently. I hope you have a good stay over here.'

'I hope so as well,' he said quietly.

He had thick grey hair, which was combed backwards. He showed no sign of balding. His nose was prominent with a brownish mole near the tip. He had conspicuous cheekbones. His ears looked a bit curved to the front with big earlobes. He was clean-shaven. I think he had a very neat personality. I felt in him a keen and discerning intelligence. I must say I liked him. I wanted to talk to him but he was very quiet and was gazing at the floor of the ambulance, he seemed immersed in deep thoughts and I decided not to disturb him.

The ambulance moved quickly on the roads, although no blue lights or sirens were on but as we approached, the traffic parted giving us way. We reached the hospital more quickly than I had imagined.

The hospital was located bang in the centre of London. The watchful eyes of two sand-coloured lion statues guarded the entrance to the hospital. The front courtyard was cobblestoned, framed by a cement footpath.

Rob swiftly jumped out to open the rear door. He helped Mr Nazir to alight and carried his suitcase. The glass double doors led to a wooden-floored reception area. Unlike, an NHS hospital, the reception was like that of a five star hotel, very bright and welcoming. The waiting area had olive green leather sofas. A bouquet of fresh white lilies was displayed in a tall crystal vase on a polished reception desk. A large, railway station style clock was mounted on the wall. The receptionist greeted us with a warm smile on her face. After the usual exchange of niceties, a form was given to Mr Nazir to fill in.

'We have all your details, we just need the contact details of your next of kin.' The receptionist said very politely.

Mr Nazir looked at me and asked, 'is it okay if I ask you to give your phone number and address?'

'That is perfectly alright,' and I wrote my details on the form.

'It's a big responsibility on your shoulders,to be the next of kin to an un-well old man like me,' he said light heartedly, and we all smiled.

'I will inform your consultant that you are here. Should I ask him to see you in an hour?' the receptionist asked Mr Nazir very politely.

'Yes, that would be perfect.'

'The porter will take your luggage and show you to your room.'

I thought that I should ask his permission to go. 'Mr Nazir, if you don't want me for anything I could leave now. Should I come to see you tomorrow?' I asked.

'Thanks for coming you may go now. It would be a pleasure to see you again tomorrow. Bye and take care.'

'Bye.'

CHAPTER 7

It was not too difficult to find Mr Nazir's room at the hospital. I knocked at his door gently.

'Please enter.'

The door opened with a soft squeak. Mr Nazir's back was facing the door; he was sitting in his high-backed arm chair. He made no effort to see who had entered the room and continued staring at the window. The curtains were fully open.

'Assalam-o-eleakum, it's me, Ali. I hope I haven't disturbed you.'

'No, not at all, you are most welcome.' He looked at me and said with a kind smile, 'Please take a seat.' His breath had a fruity odour.

I took a seat in front of him. It was quite a decent-sized room. His bed and over-table were to the left of the oxygen ducts. It seemed his bed was freshly made. The seating area in the room was on the right, which comprised his chair, a coffee table and an L-shaped sofa.

'Mum sends her regards. She'd like to invite you over for a meal at our home, whenever you feel better,' I said.

'It's very kind of her. I'm totally off food these days. I'm living only on fruit juices. Once I get a bit better I'll definitely come for food.'

It was quite a strange habit of his that after an initial gaze he would not make any eye contact but fix his gaze on the floor.

'How are you today?'

'As usual, not bad.'

'How did your initial consultation go?'

'Quite good,' he said quietly. 'Despite all hazards and ailments life cannot end before its appointed hour, and regardless of all precautions and medical surveillance it will not extend beyond its appointed hour.' His voice lacked emotions.

'I hope you get well soon,' I said. 'Dad told me quite a lot of good things about you.'

'Yes, it's very kind of him.'

'Yes, he also told me that you were very good at maths.'

'I always love to play with numbers.' A glint appeared in his eyes as he looked at me, raising his gaze from the floor. I think he liked this topic of conversation.

His answers to my questions were too short and just to the point. I was not sure whether he did not wish me to carry on with the conversation or whether this was his usual style of talking. I liked him. I wanted to talk to him and I thought I should make another attempt at conversation.

'Some people regard maths as a very dry subject. In school I used not to hate it but it was definitely not one of my favourite subjects,' I said.

'Some people may even have a phobia of numbers which is generally known as arithmophobia.'

'Really, I didn't know any such phobia existed.'

'Oh, yes, this phobia is not uncommon among students, who don't do well in their maths exams,' he said smilingly and cleared his throat. 'Maths is the most accurate of all the sciences. Galileo rightly said that mathematics is the language in which God has written the universe and if you want to understand His creation you ought to know maths.'

'True, absolutely right,' I said and was relieved that he had spoken a full sentence. 'Dad also told me that you had a very good direction sense.'

'I still have. We have become the slaves of these navigation systems and very faithfully and mindlessly follow them. I was reading in a newspaper that some accidents happen just because of these navigation systems. Someone blindly followed the system and did not read the road warning sign of a broken bridge and unsurprisingly ended up in the river.'

I could see that he was getting into a chatty mode. He was softly jiggling his keys during his conversation.

'Dad also told me that you hold some discussion forums at your home. If you don't mind, can I ask you what the topics of these discussions are?' I said and made sure to ask the question as politely as possible so that he did not get annoyed.

'Every human living on this earth has got some questions in their minds, some cobwebs in their ideas and some cobwebs could be so thick that they create deep dark alleys in their minds, and this creates an unease, a conflict in our lives. The whole idea of these forums is to spring-clean the cobwebs, to let the light come through, to make one's life easy. There is no set pattern of topics for these forums; we kick start with any questions and discussion flows.'

'So every person has to bring a question?' I said. 'Does it not put a person at a disadvantage who is too shy to ask a question?'

'You are absolutely right and sometimes this also happens that a question hides inside one's mind like a thief when confronted with an answer,' he said with a smile.

There was a faint knock at the door.

I went up to the door to open it and a nurse entered with a hint of a smile on her face. 'Blood pressure checking time.'

'Thanks,' Mr Nazir said. He slowly stood up, took off his jacket and rolled up the sleeve of his left arm. There was barely any muscle mass. A white plaster with cotton wool was attached to the inside of his elbow.

'Should I take it off?' the nurse said pointing towards the plaster.

'Yes please,' he said.

She peeled the edge of the plaster with her nail and rolled it on the cotton wool before discarding it in the bin. There was a purple, circular bruise in his elbow pit. The rope-like veins in his arm became more prominent as the automatic machine inflated the blood pressure cuff. The nurse checked his temperature with an ear thermometer.

'Everything is fine as it should be. I'll see you again in four hours,' the nurse said and before she could leave she turned around and added. 'We apologise again that due to health and safety reasons we could not allow bouquets of flowers in your room. They were really beautiful flowers, the hospital chaplain is very grateful to you for donating them to the chapel.'

'It's not a problem,' he said. 'I hope they help to uplift someone's mood, make someone's day.'

'I'm sure they would,' the nurse said.

'Please could you let the receptionist know that from now onwards all the flowers which are sent to me should be directed to the chapel and I hope the chaplain won't have any objection to this?'

'No problem Sir. I'll get it sorted for you,' the nurse said.

'Thanks.'

I was quite curious to know how he learnt mysticism at the mausoleum of Ali Hejwari but then I thought that perhaps it was not appropriate to ask about such things at our first one-to-one meeting. I did not wish to upset him.

'What are you thinking, Ali?' He said without looking at me. A shiver went down my spine. Could he read my mind even without looking at me?

'No, nothing,' I lied without thinking.

'There is no point in hiding a question, but we will talk about it some other day.'

My heart was racing. 'Can you read my mind?' I said and hoped that this question did not irritate him.

'Every living creature is a big, jumbo transmitter of waves and we all are equipped with a receiver to catch these waves but in the majority of us it remains unturned, unutilised but someone's kind attention helped me to tune in my own receiver.' His bunch of keys was making a soft jiggling noise.

'Who was this "someone"? I couldn't resist asking.

'We'll talk about this some other day,' he said quite seriously. 'I am feeling tired now, I think you should leave now. Could you please help me into the bed?'

'Yeah, sure,' I said.

He got up and held onto my hand tenaciously. His hand was cold and it felt as if I was clutching the dried branch of a tree.

He lay on the bed with his eyes closed and said, 'bye, Ali, we'll meet next weekend. Bye for now.'

'Bye, Mr Nazir, I'll see you next week.' I slowly walked out of his room.

On my God, what was that? I said to myself as I walked towards home. Dad was absolutely right about him, he was an extraordinary person. The way he looked, the way he talked and what he talked about was mind blowing. I needed to meet him again.

CHAPTER 8

'It's quarter past eleven,' Mum said, as she irately opened my bedroom door. 'What time do you have to go to the hospital today? Were you watching movies all night?' I half opened my eyes to look at her, but shut them again as she opened the curtains and bright daylight flooded the room.

'Mum….. why'd ya always do this……how many times do I have to tell you to knock on the door before you come in.' I was clenching my fists so hard underneath the duvet that my nail beds began to ache.

'…. And this sunlight…. it really hurts,' I said.

'I will hurt you even more, what time do you have to go?'

'I'm meeting HR to fill in my paperwork for the work experience today,' I said. 'I'll go there at half one.'

'You better get up now,' she said and looked around at my room. 'I want this tidied up before you go. I'm tired of cleaning your room every day. When will you grow up?'

I pushed the duvet aside, jumped out of bed and gave her a big hug. Mum was tall and slim like dad; I looked into her dark-brown eyes and said, 'It's not a mess.... This way I know where everything is.' Mum gave a sigh and looked at me with a shake of her head. 'Ok... ok.... I'll tidy it up, I promise,' I said.

She pushed me off her and said, 'Your Dad has left some letters on the console which he needs posted today. Could you post them for him?'

'Sure,' I said pointing to a box laying on my study table. 'I have to post this as well.'

'What is in it?'

'My old CDs and DVDs. I'm selling these to raise some cash to buy a new cricket bat.' I looked at her closely but Mum shook her head again, she didn't look impressed.

I quickly slipped into my en-suite bathroom.

* * * * *

It was a hazy, warm day. I noticed Carr lazily riding his bike down the road as I walked on the footpath. Carr lived a few houses down our road. He was the youngest member of the family and had three elder sisters. I had never seen his dad but I knew that his mother was a banker in the city. Both Carr and I were in the same sixth form. He was incredibly intelligent, and was in the top set for all his subjects. Carr had bright copper hair, pale, grey-blue eyes and freckled cheeks. He had this great ability to ignore people if someone tried to call him 'redhead' or 'ginger ninja', and he never lost his temper.

'Going to the post office are we?' Carr said looking at the letters and the parcel in my hand. 'I'll cycle with you.'

'Sure.'

'Have you seen anyone from school?'

'No, not really, my only contact with them is through my phone.'

'Not even any gigging with your guitarist friend?'

'Only twice a couple of weeks ago. Not much time, man. I've been back and forth to the hospital to complete paper work to start work experience at the hospital.'

'Alright...... what'll you be doing there?'

'I'll work as a porter.'

'Really, that would be fun. What will you have to do there? Will you have to take patients to the operating theatres?'

'Yes, maybe sometimes. Mainly I will be taking urgent blood samples from wards to the lab and get case notes from the medical records. Yeah, it will be busy, but I hope it's good fun. Why do you ask?'

'Well, you might have to take me to theatres in exactly two weeks' time. I'm having an operation on my nose for this nose-bleed problem, it's happening too often now. Do you remember Miss Robin,' he said with a meaningful smile on his face.

It took me back two years. 'Who could ever forget her?' I said.

It was a boy's only history class. We all loved to attend it not for the love of the subject but for the looks of our teacher. Her name was Miss Lynette Robin. She had joined the school only a couple of weeks before. Miss Robin was in her mid-twenties and was pretty like a delicately carved marble statue, smooth and full. It was not only her looks but also her mannerisms that 'wounded' us all. The way she talked, the way she walked, the way she raised her glance: it was all lethal. Not surprisingly, the whole boys section had a huge communal crush on her.

One day, when all of us were deeply absorbed admiring the beauty of Miss Robin and pretended to be attentive to her by a pin drop silence in the room, all of a sudden Carr had had a couple of sneezes after which he loudly said 'excuse me' and as expected someone said 'excused.' Then we heard Carr saying, 'Miss, I'm bleeding.' Carr walked to the front of the class. His shirt was soaking wet with blood. He was holding his nose between his thumb and index finger, blood still dribbling from his nose like an ill-shut tap. Miss Robin looked at Carr, a wave of fear appeared in her eyes and her face turned pale. She tried to clutch the table in front of her and we all knew that she was going to faint. Almost everyone dashed to catch her but only four of us including myself were successful in holding her before she could fall to the floor. The whole class gathered around Miss Robin, completely ignoring Carr and his bleeding.

'Put her into the recovery position,' Matthew said.

'How do you do that,' someone asked.

'I don't know,' Matthew replied shrugging his shoulders.

'That's how you place someone in the recovery position,' I said turning her over onto her side.

Peter and Trevor left the room to inform the head teacher but as it turned out later only Peter reached the office. Tony and Andrew looked at each other and skidded off to the toilets to smoke. The rest made suggestions of all sorts, including sprinkling cold water onto her face, to commence CPR or to perform mouth-to-mouth resuscitation and to ring 999. It seemed my knowledge of the recovery position had impressed everyone and my suggestion of elevating her legs in the air to improve circulation was met with some sniggers and winks but was immediately acted upon.

Miss Robin was gently placed on the floor. She was breathing heavily but was still unconscious. Her palms were slippery due to profuse sweating. We lifted her legs up in the air. Before this, I had never realised how difficult it was to hold up a comatose person's legs. Her slim legs felt as heavy as logs. Her skirt had folded on to her tummy. Her under garment became visible through her skin coloured tights. To my great disappointment, I developed a cramp in my hand and could no longer hold the leg, I asked someone behind me to take over from me. There was an obvious struggle to get the honours of holding her legs. The rugby team captain of our class stepped forward and stopped everyone by a gesture of his hand and said loudly, 'Back-off, everyone, back-off, just place her legs over my shoulders,' and he sat between her legs.

This is exactly the time when the head teacher came running to the class and saw a student sitting on the floor with Miss Robin's legs on his shoulders. Miss Robin soon gained consciousness with this manoeuvre but could not overcome her embarrassment of the whole situation. She was allowed home and given time off from work. But she never came back from her sick leave and handed in her resignation.

'How's cricket, mate?' Carr said, slowly peddling his bike to keep pace with me.

'The season has just started. Due to rain, we're only playing indoors,' I said. Carr was only an arm-chair cricketer and would watch every single game on TV.

'I'm sure you already know that the South African's will be here this summer,' Carr said. 'Are you gonna go see any games? Your favourite, Dale Steyn will be here, strapped in all sorts of bandages like a mummy,' he said laughing. 'I also like him. I love the aggression of a hawk in his eyes when he runs to bowl.'

'No, actually, I didn't know that the Proteas were coming. I would love to see Steyn in action. I'll ask our coach if I can get hold of some tickets. Would you like to come?' I said.

'That would be awesome.'

We reached the post-office. A girl who was riding a bike whizzed past me. She dismounted and left her bike by the disabled ramp at the post-office. As I passed her, she blew a large bubble gum balloon and deliberately popped it. I looked over my shoulder and saw Carr witnessing this. The girl, who was white, was probably in her early twenties. She had curly hair and one lock had strayed down on her forehead shaped like a fishing hook. She wore large, hooped earrings, which touched her shoulders. I didn't like this girl for two reasons: for blowing bubble gum which had always reminded me of big, yellow, slimy frogs, emerging out of nowhere during the rainy season in Pakistan, sitting on their hind legs and blowing their vocal sac during croaking – just like bubble gums. Second, I don't know but I never liked the looks of large earrings for some strange reason.

'It shouldn't take very long, will you wait for me here?' I asked Carr.

'Yeah, sure, I'll hang around.'

I was waiting for my turn in the queue. The girl was ahead of me. I could see through the window, Carr was stooping over this girl's bike.

I came out of the post-office, maybe a minute after the girl. The girl sat on her bicycle and then looked at the rear tyre, which was flat. The girl angrily walked to Carr and said, 'Why did you take the air out of my tyre?'

'I felt the atmospheric air pressure was a bit low so I corrected it from your tyre by letting air out,' Carr said seriously by taking a deep breath.

'Ha, ha …very funny. Why did you not take air out of your tyres?' she said.

'Oh, I'm so sorry. It never occurred to me,' Carr said innocently.

'Now, you go and blow up my tyres.'

'Nah....I don't wanna do that,' Carr said and commenced peddling his bike but the girl leapt like a lion and pretended to punch him in the face. I'm pretty sure, she never touched him but as always, Carr who seldom needed an excuse to have a nose-bleed, began to have one. He sat on the ground, elevating his head and looking towards the sky, pinching his nose.

'Oh, I'm so, so sorry. I didn't mean to hurt you. Did I hit you? Is this painful? Should I call an ambulance for you?' she said panicking, sitting beside him. She really thought that she had hit him and looked frightened.

'Oh yes, it hurts a lot,' Carr said, sounding different and I knew in my heart, absolutely sure that he was faking it. 'If it doesn't settle soon, you should call an ambulance.'

Within minutes, the bleeding had stopped. Carr looked at the girl who helped him to get up and he slowly walked towards his bike.

'Do you want me to fill your ....' Carr deliberately hung his sentence.

'No, no, I'll go myself.'

'Can I see you this evening?' Carr said to the girl with a grin on his face.

'If you really wanna,' she said and blushed.

'I'll come to your house at six.'

'Sure.'

The girl began to walk with the bike in the direction she came from.

'Do you know her and where she lives?' I asked Carr.

'Of course, I do mate. She is Lucy. I've been after her for so many days. If you wanna pull a bird, you got to chase her with your mind and soul, persistence is the key here,' Carr said chirpily.

'And have a nose-bleed,' I added.

'Yeah, I have that added advantage, every little helps.'

'But that's gaining sympathy, nothing else.'

'That's how you start, mate. You've got to do all sorts of things, pull every single trick from your hat and that's exactly what you're lacking. I've been with over two dozen girls and how many have you been with?'

'None and I don't care either. Also I don't wear any hats,' I said quietly.

'No need to get angry, man. Just chill and listen to me. Mother Nature hasn't helped you either; you haven't got any elder sister that's why you don't know how to relate with girls,' Carr said, habitually pinching his nose and paddling his bike away.

I looked at my wristwatch; there was still an hour and a bit left to get to the hospital. I thought it would be best if I went home first, had something to eat and then went to the hospital. I began to walk towards home. The magical spell of sunny English summer had turned the bare, leafless boughs of tall trees on each side of our road to emerald mantles. The sun began to shine cheerfully in the sky and the air was noticeably warmer which made the walk more enjoyable.

'A beautiful day,' said a middle aged lady, pulling on the lead of her little dog that seemed extremely interested in sniffing the ankles of all passers-by.

'Yeah, very nice,' I said, still in my thoughts. Was Carr right in making those remarks about me? Maybe he has had that many girlfriends or who knows he maybe just bluffing. What does he regard himself as, a perfect connoisseur of friendship with girls? Was he being brutally truthful or wanting me to be jealous of him?

'Lovely morning,' an old man smoking a pipe said, producing spiralling grey smoke. 'Have a good day.'

'Yeah,' I murmured and thought what's wrong with people today? I knew very well how the day was. I was not blind or devoid of visual senses. I'd like to have the sort of day I want. I didn't need any suggestions, you go yourself and have a good day and leave me well alone.

Why was I so snappy? I asked myself. I didn't think having a sister or sisters would have made any huge difference to my relationship with other girls. I'm the way I am. But still I felt an undercurrent of anger swirling inside me, choking me slowly. Had I unknowingly attached Carr's comments to my conscience like spiky, thorny burrs get attached to sheep's wool, unintentionally during grazing? Why had I taken Carr's remarks so seriously? I need to park my anger, shake those burrs off and look and think clearly.

I was almost home. I admired the graceful front of our house from a distance. We had always felt that our home was a bunch of good luck thrown our way. As far as I remembered, we had always lived here. It was a corner house off the main road, tucked behind some dense Yew trees. Dad once told me that Yew has medicinal usage and a very useful chemotherapeutic agent is derived from its bark to treat breast and some other cancers.

I looked upwards and saw a jet flying, appearing like a dot in the background of azure sky, leaving a long trail of white vapours. Unlike some of our relatives living in Hounslow, we had never experienced any aircraft noise pollution. We all loved the house and the area. It was too conveniently located for Dad's hospital, which was only three and half miles away. Despite London's rush-hour traffic, he had been never late to work or to attend an emergency call. Also to the credit of dad's abilities, he had discovered several short-cuts to and from the hospital like a road-savvy taxi driver.

The house was usually quiet for that time of the day. It seemed Mum had gone out and Bari Ammi was still upstairs, perhaps doing her *Tasbih*. I went to the kitchen, which was now neat and tidy after the breakfast activity. The dishwasher was making a soft whirring noise. I smiled as I looked at the dinner table – Mum had made a sandwich for me. How did she know that I would come back? I thought obviously maternal instincts. I picked the sandwich up, grabbed a can of Coke from the fridge and was soon sitting in front of the TV in the living room. I had almost forgotten what had happened in the morning as I was able to flick to a channel where a live cricket match was showing.

CHAPTER 9

I came to meet Sajid at his hostel room and saw him coming out with a person whom I had never seen or met before, he was wearing a black three piece suit. He was rather short in stature, slim built and bore a trifling moustache. There was a pleasant smile on Sajid's face when he saw me walking towards him and he said, 'Excellent timing, Ali. Let me introduce you to Mr Omar, he has recently been appointed as a lecturer in history at our uni and he just gave an excellent talk about the world a decade after 9/11. Mr Omar, this is my best friend, Ali. He is awaiting admission to medical school. The medical profession runs in their family. His father is an eminent doctor here.'

Omar warmly shook hands with me. I could feel his piercing gaze on me. 'Nice to meet you Ali. It seems you missed the talk. Never mind, we're going to have some exchange of views, question and answer sessions in the seminar room. I hope you will be able to join us,' Omar said and looked at his wrist watch. 'Oh, it's nearly time to start the discussion forum. We have to go now. Ali, are you going to join us?'

'Yes, I could,' I said.

Sajid and Omar led the way to the seminar room after walking through beehives of corridors and opening several doors. The seminar room was average-sized and its chairs were arranged in a semi-circle. I thought the seating arrangement was peculiar, showing an extreme degree of inefficient utilisation of space. The white-board on the wall displayed the computer projection of the title of the talk in white font against a blue background. All seats were occupied and there was a buzz in the air. There were three entrances to the room. I took a seat near one of the doors from where I could see the whole of the crowd and also in case the discussion got boring I could escape unnoticed.

'Are these all history students?' I asked the person sitting next to me.

'No, no. It's an open invitation meeting, open to anyone interested in the topic.'

There were more than fifty people in the room. The majority of attendees appeared to me as university students from Middle-Eastern countries and some from Nigeria or Somalia. There were only two girls in the whole audience; one was wearing a black and the other a red *hijab* with glittering embroidery. A couple of people in the audience looked old enough not to be students.

Omar walked slowly to the centre of the circle. I could feel something strange, something very odd about Omar. The permanent smile on his face appeared hollow tome. He was looking at people with his intense gaze as if he was trying to read their minds, perhaps checking their loyalties.

There was absolute confusion in the room but one thing was quite clear: emotions were running sky high.

'So what do you think, more than ten years after 9/11? Has the world changed?' Omar asked.

'It's a dead question, what's the point in asking?' around-faced boy wearing golden frame spectacles, sitting in the front row replied rather harshly.

'I take your point,' Omar said appearing a little embarrassed by the response. 'Let me put it in a different way, is the world a safer place now?'

'No, no, certainly not,' the girl in the black hijab said and waved her right hand in the air and continued, 'whose life is adversely affected after 9/11? Not an American's life, they are still trudging around carelessly, without any fear in their homeland. It's the life of people in Baghdad, Afghanistan and Pakistan that is affected. They are housebound with fear of explosions. They are not even safe in their places of worship. These are the nations who have borne the brunt of 9/11, not the Americans. The world has become a more dangerous place after 9/11.' I was impressed with the confidence and eloquence with which she said that.

A person whose scalp was glistening as if it had been oiled with mustard oil, with a short snow-white beard and shaved moustache had his arm up in the air to seek permission to ask a question.

'Yes, you Sir,' Omar pointed at him like a traffic policeman.

'Did the Americans ever ask themselves the question: why did 9/11 happen to them?' There was a sardonic edge to his voice.

'Was it a reaction of hatred towards America?' someone replied with a question from the back row.

'Muslims had long tolerated the injustice by Americans in Palestine, Beirut, Burma,' someone's talking was cut off.

'There has been a lot said and heard that a terrorist or suicide bomber from someone's point of view could well be a freedom fighter from another.' This comment came from the other end of the room.

'This concept of killing yourself and other people for your own cause, is a fairly new idea. It's a noble way to give your life. It is worthy of praise not to be looked down upon,' the boy sitting next to me said in his Nigerian accent.

'No, it is not.' Omar raised his right hand to quieten the crowd and said, 'Oppressed fighting against the oppressor has always done this. Samson was probably the first person to act as a suicide killer in the history of mankind some 1200 years before the birth of Jesus Christ. I am sure you are all aware that he had some supernatural powers and he brought down the whole place by pulling down the pillars which were supporting the arena, killing himself and some other 3000 people, thus wiping out the whole leadership and administration of that time.'

'That's interesting information.'

There was absolute mayhem after this. Questions were thrown at and answered by anyone. Omar made no effort to control individuals and I felt that was the way he wanted to conduct the session.

'I still think 9/11 was an inside job.'

'No, no, conspiracy theories are long dead and buried.'

'If it was not an inside job why was an enquiry not set up? It's been 10 years.'

'How can amateur pilots crash planes into buildings? They learnt flying on simulators and light aircraft,' the bald person said menacingly.

'My uncle is a jumbo jet pilot,' a slim boy who had the looks of Jesus Christ with golden brown hair, beard and moustache stood up and seemed to be addressing everyone by looking around. 'He says it is quite possible to learn flying on modern simulators and it is also possible to crash planes with pinpoint accuracy with the modern navigation systems.'

'Your uncle is a liar. Why do light aircraft pilots need hundreds and thousands of hours of flying experience before they are allowed to fly jumbo jets? Your uncle is lying, probably because he is an American agent as well.' I could not see who said this but there was an element of delirium in this voice.

'Yes, yes, shame on American agents.' A middle-aged person wearing a shining black *jellaba*s tood up on the chair and danced with both hands in the air. The bald person who was sitting next to him said something in Arabic, pulling his *jellaba*. But this person would not stop and continued. 'America bombed Iraq and could not find weapons of mass destruction. They bombed thousands of innocent Afghanis to kill one person, who was not even found where he was supposed to be found. To kill a flea you do not burn the whole of the carpet.'

'Americans claimed that they didn't kill any innocent women and children but they did,' the girl in the red *hijab* said.

'Can I make a point here? Why do they say that they didn't kill any women and children? Is it legitimate to kill men? I'm sorry but this is reverse-sexism,' the round-faced boy said with a smile.

There was a huge roar of laughter and I thought the ceiling might come down.

'America is a liar. Americans are the biggest terrorists. Shame on Americans. Go to hell, Americans; go to hell face-first Americans.' The person standing on the chair would not sit down.

What a bunch of nutters, I thought. Omar didn't seem to me to have done a good job as a facilitator of the session or maybe that's the way he wanted to run it.

'No, no, America had to do this. The attack on twin-towers was an attack on their world supremacy, their authority. They had to prove that they are the supreme power of the world. They had to show their military muscles and might to the whole world and quite cleverly they chose the two countries that could not retaliate— at least that is what they thought initially.' Sajid had stood up and said this emphatically. There were cheers and clapping.

'Will there be an anniversary of 9/11 in another 10 years or 25 years?' Omar asked.

'Do you want to know my prediction?' A person who was broad and tall like a rugby player got up and said this in his middle-eastern accent. 'There won't be any anniversary of 9/11 in twenty years, because America won't remain the world super power over the next twenty years. The power poles are shifting. Remember my words, write them somewhere, make a note. America will shrink to a lame country in the next twenty years *inshallah*. This is their destiny and they have to face it.'

'Is this your prediction or wishful thinking?' A boy from the front row said and there was frantic laughter all around.

'All the misery and disorder in the world is because of the politicians of the west. They are the biggest terrorists. The leadership of the west needs to be changed. Not one or two, all of them,' I could hear Omar saying enthusiastically.

'Yes, yes, that is truth,' someone else shouted.

'A new breed of politicians needs to appear to bring justice to the world. Justice, peace and equality to all colours, creeds and religious beliefs of people. The United Kingdom is the country where this revolution could begin,' Omar said.

'Why UK?' someone asked.

'Because, people living here have a thought process, they know how to deal with the change. Change is never easy but I feel our chances of bringing a change to the whole of the world are most promising in the UK. Long live the UK,' Omar said.

Everyone in the room was jazzed up. There was non-stop clapping all around and the room was filled with the roars from the crowd. I praised myself for taking the decision to sit near the door and quietly slipped out of the room.

What was that? I thought as I walked back home. Why does the irrational side of people come to the surface in a crowd? Do the collective emotions set the fuse for absurdity? Omar did not make any effort to bring calm and order to the gathering. I'm sure as a teacher he knew what to do in such situations, so was he doing this for some reason? Has he got some deep-seated hidden agenda? Oram I turning into a cynic? Why am I searching for the dark side in other people's personality? Is it possible that I'm the one who has got a problem, not others?

CHAPTER 10

I had been to the hospital several times before, but today I felt butterflies in my stomach as I approached the reception. 'Excuse me,' I said clearing my throat and handing over the brown envelope containing my acceptance letter to the receptionist. 'I'm Ali…. I'm starting my work experience today….'

'Thank God you're here,' she said before I could complete my sentence. 'Bob has already rung several times…… asking about you.' She wore an assortment of finger rings and all her nails were painted in different colours like a rainbow. She sat on a wheel chair. She stabilised the phone receiver between her shoulder and cheek, leaned down to open a drawer and passed me a thick brown envelope and said. 'This is your ID badge and swipe card. This is a communal ID badge; you'll have to write your name on this sticker.' She paused and spoke over the phone, 'Hi, this is reception. Could you please let Bob know that his apprentice, Ali has arrived…. Cheerio.' Her multi-tasking skills were impressive.

'Thanks,' I said.

'Please take a seat,' she said pointing at a row of fixed plastic chairs. 'Bob is on his way.'

As part of my work experience, I was posted to the operating theatres and the Gynaecology ward. A porter called Bob was in-charge of me. I could see someone walking towards me, taking long strides, and he warmly shook hands with me. 'Nice to meet you, I'm Bob,' he said smiling. 'Don't look so nervous man, you are here for work experience as a porter not to do brain surgery.' Bob had grey stubble, a nose piercing and wore a red headscarf reminiscent of the pirates of the Caribbean. Bob knew Dad and said, 'I knew Taj when he was a surgical registrar here…he was a very down to earth person even at that time and he has not changed at all after becoming a consultant….bless him……..he looked after my mother's heart a couple of years ago and I tell you …she is a woman not easily pleased… but is very happy with your dad.' He laughed and continued, 'I wanna make your work experience light and easy… and of course enjoyable…… you'll be working in tandem with me…to bring and take patients back to the women's ward. In the afternoon, spend some time in the Gynae ward to see how it works…any problems, report to me and I'll fix it for you… We'll go to theatres now,' he said and started walking towards the stairs sign. 'I only take lifts with patients; otherwise I walk up and down-stairs. We are going to the fifth-floor, you're a young man, hope you'll be OK?'

'Yeah, yeah, not a problem,' I said.

Bob seemed to know the system very well and was able to work enthusiastically and efficiently. He appeared as a 'problem solver' to me and was extremely popular among all the staff.

After bringing a couple of patients back-and-forth from ward to theatre, Bob seemed convinced of my abilities to do the job without much supervision and said, 'you bring up the next patient. I'll just slip out to have some 'fresh air'.' He said 'fresh air' by bringing two fingers close to his lips in a cigarette smoking fashion.

All nurses wore a navy-blue uniform with white hems. I wanted to hand over the slip with the patient's name on it to the staff nurse in-charge, Elizabeth, who was talking to another nurse and her back was towards me. 'There is an airline patient in room six. She was brought in at three or half three in the morning with profuse vaginal bleeding. She was seen by the Professor and planned to go to theatre at the end of his list.' She unfolded a piece of paper and read from it. 'She is seventy-eight and was travelling alone from New York to Singapore and had sex with some fella on the plane and began to bleed so heavily that the plane had to land at Heathrow.' The other nurse's eyes widened and she said, 'Blimey.' I could feel my face blushing. The staff nurse in-charge continued, 'She was examined and found to have a crescent shaped tear near the top-end of her vagina.' She stopped and said, 'What else do I need to tell you….. Her obs are stable now. She is fasted, changed into a gown, consented and all her bloods are sent.' I'm sure my face would be looking pale hearing this and hurriedly hand over the slip to the staff nurse.

'Ward G, bed 5 and nurse is with her right now,' she said pointing her hand.

'Thanks,' I said and before I walked in the direction of her hand I said in a low voice, 'This is not the patient you were just talking about?'

'No, no,' Nurse Elizabeth smiled, 'the one I was talking about is in a single room, she won't be going to theatre until late in the afternoon. The patient you have come to collect is in the ward.'

The patient for theatre seemed ready in her gown and white anti-clot stockings.

'Good morning, I'm Ali. I have come to take you to theatre,' I said.

'Thanks,' the nurse looking after her said. 'She could walk to the theatre.'

'Great,' I said. 'Should we go?'

'Can I take my book with me in case I have to wait?' The patient appeared quite articulate.

'I don't think that would be advisable as there should be no waiting and you may lose your book upstairs,' the nurse said.

'Ok,' the patient reluctantly placed her book on the side-drawer.

'It's a minor operation, you'll be back soon,' the nurse said cheerfully to the patient.

The patient listened to the nurse with absorption and in a quiet voice imparted a fire-cracker of intelligence. 'In my opinion, the definition of a minor operation is one that happens to someone else, I won't belittle my operation by calling it "minor".' We smiled affably.

At lunch time I met Uncle George on the way to the hospital restaurant. Like always, he was pleased to see me. He enquired about dad, mum and Bari Ammi. 'I usually don't have lunch but I'll buy you one,' he said.

'How is your day going?' I asked placing my dinner tray on the table.

'As usual,' he replied. 'Seeing patients, meeting with trainees.' He paused; his forehead creases deepened and he said, 'What do you think Ali, why do people seek advice?'

'I think…. people ask for advice when they aren't sure what to do ….. and when they would like some guidance from someone more experienced, wiser and sincere,' I said.

'So you think people take advice because they are undecided in their minds?' George asked.

'Yes….I think so…… If they had decided why would they ask for advice?' I said.

'Emm…nothing is less sincere than the way people seek and give advice. I'm very dubious about this whole process. I think the person asking for advice has already made a decision in their minds and they just wish for approval of their decision and to transfer responsibility for their conduct onto the advice giver.' George looked around and continued. 'For example, a trainee came to me this morning asking my advice about something. When I was talking to him, I could see a train of thought in his eyes. He wasn't listening to me; he was just 'picking-up' what he wanted to hear.'

'I'm sure this is your experience with more than one trainee,' I said.

'I've been a consultant for over seventeen years and have seen hundreds of trainees and it is not exclusive to the trainees, everyone does this.'

'And what about the advice giver?' I asked, enjoying his conversation.

'The advice giver usually feels flattered inside with the confidence that has been placed in him, although most often the advice he gives is calculated to further his own interest or reputation alone.'

'So, you're saying there is not much point in taking advice?'

'No there isn't. Having said this, there is no harm either as long as you understand what I have just said…..and also don't forget to take advice from you, your own-self.' George said looking at the clock in restaurant, 'I've got to go now. I have a clinic starting in five minutes….and listen it was lovely to meet you. I'm away on my holidays from tomorrow for the next two weeks and then on study leave for a week. Perhaps I'll see you after that. Take care.' He warmly shook hands with me and swiftly disappeared into the corridor.

I couldn't think of any meeting with George when I hadn't heard something new from him.

As soon I came out of the restaurant I was bleeped from the ward to carry some urgent blood samples to the pathology lab.

'I suppose the pathology lab is well sign-posted,' I asked a nurse who appeared free to have my attention. She had a plain body. Her breasts and hips protruded minimally from her short statured body. The foundation coat on her face extended to her neck. She had emphasised the M of her thin upper lip by sensible application of lip-liner and lipstick. When she blinked, her artificial eye-lashes became noticeable. She had carefully tied streaked hair on her head like a hot-cross bun in a fine net. I may be wrong but it is quite possible that she might have spent a good part of her waking time in front of a mirror before coming to work.

'Didn't they show you where the lab is during the induction?' she asked and stood by placing her hands on an area of her body where hips should be located.

'What is "induction"?' I asked in reply and read her name, Margaret on her left breast-pocket beside her upside-down hanging nursing-specific watch.

'Induction is supposed to take place on the first day of your work to show you where what is. If you haven't had one, I've to fill in an incident form for that.'

'Nurse,' a stripy dressed health-care assistant said to draw Margaret's attention. 'The patient from Ward G bed 2 slipped in the shower, but she is ok. I thought I'd just let you know.'

'Ok. I'll fill an incident form for that as well,' Margaret said.

'Sorry Margaret, what's an "incident form"?' I asked.

'It is an electronic form which we've to fill in for anything which goes wrong in the hospital to prevent this happening to anyone else.'

'But what will an incident form do to prevent patients slipping in showers? This can happen anywhere, even at home.' I couldn't resist asking the question.

'I know it's daft but we have to, in case a patient makes a complaint,' Margaret said.

The way to the pathology lab was very well sign-posted. I also met Bob in the corridor who gave me detailed instructions on how to reach the lab. While Bob was talking to me, a middle-aged man in stripy pyjamas came and stood beside us. He stroked the ground twice with his walking stick to draw attention and said to Bob in a loud voice, 'I'm fine, how're you?'

'I'm fine too,' Bob said looking closely at him. Long golden-brown hair curtained his pale, limpid face. 'Do you want me to take you to your ward?'

'I can find my way, I need no help.' He cleared his throat, paused and said, 'Some days, I hate this world, I hate everyone.'

'Join the club,' Bob said smiling.

'Some days, I feel I want to pull my trousers down in public and piss on everyone,' he said very seriously.

'I can understand the feeling,' Bob said. 'You need to drink loads of cups of tea before you can do that. Should we take you to your ward?'

'I wouldn't mind a cup of tea,' he said and started walking with Bob who winked at me.

The lab was just outside the main hospital building. I placed the specimen in a box which read 'Urgent' and was about to leave, when I heard someone saying to me in a somewhat angry tone, 'don't just leave them there….enter them on the computer.' My heart jumped to my mouth. I looked back and saw a middle-age man in a white coat which was stained with various colours, pointing his grubby finger towards the computer.

'I'm sorry. I wasn't aware….. I just started my work experience today. Could you show me how to do this?' I said looking at him. He had unkempt grey hair.

'I don't have time to train you…take them back…… and ask someone to bring them back who has a pass-word to enter them in the computer,' he said brusquely.

'There are urgent bloods …I was told….'

He cut me off in the middle and said, 'Every flipping thing is urgent in this hospital, what am I supposed to do?' His voice trembled, 'this fucking "lean management" is just meant to get more work out of me for the same wages, same hours. Can someone tell those morons in hospital management that what worked in a Toyota factory cannot work here, in a hospital. How can they even compare a factory with a hospital? They're nuts. What could be fucking "urgent" in a factory?'

'I'm so sorry,' I said, my heart was still beating fast. 'I think you're absolutely right. A factory deals with metal and what not and a hospital with humans, both aren't comparable to each other.'

'Yeah, but who could tell this to the hospital managers? They're absolutely bonkers,' he said and I could see his facial expressions softening towards me a bit. 'Don't you worry; I'll enter these bloods on the computer for you. You can go now.'

'Thanks.' I said. I was thinking on the way back that this person was profoundly unhappy about something which had been recently imposed on his work pattern. He was not a bad person at all; he was just over-worked and not coping well with this new way of work and found me as an opportunity to ventilate his anger. As it was generally said that change was painful; perhaps change was more painful when there was an attempt to convert hands before hearts.

I received a text from Carr. He had had his operation two days before but needed another the same day to stop the bleeding. I walked upstairs to the ward where he was. Carr was lying flat on his bed, eyes closed. His nostrils looked bigger than usual and a white bandage, which had some blood staining seemed tightly, packed in them. His face appeared swollen and he had to keep his mouth open to breathe. The top of his side-drawer was jam-packed with 'Get Well Soon' cards.

'How're you, mate? I knew you were greedy for things but never knew you would ask for two operations,' I said light-heartedly.

'No, it wasn't my choice,' he said slowly opening his eyes and pointing to his nose. 'Looks like I'd a two-stage procedure. I was supposed to have this nose job done as a day case but when I came back from theatre here to the ward, this bleeding would not stop. I had to be rushed back to theatre again in the evening and had another operation to tie this leaky vessel. I don't know why they didn't do that at my first operation?'

'I have heard that every operation can have complications but the good thing is it's fixed for you,' I said.

'I don't mind complications or staying in this ward, what I mind is that there's not a single good-looking nurse over here to cheer me up. If I stay here any longer, you might see me going to the church even when it's not a Sunday. They've only employed "angels of death" on this ward to scare the life out of you. I just keep my eyes closed here.'

I had to suppress my laughter and tapped his shoulder, 'So when will you be discharged home?'

'I'm just waiting for this nasal pack to come out and my take-home medicines to arrive from pharmacy, and I'll be on my way.'

'If you're here till five, I could give you a lift back home.'

'Mum is coming to pick me up. I'll text her when I'm ready. Thanks for the offer.'

'Ok, I'll see you around.'

'Bye.'

'Thanks, Ali.'

Back in the ward, there was a flurry of activity. Consultants along with their teams were going round. Some were explaining operation findings and discharging day case patients to their homes.

I followed one of the junior doctors to a cubicle to observe the consultation. The consultant, Mr Smith told the middle-age, anxious-looking lady, 'I had a look at your MRI scan. You've got a circular mass in your tummy and you'll need an operation to remove it.' Mr Smith had short stature, curly grey hair, a rotund face, an over-hanging double chin obscuring his neck and it appeared that his head was directly attached to his torso. He was wearing a navy-blue silk suit; two red embroidered braces supported his trousers over his full-term pregnant woman-like belly. Mr Smith also appeared a 'circular mass' to me.

At the nursing station, Staff Nurse Elizabeth said, 'Prof Hopkins, I've had several phone calls from the airline about your patient.'

'The one who came from Heathrow this morning? Is she ok post-operatively?' Professor Hopkins asked.

'Yes, she is perfectly fine. I had a look at her pad about half an hour ago. It was totally dry. There is no bleeding at all.'

'Good. She can be discharged.'

'Professor, the pilot would like a letter from you stating that such bleeding will not recur during her onwards flight,' Nurse

Elizabeth said.

'Well, my letter will do nothing; it all depends on the vigilance of his crew,' The Professor replied and we all laughed genuinely.

'Hi, Professor, how are things?' Mr Smith said passing by the nursing station.

'All fine. Congrats. I heard you've managed to persuade Gynae Directorate to buy you a million pounds worth of the da Vinci robot.'

'Well, they had no option. My belly won't let me reach patients on the operating table,' Mr Smith said stroking his tummy.

'It would have been cheaper for the hospital to employ a personal trainer for you,' Professor Hopkins said smiling.

'Hush, don't give them ideas,' Mr Smith said. 'I don't have to come to hospital on my operating days anymore; I could operate from my bed room. Cheerio.' He waved at us all and left the ward.

'Joking aside,' the Professor said looking at me, 'Mr Smith is an excellent key-hole surgeon and I'm pleased the hospital has made the right choice. Robotic surgery is the future of surgery.'

Suddenly, a fire alarm went off and fire-doors clunk-closed automatically. Surprisingly there was no urgency on anyone's faces. Professor Hopkins mumbled as he walked off the ward, 'Someone burning the toast again.'

It was almost five and time to go home. I quickly walked down stairs from the fourth floor. Several patients, their relatives and some staff had gathered outside the hospital at the fire assembly point. Soon the fire-engines arrived and the fire-crew clad in yellow jackets and helmets jumped off and quickly entered the hospital building. I took a short cut through the car park to come to the main road. I saw Carr's mum's car whizz past. I felt sorry for Carr, as his discharge from the hospital might be delayed due to this fire alarm chaos.

As I was driving back home, I was thinking why were the intimate acts of some people made public? I was sure, that seventy-eight year old lady was not the first one to have sex on a plane. The picture of that middle-aged man who hated the world appeared in my mind. I felt sad for him. What makes people go crazy? Is it genetics or environment or both? I admired the way Bob handled him. I could also imagine Staff Nurse Margaret leaning over the computer and filling some more incident forms on trivial matters. Anyway, it was an interesting first day of my work experience.

CHAPTER 11

Sajid's name appeared on the screen when my mobile rang.

'Are you in?' Sajid asked me as I pressed the green button.

'Yep.'

'Are you free to come with us?'

'Where are we going? When?'

'Now, we're just pulling up outside your house, jus' come out.'

As I stepped out of the house, an old looking, light blue Ford Escort stopped at the front. I didn't recognise the person in the driving seat. He had a dark skin tone and a big square head with very short curly hair. He was probably in his early twenties.

Sajid introduced me to the driver. 'This is my friend Ali. He'll be going to medical school soon.'

'*Mashallah*, nice to meet you,' he said. He had a gap between his front teeth. 'Please come in,' he leaned backwards and opened the car door from inside.

As I sat inside the car, a smell of dust, leather and engine oil filtered to my nostrils. There were Arabic newspapers spread on the back seat. I gathered the newspapers up behind the passenger's seat and made room to sit. The car hiccoughed twice, jolting us forwards and backwards before purring smoothly along the road.

'Sorry for the junk. Every day I plan to clean the car, but days come and go so fast in this country.' He spoke English with an Algerian accent.

'Don't worry,' I said. 'Where are we going?' I asked as the car drove off.

'Just chill man, you'll find out soon,' Sajid said as he smiled.

I looked around at the interior of the car, which was hardly meant for chilling. The cloth seat covers had worn through in several places and light brown sponge was showing. The plastic door cover was hanging off and revealing the wires to the electric windows. There were no floor mats. An empty, crumpled packet of crisps and a plastic water bottle were lying on the floor; the bottle was rolling around with the motion of the car.

The driver of the car seemed to know Sajid well as they were talking about their school football team and other stories from the past. The car was moving out of the residential area of the city. I couldn't recall whether I'd ever been to this part of London before. The road turned into a rutted dirt track with tall trees on both sides which were hugging at their tops. After a jolted journey of maybe half an hour suddenly we were in front of a house-in the middle of nowhere.

I felt sick as I got out of the car. A roofless shell of a house with boarded up windows flanked the house. The noise of car doors shutting made a kit of pigeons fly up from the derelict house. The door of the house we were about to enter was ajar. Green paint was peeling off it revealing a black undercoat. A bearded man opened the door as soon as we stepped out of the car as if he was eagerly waiting for us. I immediately recognised this man: he was Omar. He was clad in a pale coloured *jellaba*. He said, in the softest accent, '*Marhaba*, my friends, welcome my friends, welcome to my house.' He warmly shook hands with me; his hands were chubby with knotty fingers. He was extremely observant as he said after glancing at me, 'you do not look well, my friend. Can I get you something?'

'No thanks, I'll be fine soon enough.' I felt a bit embarrassed.

Omar hugged the driver of the car and Sajid warmly, kissed cheeks, and led us into the house. It had the smell of a shut closet. The front door led into a small sized room. There was a study table with a laptop on it. There were papers scattered everywhere. In one corner there was a single bed which was not made. A heater with a gas canister was lying next to the bed. Dark-black speckled mould was growing at the junction of the walls and the ceiling. There were a couple of rows of empty shelves on one wall.

Omar had a faint scar between his upper lip and nose. He had wiry grey hair. He had a bout of coughing which made his face look purplish and his eyes congested. Once settled with his cough he brought out an inhaler from his pocket and took a deep breath from it.

'Gentlemen, what can I get you? Tea, coffee, coke? I am afraid I only have three options for you,' Omar said and again I felt his smile to be artificial.

'Can I have a glass of water please?' I seemed to have stretched his number of options.

'Yes definitely.' Omar opened a small fridge next to the study table and got a water bottle out for me. He handed me over the bottle and a white plastic cup.

'Thanks,' I said.

'You look better now, how do you feel?' Omar asked me.

'I'm fine now, thanks,' I said. I was uncomfortable with his piercing gaze.

Sajid and his friend opened their cans of coke and started sipping.

'How is your dad's charity work going?' Omar, who seemed always to be smiling, asked me. There was a dark, oval *sijddah* mark on top of his forehead.

'Fine,' I was surprised by this unexpected question. 'Do you know my Dad?'

'I know all the good people around here.' Omar said and both Sajid and his friend laughed.

As far as I knew, Dad had a habit of not letting other people know when he went out to do charity work, but perhaps Omar knew Dad from the hospital, I thought.

'And how is your work experience going on at the hospital?' Omar asked me.

I was surprised again at his question, how he knew all this and I looked at Sajid who was tilting his Coke can and staring at it as if he had never seen a Coke can in his life before.

'It's going well. I'm working as a porter at the hospital. There is loads of running around the place.' Words came out of my mouth as if I had just learnt how to speak.

'I know that,' Omar said in his usual soft voice. 'Well my friends,' Omar's gaze fell on each of us. 'Without more ado, I would like to explain to you the purpose of our meeting.' He looked very serious.

He took his mobile out of his pocket and raised it in the air and said, 'Please switch off your mobiles, I want no interruptions,' and he placed his phone on the table, he looked stressed.

I looked at Sajid and his friend, who took out their mobiles, switched them off and placed them on the table as well. I did not like the demeanour of this meeting. I took my phone out of my pocket, put it on silent. I looked at Omar who was pacing up and down the room. I looked down and quietly set the mobile on voice recording and placed it upside down on the table, closer to me, in case I had to cover it with the palm of my hand.

'It's disgusting to see what is happening to Muslims in Iraq, Afghanistan, Palestine and Chechnya. Hundreds are slaughtered every day, every single day. Why is Muslim blood so cheap? Why are we so helpless, but remember God's help comes only when we help ourselves. We have to do jihad in the cause of Allah.'

Omar's voice became deeper, pools of splutter formed in the corners of his mouth and beads of tears began to roll over his beard. He began to cry like a baby with a wet nappy. Mini hiccups interrupted his cries, moving his chest up and down. Honestly speaking, I found all this extremely amusing.

Both Sajid and his friend got out of their chairs and compassionated Omar by putting an arm over his shoulder and Sajid's friend said. 'Don't be upset, ultimate success will be ours, we're all with you and above all God is with us.' Sajid poured the remaining water from my bottle and handed over the glass to Omar who gulped it down his throat in a single go.

Omar wiped his eyes with a tissue and then blew his nose hard into it and said. 'Brothers, we can do something, look at the history of the world. Who is behind all these wars and killings?'

I didn't know whether it was a question posed to us or it was a part of his conversation, I looked at him with a blank face.

'Always, always it has been bloody politicians.' Omar himself replied to his question, ran fingers through his beard, producing a sound like scraping the back of a horse and said. 'We are not helpless, not lame but can make the leadership of this country lame. These self-proclaimed, greedy leeches, who have been behind all these decisions to kill our Muslim brothers, need to be replaced with a new breed of honest politicians. It is our religious duty to take part in jihad.' He paused and looked at us as if he was trying to gauge the impact of his speech on us.

'You need to promise that whatever you hear now, will not leave this room.' He quickly moved to his table and grabbed a book and said, 'You all have to take an oath on the Quran that whatever I say now you will not tell to anyone, not even your parents not even the people you love most.' I was taken aback with this dramatic development and was not sure how to react.

Omar placed the Quran on the table and asked us to place our left hand on it and to raise our right hand and the oath was taken. I could feel a quickening of my pulse. I knew that something pleasant could not possibly happen after this occurrence. I looked at Sajid who appeared calm.

Omar said, 'The only way we can improve the situation for our Muslim brothers is by restricting the current Prime Minister of this country. This idiot has carried on with the policies of the past prime minister. These bastards are now going to pass a motion in the coming weeks in the House of Commons, which would give powers to the Prime Minister to allow an attack on any country in the world without approval from their cabinet. Of course brainless Americans will follow this motion in the Congress but we have to foil this bill.'

'How are you going to achieve this?' I couldn't resist asking this question.

'By making them ill, very ill, so they could not cast their votes.' Omar said, and my heart sank.

'Have I been sucked into a terrorist plot here?' I thought to myself. I could hear my heart beat in my ears.

'No, terrorism is not the answer to this problem,' I said in a loud voice. 'I will not become a party to any killings; I want to leave now, right now.' I stood up and started walking towards the door.

Both Sajid and his friend immediately stood up and ran after me and said, 'Just listen to him first. We aren't killing anyone. Listen to his plan first and then if you decide not to join us, then you may leave.'

'So you already know the plan, Sajid? You already knew why we're here? Why didn't you tell me?' I could hear my own voice trembling with anger.

'Calm down, man, calm down,' Omar said. 'Do you need more water?'

'No I don't,' I said forcefully.

'Please first listen to Omar's plan, I beg of you, please,' Sajid said.

'Brother, feel free to leave but remember the oath you have taken on the Quran,' Omar said.

'Please stay and please listen to Omar's plan and then if you decide not to join us you may leave. We aren't gonna kill anyone,' Sajid's friend said.

'OK, tell us your plan,' I said.

'That's more like it.' A smile re-appeared on his face. 'My plan has got no hi-jacking of aeroplanes and thank God for that, I have a phobia of flying,' Omar said. 'No bomb blasts, no shooting, no killing of innocent people, no suicide bombing and no ordering of explosives.'

Omar's eyes were fixed on my face. I knew he was trying to lighten the heaviness of the meeting.

'My plan is very simple. I can share a glimpse of our plot with you. The details of the plan will be given to you in a later meeting. A highly deadly strain of bacteria called E Coli O157:H7 will be used to contaminate the food supply of the Houses of Parliament. This bacteria is so deadly that you need less than a hundred bacteria to make a person ill. The bacteria are kept under lock and key at microbiology laboratories at some highly selective hospitals. The bacteria can cause severe diarrhoea to a degree that patients might need intensive care treatment in hospital. I have a friend who provides catering to the Houses of Parliament and he has already agreed to join us in this jihad.' Omar paused for a moment and said. 'Can you imagine MPs dropping like flies by shitting themselves on the toilet? A considerable part of the leadership will be in toilets or in hospitals so this motion of attacking any country in the world will not go ahead. We'll achieve our aim like this.' He made a sharp noise by clicking his thumb against his middle finger. 'No sniffer dog can catch you, no detector can detect these lethal bacteria. What do you think of my plan, ingenious, isn't it?' Omar looked around with achievement in his voice.

'But if these bacteria are kept in a safe how do you plan to steal them?' I deliberately used the word 'steal'.

'Good question,' Omar said. 'We know someone working in the lab that has access to this dirty bug and will pass it onto us in a tightly sealed envelope which will be delivered to our friend working in the House of Commons the same day. Please do not call it stealing. We are doing this for a higher cause – jihad, not for any worldly gains.'

'I'm wholeheartedly with you. But can I clarify something?' Sajid said to Omar.

'*Masallah*. Yeah, sure, please go ahead.'

'Are we not presuming here that all MPs eat in the Parliament restaurants? It is quite possible that many MPs would eat elsewhere. Also by the looks of their double-chinned faces and downwards protruding bellies, not many in my opinion, would touch salads and would prefer alcohol to food. It is quite possible that large numbers of MPs may not be sick due to this infection and this important vote would either be taken with fewer MPs present or might be postponed for a little while,' Sajid said.

'I know these possibilities and I've thought about them. I think the most likely outcome of this infection would be that the vote will be postponed and soon there'll be the MPs summer break. Six weeks is a long time in politics. I would regard this as success; our *Fatah-e-mubeen*. The important thing is to instil fear in them. Make them scared. This would be our achievement.'

'What is expected of me in this plot?' I asked.

'Not much, not much at all,' Omar said. 'The hospital where you are doing your work experience has the laboratory with this dirty bug. A friend of ours works in this laboratory and he will give you an envelope and the only thing you have to do is to take that envelope to your friends waiting outside the hospital gate.' Omar pointed towards Sajid and the driver. 'Your job finishes there, that is all we expect from you. Is it too much? According to our calculations it should not take you more than three minutes to hand over the envelope outside the hospital. Only three minutes. We will let you know a route between the lab and the hospital exit which has no CCTV surveillance. Just imagine, your three minutes could change the fate of the whole Muslim world. The suffering of our Muslim brothers could evaporate in just three minutes of your time. Please, do not disappoint me. Please, please we need your help. Jihad is a religious obligation on us all. It is our duty, we cannot shy away from this responsibility and hopefully God will reward you in this world and hereafter. God bless you. Please promise you will help us?'

'I need some time to think about it. It's a big undertaking.' I said. 'At the moment, I'm not too sure it is the right thing to do.'

Omar looked at both Sajid and the driver. Sajid said in an excited tone and rubbing his hands together, 'Bloody marvellous, that would be fun. MP's pooing their guts out. Count me in, I'm with you. I'm sure Ali would agree as well.'

'I'm with you,' Said Sajid's friend who was continuously biting his nails.

'Good, very good,' Omar said, 'any questions?'

'Can we harm ourselves with this disease?' Sajid's friend asked in a timid voice.

'Good question. No, but obviously we've got to be careful,' Omar said.

'So you want to kill the present Prime Minister and MPs.' I asked.

'No, no, we don't intend to kill anyone. It's a major sin,' Omar said by holding the right ear lobe with his left hand and the left earlobe with his right hand, making a cross of forearms over his chest, 'but if someone dies it's God's will, it's their hard luck.'

'If the current Prime Minister dies as a result of your infection, what is the guarantee that the next prime minister and MPs won't do what the current PM and MPs are doing? We may be in the same situation again, aren't you just delaying the inevitable?' I said.

'No, no that is being pessimistic. As I've said earlier, the important point is to show them that we are capable of inflicting harm. Don't underestimate the power of the fear factor to keep them on the straight path and that is only possible if we could show them what we are capable of doing.'

'Are you willing to join us in the Jihad?' Omar asked me, there was jitteriness in his tone and I thought he might lose his temper any second.

'I'm not too sure but will let you know,' I said.

'Please remember the oath you have taken on the Quran,' Omar said without looking at me. 'If you break the oath, desolation will rain down on you and your family, it's a holy pact you have made.' He looked around again. Anger was evident from his face and voice. 'I know you are a good Muslim. I'll pray to God so that he gives you courage to help other Muslim brothers, and God bless you,' Omar said. He seemed to have gained his composure now. 'Thanks for coming, gentlemen. Please wait for further instructions. Have a safe journey.' Omar stood up and opened the front door for us. 'See you soon.'

As we came out Sajid said to his friend, 'I know a shorter route back. I could drive.' And without waiting for a reply from his friend, he took the car keys from his hands.

I had to make an effort to conceal my anger. Why did Sajid have to involve me in this?

'Bruv,' Sajid's friend said to me, 'Please don't take this mission as negative, we should be grateful to God that He has given us an opportunity to do some good for this *ummah*, please think of this as a blessing.'

'I will think the way I want to think,' I said harshly. I looked at my mobile: twenty seven minutes and three seconds of voice recording had taken place, and unexpectedly mum's picture appeared on the screen.

'Hi Mum, yeah….I'm on my way home… see you soon, bye.' I said.

'I'm sure you will be a clever doctor. If you had not reminded me, my mobile would have remained switched off for days,' Sajid's friend said.

I was relieved that no one had noticed my mobile. Both Sajid and his friend remained silent for the rest of the way. I didn't think Sajid was taking a short cut route back home but he did drive at a speed showing some urgency.

CHAPTER 12

My mind sagged around the same thoughts again and again, like a Ping-Pong ball bobbing up-and-down, up-and-down all the time. Although, I was quite pleased not to be contacted by Sajid but I was unable to take my mind off what had happened earlier this week. After this mind-numbing meeting, I had been wrestling with the ideas of morality, religion, religious obligations, my conscience and the consequences of breaking an oath taken for my family and me. I felt stuck in a quicksand, slowly sinking in; stranded and helpless. I was missing Dad; this matter would have not been that hard for me if he was around. I could have consulted him, could have taken his advice. Speaking to Mum could only make the matters worse. She would probably shoot her blood pressure sky high and suffer another stroke which could only add to our problems, not solve them. Another option was to speak to George. He would be a sensible counsel, but should I disturb him during his holidays in Scotland?

'Don't you have to go and see Mr Nazir today?' Mum entered

the room and broke my chain of thoughts.

'Oh yes, I nearly forgot it,' I said and sprang out of my bed. Hopefully my meeting with Mr Nazir would be able to help me to shake off the most dreadful meeting of my life. The desire to forget it was so great that in the next hour I was hurriedly climbing the stairs of the hospital, taking two at a time to meet Mr Nazir.

As usual he was sitting in his high-backed chair; an infusion of milk-like fluid was being given to him. The drops were falling in the chamber of the drip, causing a mini-splash before running into a tube to his vein. He looked weaker than the previous time I had seen him, dark circles had appeared under his eyes and his nose now appeared a bit more prominent on his face.

'Good to see you Ali,' he said. His voice had not changed its tone despite his illness.

'Thanks. You look good today.'

'Yeah, I feel a bit better today. I still haven't got any appetite but this protein feed is keeping me alive, at least for the time being. Anyway, I think this is how life is going to be from now onwards. You tell me what you wanted to ask me last time.' He was straight to the point.

'Hope you'll get well soon,' I said. 'I was just curious,' I said hesitantly, 'Dad told me that something strange happened to you at the Mausoleum of Ali Hejwari and if you don't mind, could I know about this? I was quite intrigued to hear it.'

'It wasn't a strange happening. It was the start of a journey of journeys, journeys in self-awareness,' he said quietly.

'The reason I was so interested in this was due to the fact that one is chosen by someone, selected by someone before the process begins.' I said 'someone' by the comma shaped movements of index and middle fingers of both of my hands. 'How is one selected, who decides the eligibility, the suitability of the person for the process?'

'I think that was my destiny,' he said. I could see friendliness in his eyes. I remained silent to encourage him to expand on his answer but he continued his gaze towards the floor. I felt like a thirsty crow that was flying here and there in search of water and eventually found a utensil with water in it but so shallow that he could not reach it. As the crow in the story came up with the ingenious plan of throwing pebbles into the pot until the water rose and quenched his thirst, I also decided to throw pebbles until the water rose, to keep asking questions from Mr Nazir until I got some answers. Unlike the crow in the story, I wasn't sure it would work but it was worth a try.

'So where do these journeys of self-awareness lead to?' I threw another pebble.

'To the truth, the one and only reality.' His answers again had an economical use of words.

'How do you reach the truth?' I asked. I was in no mood to give up that easily.

'One has to have an extreme degree of eagerness, an immensely strong desire to search for truth and then someone has to lead you there,' he said.

'Why do you need "someone", can't you learn it by yourself?' I was very surprised to hear this.

'No, it is not a DIY job. No matter how many times you read that thick textbook called *Grey's Anatomy*, you cannot learn how to remove someone's appendix, you need to learn it from someone. You have to submit yourself to someone as an apprentice.'

'So in your opinion to be a student of "searching for the truth" is like learning to perform surgery?' I said light-heartedly.

'Oh, yes, most definitely and as serious a matter as learning to perform surgery. If you learn something, which you should not, you can easily harm yourself or others. That is why it is very important to be under direct supervision just as in surgical training until the teacher is fully convinced that one can operate independently.'

'Really,' I said and felt my eyes popping out in amazement. 'Who was your teacher?'

'No, I cannot tell you his details or whereabouts because it is not relevant to you.'

'Can you tell me how to spot a true teacher?' I asked, as I wanted to know more about him.

'Yes, I can tell you some of the characteristics of these masters or friends of God or whatever names you want to call them. It is very difficult to fully describe these masters. They live in a world where consciousness and wonder exist side by side, where madness intermingles with awareness. To them the past, the present and the future are a seamless flow of time. They know the meaning and significance of things.'

I felt mesmerised by his speech. My strategy had worked. He continued.

'These masters, who are lost in their quest for the self, emerge from the fountain heads of knowledge and reach such a terrifying wilderness of self-awareness where there is no union with the object of one's desire and no separation from it either, where there is no one they call their own and no one who they can regard as a stranger. These masters are not troubled by the possible and the impossible. They converse with silence; they listen to the heartbeat of sand grains. They understand the 'unreality' of 'reality'. Their eyes are fixed on the interiority of the being and the existence. They can see, in a drop of water, the rolling sea and in a grain of sand, the whole desert. They regard both the raven and the peacock as manifestation of the same epiphanic reality. They acquire the awareness of death from life and the consciousness of life from death. They themselves are the ultimate question and the answer at the same time. They laugh without any justification and weep without any reason.'

It was the first time ever I had had such a long reply from him. The soft jingling of his keys gained momentum with his speech. His gaze was locked to the floor.

'What did your teacher teach you? It must be very complicated,' I said.

'No it was all very simple in the beginning. You start your lessons with love and care for all living creatures. To eat pork is disallowed in our religion but to do a dressing to a wounded pig is a matter of *sawab (a good deed)*, to love and to serve God's creature brings you closer to the creator. Yes, the learning modules do become complex as the learning capability of the apprentice increases, just like in surgical training one is expected to learn complicated surgical cases in the final year of the training. It also happens sometimes that no module is taught, no information is imparted but the mere nearness of these masters sparks off a change in you, exactly as a piece of iron when placed close to a fire blazes like fire itself.'

I was enjoying this conversation and wanted to listen to more of him but there was a knock at his door and two doctors and a nurse entered the room. One of the doctors, who looked to be a consultant, had an air of authority in his manners.

'Good morning, Mr Nazir,' the senior doctor said pleasantly and warmly shook hands with Mr Nazir.

I stood up and said, 'I think I'll wait outside.'

'No, no, please remain seated,' Mr Nazir said and also gestured with his hand. 'What's the news, Doc?'

'I have your blood results. They are still showing abnormality in your liver and kidney functions but the good news is that they aren't getting any worse. I was told that you had some breathlessness last night. How're you feeling now?'

'I'm feeling OK. I don't know what happened but I was sitting in this chair and suddenly became breathless.'

'Well your ECG and the ultrasound of your heart did not show any abnormality but we'll run some other tests on your lungs to ensure that you are not throwing off any clots into your lungs.'

'OK.'

'We'll also repeat your blood tests tomorrow.'

'I'll look forward to that,' he said smiling.

'Ok, we'll leave you in peace. I'll see you tomorrow,' and the team left the room.

'Some more blood tests,' he mumbled, 'as if it is going to make any difference.' He stopped and cleared his throat and said, 'So Ali, what else do you want to ask me?'

'Could you tell me something which your teacher had told you and you found most amazing, something very special?'

'Everything was special, exclusive, worthy of learning,' he said.

'Anything which many people are not aware of?' I asked.

He smiled broadly and said, 'You are being curious.'

'Possibly,' I said. 'I like to learn new things.'

'People only learn for two reasons,' he said in his usual manner. 'One, based on self-interest, makes us want to learn what may be useful to us. Another, based on pride, comes from a desire to know what others don't. I have a feeling your curiosity is falling into the latter group.'

'I'm sorry....maybe you're right... but I thought it would be good to know something of which other people may not be aware,' I said and felt a bit embarrassed by his spot-on analysis of my thoughts.

'The desire to impress others with your knowledge or to belittle them and to beat them up with your stick of awareness and understanding of things needs to be curbed. This is an important lesson for you to learn today,' he looked closely at me and said, 'I'm sure you will be considerate toothers in every respect.'

'I promise I'll be,' I said.

'Well, I know you will. I can tell you something which many people are not aware of.' He said this while leaning his face closer to me. 'At any one time, there are four thousand friends of God present in this world. This number remains constant. When one dies some other is promoted to the empty place. These friends could be men or women, some are aware of their office of being friends of God and others may be doing their job without this knowledge. The gravitational pull remains functional because of these people: the soft caress of a summer breeze, the serenity of moonlight; the changing seasons; vegetation springing from barren soil. The honey bees collect nectar just because of these people.'

I was deeply amazed to hear this and I wanted to ask Mr Nazir whether he was one of them but I knew that certain questions are best not asked and this question was certainly one of them.

'You mean to say that the life of seven billion people on this planet depends upon these four thousand people?'

'Yes, that's true. Can we talk about something else?' it was obvious that he wanted to change the topic.

I shifted in my chair and threw another question at him. 'Why is everyone so unhappy in this day and age?'

He was resting his chin in the palm of his hand and started talking. 'Today man is up against a bizarre predicament. His very attempt to ensure security for himself has resulted in making him even more insecure. The storms of nameless anxieties blow out one by one the beacons of hope and enlightenment. Knowledge is on the increase and is available to more and more people. But as the libraries overflow with books and people are carrying thousands of electronic books in their back pockets, the heart is becoming emptier of compassion, understanding, peace and tranquillity. Our craze for the acquisition of life's comforts is like a strangulating creeper choking our thoughts and feelings.'

He took a breather and pointed with his index finger towards the jug of water. I poured some water and handed him over the glass. After taking a couple of sips he continued. 'If Socrates was reborn now he would be forced to drink hemlock again. Feelings are dead now. Today's tragedy is that tragedy itself is dead and no one can spare a moment to mourn its demise. Machines have robbed men of their decency; they are able to receive messages from a distant planet but are unable to read the face of a person just sitting in front of them. There is so much light that the vision cannot function. Everyone is living a multi-purpose life with conflicting demands so how can one be happy?'

'Is there any simple recipe for happiness?' I asked.

'Very simple. Happiness is never found in its pursuit. It is only found in the pursuit of giving up yourself to give to others.' He stopped to drink water again and continued with his eyes shut. 'The problem we are facing here is that we do not like what we get and the irony is that we do not get what we like. If we begin to like what we get here, it will make life very easy.'

'Everyone is running after money. Is it the rat race making people unhappy?' I wanted him to continue to talk on this topic.

'There is no harm in keeping money in your pocket but do not keep it inside your heart, do not fall in love with money. Keep it like a slave not your master.'

I smiled at the way he expressed his opinion.

'Wealth does not just mean that you should have money in your pocket. Your eyesight is wealth, the idea flashing across your mind is wealth, the feeling filling your heart is wealth, and your life itself is wealth. So do not worry too much about wealth, we all are born wealthy.'

I was completely swept off my feet by the way Mr Nazir talked. It felt that he had been musing over all these matters a million times. His keys jingled and he continued.

'Every man's living is secured in some part of their body. For instance, a writer's livelihood is seated in his understanding and powers of observation – in his pen, an orator in his tongue, and a singer in his melodious vocal cords. It is true to an extent that some people's face alone is their fortune. Similarly, some find their subsistence in the strength of their arms, others in their deceitful use of their brain cells and yet others in their invalidity. Innocent babies get their sustenance through their own innocence. In several countries even sex forms a part of economics. In short, man serves his belly by means of some part of his body.'

I had read so many books, listened to so many discussions but had never heard such philosophy before. He sipped water again and continued.

'The question to ponder is that who is it who gives an idea to a writer to write? If anatomically all vocal cords are similar why are some melodious? The weight and the dissection of Einstein's brain did not show it different from any ordinary human's brain. Apples have been falling from trees for hundreds and thousands of years and men have seen this phenomenon but why did only Newton discover gravity? Why Einstein why Newton? I feel there is an element of selection. You are selected to do a job, like your Dad is selected to treat sick human beings.'

He opened his eyes and fixed his gaze again at the floor.

'Is it true that a spiritual person can see and tell about the future?' I asked.

'They can but they tend not to. The important bit in life is the present, if you learn to live in the present time, your life become easier. Contentment is, in fact, coming to terms with your present life.'

There was another knock at the door and a nurse entered the room.

'I'm awfully sorry to disturb you, I thought I would just let you know that as you suggested, I had spoken to the fund-raising committee of the Children's Hospital. They are willing to sell the bouquets of flowers as charity to raise money for the new neonatal unit.'

'That's excellent. I'm grateful to you for your kindness,' he said.

'You must have a lot of well-wishers. How many bouquets have you received?' I asked.

A smile appeared on Mr Nazir's face and he looked towards the nurse.

'Well, in sixteen days, so far we have received….' she stopped like the host of an award ceremony, 'one thousand seven hundred and fifty two.'

'Wow.' My mouth opened with surprise and I said, 'It's almost more than a hundred each day.'

'Yes, our Mr Nazir is very special and he deserves every single one of them,' the nurse said.

'I'm not sure about that but I can tell you there are more to come than those you have received so far,' he said.

'That's not a problem. Now we have a system in place all fresh bouquets will be diverted to the Children's Hospital but we will keep an inventory of the numbers and names of people sending you these, for your information.'

'Thank you very much,' Mr Nazir said.

'I'll see you soon,' the Nurse said as she left the room.

'It seems you have a huge number of followers back home. I assume people attending your discussion forums are flooding you with these bouquets?' I said.

'The majority of people who come to my Thursday forums barely have enough money to make both ends meet,' he said.

'So who are these people who are sending you these?' I said with obvious surprise in my voice.

'I don't know,' he said. 'Ali, can I be left alone now. I'll see you next week.'

I was slightly disappointed at the abrupt ending of our meeting but it was a good meeting. I was pleased that I could meet him again. I shook hands with him and quietly left the room.

CHAPTER 13

My mobile rang. 'Have you made-up your mind to join us?' Sajid said as soon as I answered his call; I knew he wanted an affirmative answer from me.

'Maybe, maybe not,' I said.

'You and your fucking indecisiveness,' he said grinding his teeth. 'Come on... It's a golden opportunity to help our Muslim brotherhood. We may not get this chance ever again in our lives. Don't waste your time mulling it over, just be positive. Be brave. Can you not spare five minutes of your time? You have the whole wisdom of Aristotle and can't decide this small matter.'

'Ok, ok. Perhaps I will, but the whole plan looks unworkable to me.' I said.

'Unworkable? My foot,' Sajid said sounding a bit irritated. 'Unless you know the whole plan how can you regard it as impractical? We must go and listen to the finer details and if you still find any flaws with the plan then you should make suggestions for improvement. I'm sorry I don't think it is fair to criticise the plot until you have fully heard it.'

I must admit, I was not comfortable with a second meeting with Mr Omar. Sajid was insistent to the point of bullying me to attend the meeting. I wanted to say 'no' to Sajid but could not. Not being able to say 'NO' had been my weakness for a long time. I was unable to get on top of this.

Sajid drove me to the towering flats close to Waterloo Station. The daily commuters were hastily coming in and out of both train and tube stations. There was tiredness and signs of relief on people's faces that the day had ended. After a couple of minutes' walk we reached a gated entrance to the flats. Sajid pressed the buzzer and before he said anything a voice came from the speaker: 'Come to the 10th Floor, Flat Number 10 and I'll open the door for you.'

Before entering, I could see a breath-taking view of London. I was sure the night view of London's city lights would be splendid from here.

A soft knock at the door revealed that it was already open.

It was a very small room, which was full of hazy cigarette smoke,and it was difficult to make out who actually was in there. It took me a couple of minutes to acclimatise my sight. There was a long dining table in the middle of the room and Omar and a person who was later introduced as Sharif were sitting around the table. There were two other people sitting with them who had covered their faces with tea-cloth-like scarfs and only their eyes were visible. Initially, I was not too sure whether they were covering their faces to conceal their identity (which later proved to be the case) or simply protecting themselves from the cigarette smoke.

Sharif appeared to be in his late forties. His swarthy skin was stretched across his jaw and looked thick and leathery. It seemed he had not shaven for days. He was smoking cigarette after cigarette, lighting one from the butt of the last. He was sucking deeply on them, creating deep pits in his cheeks. I was already feeling nauseous.

'Tea?' Omar asked us all. Sharif raised his hand. No one else wanted tea and the men with covered faces couldn't have it even if they wanted. The complete silence in the room was interrupted by the growls of the boiling kettle. Omar stirred a spoon sharply in the mug, took the tea bag out and placed it on top of a mound of rust coloured dried tea bags near the kettle. Omar placed the mug in front of Sharif and said, 'Thank you very much for coming. I'll first introduce you to Mr Sharif, who works in a microbiology lab in a hospital not very far from here, and he will tell us the details of the plan which I have already briefly shared with you. It is obvious that this meeting is highly confidential. Over to you, Sharif.'

Sharif cleared his throat a couple of times like an old car failing to start and then eventually said, 'Thanks, Omar.'

'Please switch your mobiles off and put them in here.' Sharif pointed towards an empty fruit basket.

I looked at Omar's face, my heart jumped to my mouth. Had he come to know about the voice recording on my mobile? His face looked completely expressionless. I thought it was best to look away.

'Have any of you heard of E Coli O157: H 7?' Sharif asked.

'Yes, we heard from Omar about it last week,' I said in a quiet voice.

'No problems, I'll explain. E Coli O157 is a deadly type of bacteria. Infection from it is quite rare. When an outbreak of O157 happens, it becomes a real emergency. If these bacteria are suspected in a patient's stool, a sample is sent to a central laboratory here in London to confirm the diagnosis. This confirmation usually comes within seven days and we have to destroy the bacteria in our lab once the diagnosis is confirmed.'

'Does everyone die as a result of the infection?' one of the scarfed faces asked.

'No, not really,' said Sharif. 'There are 650 MPs in the house of Commons. Say if we manage to infect 300 with O157, one hundred and twenty would need admission to the hospital, possibly 60 would have kidney failure and it is possible 12 would die as a result of the infection.' Horizontal wrinkles appeared on his forehead which he scratched with the fingertips of his left hand as he said, 'These figures which I have just quoted are from the various outbreaks comprising of all age ranges and I have a feeling that the results from our plan would be far worse or better should I say, as the average age of MPs is 50 and this age group is more susceptible to bad outcomes from the O157 infection.' Sharif was now talking passionately and spit was flying off his mouth. His enthusiasm to harm MPs scared me. I was deeply worried.

'Omar told us there is no killing involved in the plot,' I said looking at Omar.

'Correct, our intention is to cause the vote to fail, but if someone does become seriously ill, they are just plain unlucky. Please let me finish first,' Sharif said by banging his fist on the table. 'We plan to contaminate food for three consecutive days and that should have the desired results.' The crow's feet deepened beside Sharif's eyes as he said this with a smile on his face.

There was a heavy silence in the room.

Sharif dropped his cigarette into his tea mug,there was a hiss and a faint, wavy smoke arose from the mug.

'I'll make sure that I isolate O157 from a patient of 40-50 years of age. As I have mentioned earlier, I'll have to wait for the confirmation.' He leaned backwards on his chair which creaked. A wreath of cigarette smoke appeared from his mouth as before, which slowly dissolved in the air.

'We might have to wait longer. As you said it is a rare infection and you may not be able to get hold of the bacteria for years,' Omar said. 'We can't afford to wait; we have to carry out our plan by the 10th July. This crucial vote is due to take place on the16th. So we have got exactly three and a half weeks. We have to prevent this vote by MPs non-attendance and anyway after that MPs will go on their summer recess until September. If we are able to do this, I would regard it as a slap in the face of this bill and an explicit success. *Inshallah,* God willing with your help, this will happen.'

'What is the incubation period of this bacteria?' Sajid asked.

'The incubation period is 3 to 8 days,' Sharif replied.

'In that case we have to start dressing the food by the 10th July. We cannot delay it,' Omar said and the lines on his forehead deepened.

'Well, hopefully I'll get the bacteria from my own lab but failing this, I might have to pluck it from the central lab. This could be risky, as it is kept in a safe place over there and there are regular police checks to ensure no one has had access to the O157, but let's not be pessimists. Hopefully I'll have O157 from my own lab in the not too distant future.'

'Ok, what happens when you get hold of O157?' the other scarfed face asked.

'Well, the bacteria will be transported in a small broth bottle to our friend in North London. What he has to do is to turn on the kitchen oven to 60 degrees centigrade for only 5-7 minutes and empty the small broth bottle into the larger one, that's it. After a few hours, the bacteria will multiply and would be ready to be served on cold salads,' Sharif said by making a V sign with his nicotine stained fingers and having a fit which appeared a mixture of laughter and a chesty cough.

I could feel shivers running down my spine. I looked at Sajid who appeared cool.

'How will you confirm the bacteria have actually grown? Is it like making yoghurt from milk?' Omar asked sounding extremely excited to hear the plot.

'Great question. The colour of the broth changes when bacteria grow and will be much denser than a broth bottle with a few bacteria. After that what is required by our friendly chef is to gently sprinkle the cultured broth on the salad dishes. The bacteria will be killed off on heating food or microwaving.' Sharif sounded excited and I really felt sick.

'How big would the broth bottle be?' the others car fed face asked.

'Smaller than a nail varnish bottle, approximately 2 to 3 inches long. It should easily fit into any pocket without being noticed,' Sharif said chirpily.

'I think, this is a brilliant, very well thought-out plan. What I like most is that it does not involve carrying heavy backpacks, no fear of sniffer dogs catching you. It's simply epic,' Sajid said looking at me.

'Thanks, Sajid.' There was a twinkle of achievement in Omar's eyes. 'Any questions gentlemen?'

'Where is the toilet?' I asked.

'The last door on your left.' Omar pointed towards a door.

I hurried towards the toilet. A scarfed man got up from his chair and physically stopped me at the door. 'I need to go first, I've got IBS.'

'What?' I couldn't understand what he'd said in his muffled

voice.

'Irritable bowel syndrome,' he replied, chewing-on every word and sounding irritated. He didn't lock the toilet door and I could hear his posteriors slumping upon the toilet followed by an explosive and abundant usage.

'You may go inside... entirely at your own risk,' he said as he came out, wiping forehead with toilet paper.

The stench inside was unbearable; I pinched my nose and opened the toilet window to breathe in the fresh air. The toilet door swollen by dampness, juddered at its hinges and would not close, leaving a large slit through which I could hear the conversation. The toilet was without a seat and water was continuously leaking from the cistern down the loo. A large section of wallpaper had come off and flapped like a triangular flag.

This was pretty serious stuff, both disability and death to MPs was on the cards. I had to untangle myself from this plot, but how? My throat went totally dry. This very question could cost me my life. Despite cool air coming from the window, I could feel sweat flowing over my face.

CHAPTER 14

I think the plot had malignant intent. There was a one-in-four chance of death. A cursory search over the internet revealed a mortality rate up to 25% after E Coli O157:H7 infection. I didn't think that Omar and his microbiologist friend were that idiotic not to know this risk. Were they trying to hide this figure from us to snare us in their plot? Did they really think us so stupid that we would believe anything they told us? Were they still living in the dark ages and did not know that we carry mountains of information in our pockets in the form of mobile Internet? I had heard the voice recording of the meeting over and over again and at no stage had Omar said that the intention of the plot was to kill. Could he be naïve? I thought but I could not convince myself of that. I absolutely abhorred the whole idea of taking an oath over the Holy Book. I wanted to speak with someone but was also worried that I or my family might face vengeance as a result of my breaking the oath. Dad was doing charity work in a politically volatile region where opposition groups did not hesitate to kill charity workers. Both Bari Ammi and Mum had just recovered from strokes. I didn't wish any harm to come to my family because of me. I felt my eyes were bulging with tears. What should I do? I should make the utmost effort not to breech the vow, I thought. I would have a guilty conscience if any harm came to my family because of me. Life won't be worth living. Should I speak to Sajid and tell him my views? He would most probably first call me a chicken, then show his belligerence towards my thinking and taunt me that my way of thinking was the result of my sheltered life. Should I give way to peer pressure to join in the plot? Should I take advice from Mr Nazir? That would be best but then there was this issue of my oath, so what should I do?

Whenever Dad agonised on any issue, he would 'walk the issue' by going out on a long walk. Dad used to say that this walking helped him to concentrate his thoughts, helped him to understand the problem and the possible solutions to a problem. George used to make fun of this habit of Dad's and said that his grey-matter was mislocated in his ankles.

I also decided to 'walk the issue'. I put on walking shoes and immediately left the house.

I came out of Baker Street tube station and turned right on Baker Street towards Regents Park. I remembered Mum and Dad used to bring me there for picnics when I was little. So many years had passed since.

It was warm and humid after the rain. The water on the wet footpaths was evaporating like steam. The underground 'lost property' office, which was located immediately after the turn, had no claimants. The man in charge was seen hiding behind an opened newspaper, and only his fingers were visible. In front of the Sherlock Holmes museum, two tourists were having their picture taken with the gate keeper, who was sandwiched between them; their arms were on his shoulders looking like real chums. A middle-aged lady from the café was wiping the rain from the aluminium chairs on the footpath. As she leaned forward the deep cleavage of her buttocks became visible. The zoom lens of a tourist's camera popped out and he took several pictures of the bare bottom of the lady amidst wild laughter. The lady continued her work oblivious to the photography of her backside. 'Why is it not illegal to take random pictures of people in public places?' I thought.

Can Omar and his friends really sabotage the parliamentary motion on attacking any country in the world by carrying on with their plot? I thought as I waited at the pedestrian crossing. If there were not enough MP's available to vote then that did not mean the vote would fail,or would it? I did not know the answer.

'Wait for the green-man,' a woman who was pushing an empty push-chair shouted loudly at her toddler. A sullen look appeared on the child's face whose free movements were suddenly halted.

'He looks quite independent,' I said to the lady.

'Too independent sometimes,' she said. She looked a bit embarrassed, as she noted that she had caught the attention of all waiting at the crossing.

I had no doubt that Sajid had at least some knowledge of the plot before we went to Omar's place. Why did he not tell me? Was he worried that I might not agree to join if I was made aware of the plot beforehand? If this was the case, it was deception, blatant trickery to suck me into the plot. Was it planned that way or had it just happened by mistake? I didn't know. Omar knew exactly the role of everyone in the plot, but had he communicated this to Sajid?

A jogging lady whizzed pass and left a trail of fragrance. She was wearing a black top and trunks which were so tightly clasping her body that her feminine bulges and curvatures were evident without any strain on the imagination.

I had always liked to look at the trees. Like humans, I think each tree has got its own beauty, its own personality. Unlike humans, trees are not devious. They just do what they are supposed to do: look after us both physically and psychologically. I was walking slowly and was trying to re-play the whole of the meeting in my mind. The sunlight, filtering through innumerable leaves still felt warm on my face. I was walking on a footpath which was wandering across the carefully mowed green lawns. Did Sajid tell Omar about my work at the hospital? Or could it be his friend at the lab? Was I being watched at the hospital? The mere thought of being watched sent a chill down my spine. What I needed to disentangle was this: who was the mastermind of the plot, Omar and Sajid or only Omar? If it was a joint plan of Omar and Sajid then perhaps I could speak to Sajid and try to wriggle out of it. But if Omar was the mastermind of the plot then it would not be possible to come out of this unharmed. I was stuck in a shit-hole, I thought. I wished I was a tree on a bank of a canal, carelessly producing oxygen and did not have to go through all this. The voice of Mr Nazir echoed in my ear. 'You are selected for this'. This phenomenon of 'selection' was beyond my comprehension but I had a feeling it was indeed a dangerous business, a deadly one. Without your willingness, your consent you were 'chosen'. I wished I wasn't.

I wanted to re-discover the picnic spot of my childhood times. It was on a gentle slope under a tall, dense tree whose stem was bent like a letter S. The tree was located near the lake. I used to sit and play with Mum on a blanket and Dad would go for a walk. I thought I had reached the picnic spot, the slope was there, the lake was there but there was not that tree. It seemed either that the tree had fallen or been cut down to extend the footpath. I felt a bit sad not to find the tree. Dozens of people were lying on the slope, soaking in the orange sun. One, two, three, four. I counted the people sunbathing. A mortality rate of twenty-five per cent meant every fourth person infected could be dead as a result of the infection. Something churned inside me. People lying on the slope got up on their elbows to see a white swan in the lake which was stretching and flapping its wings to intimidate a black swan, who honked like mad.

A large, circular flowerbed, blooming with bright red tulips gave the look of a blaze from a distance. Another plot had violet, azure and golden flowers added to the magic of the early evening. I bent to smell a pink rose-flower which was bigger than the palm of my hand and noticed small pearl-like rain-droplets on its petals; a sunbeam was turning these gems into yet more glittering white. This carefully tended natural beauty sent a wave of happiness to my mind, enthused a spirit of well-being, adding another reason to live on this earth.

A young couple were sitting on a wooden bench, under the shade of a tree, talking, looking down at the lake while their small dog on a long lead was scampering around, panting and sniffing the heels of passers-by.

Two teenagers went zigzagging by on their roller skates. Loud music was emanating from them, one of them was pulling on something which initially I thought was a trolley suitcase but later I realised it was a speaker which was attached to their iPhone. Life is so easy and fun for some I thought.

I needed more information, answers to my questions; an amble in the park was not enough. I should ring Sajid to clarify how much and what else he knew about the plot, I thought, reaching for the mobile in my pocket. 'Hi, Sajid, it's me, what are you up to?'

'Just chilling, where are you?'

'Just came for a walk here in a park,' I said. 'Sajid, I think we're screwed up. Did you know the infection with this bug could be fatal?'

'No, I didn't but that's their bad luck I suppose.'

'The bug can kill one in four people.'

'Really?' Sajid said while laughing. 'That would be a blast, epic.'

'You knew the plan before we went to Omar's place?' I asked.

'No, honest to God. I only knew that Omar wanted to stop the vote in parliament but other than that I knew nothing.'

'What else do you know, which I don't?'

'No…. nothing…Honestly.'

'So you are not worried that people might get killed?'

'You call them people. They are worse than animals. Stuff them. Ali, I got to go now, I'll ring you later. You carry on with your walk. Good boy. Bye.'

'Bye.' I said.

So Omar was the mastermind. The situation looked ugly.

I continued to walk. To break an oath, a covenant, how bad could it be? Could it really bring bad luck to you? Or was it just an urban myth or an instrument to blackmail us? Was it just used to ensure compliance and obedience? God is merciful to his creation, how could He bring rage onto his own creation especially when someone was trying to shield behind his book to harm his creation? Surely, this couldn't be right. Omar was just using this ploy to get us on his side. Another idea flashed up in my mind. I had taken the oath not my mobile. I should just let the voice recording run to Mr Nazir. I felt a broad smile appearing on my face. Suddenly the whole weight lifted off my mind and I felt light as a kite in the sky. It was time to celebrate and in the next minute I was standing in a queue to buy an ice cream.

CHAPTER 15

I hurriedly climbed the steps to Mr Nazir's room. I was praying in my heart that he was not asleep or feeling unwell. I was becoming a hostage to the whole idea of the plot, I was thinking about it all the time. The burden was getting me down. I wanted to know the answer, if possible, today. I was clasping the mobile firmly in my hand, which was getting moist due to my nervousness rather than the physical activity of climbing up the staircase. I made sure that the mobile was fully charged before coming to see him; I didn't want any technical hiccups to add to my torment. After my last meeting with Mr Nazir I was absolutely sure that he would know exactly what to do in such a situation. It wasn't that I was reverent towards him; I knew in my heart that he was the right choice.

I gently knocked at the door of his room. 'Mr Nazir, this is Ali. Could I come in?'

'Most definitely, please do come in,' he said.

As usual, he was staring out of the window which was partly

open. The room appeared a bit darker as no lights were on; the sun had taken refuge behind the gloomy clouds. He appeared fatigued, thin and pale as if he had aged considerably during the past few days.

'Assalam o elakum,' and to cheer him up I said, 'you look better today.'

'Thanks,' he said in a very low voice, slowly raising his gaze at me. 'You are a very nice person. You haven't learned the art of telling lies with conviction.'

I smiled to hide my embarrassment and felt as if I had been caught stealing.

He continued: 'I feel the final destination is not very far. I know this now but knew it before as well. I didn't want to come to this country for any treatment because I knew, in my heart that no treatment was going to work for me, not in this country, not in any other country.' He stopped and moistened his lips and said, 'I am reaching the end of my present journey. Everyone who has come here has to go one day. I'm not worried about that but what I don't understand is why I agreed to come here for treatment. Perhaps nature wanted me to be buried here or there is some other reason or purpose which I am failing to understand. There is never any useless action here in this universe, it is our lack of insight or understanding about events that we regard as useless.'

'We all need you and wish you to be healthy soon. You're in our prayers,' I said by getting up. 'Do you mind if I turn the lights on?'

'Please do so,' he said looking at me. 'It looks as if something is bothering you. What's the matter Ali?'

'It's very difficult to hide anything from you, Mr Nazir. You can read the mind, heart and even the soul,' I said light-heartedly. 'Yes, there is something about which I need guidance.' I placed the mobile on a small coffee table in front of him and said. 'Mr Nazir,

I need your help, your advice.' I could hear my voice getting deep with emotion. 'If you are not feeling too tired or unwell, can I ask you to listen to the recording of a meeting? It is something which has been twisting my soul for the past two weeks. I am unable to decide what is right or wrong but what I am one hundred per cent sure of is that your advice would be most useful to me.'

'Sounds very serious,' he said and raised his gaze from the floor and looked at me with his penetrating glance. His eyes appeared like white lotus flowers floating in a dark pond. 'What is this about?'

I told him about the clandestine meeting and how I recorded it. He said looking thoughtful, 'Ok, let's hear what you have recorded.'

I got up and checked that the room door was properly shut and played the recording of the meeting. Mr Nazir kept his face resting on the palm of his hand with his eyes closed, occasionally he was looking at me as if he was trying to assess me by my facial expressions. He listened to twenty-seven minutes and three seconds of recording without saying anything and remained silent for quite some time afterwards as if he was trying to absorb the information.

The silence in the room was getting painful for me so I plucked up the courage to break it and said, 'What do you think of the oath we took?'

Mr Nazir looked at me again and I could feel his kind glance over my face. 'If someone is trying to bind you in an oath with a holy book then it is almost certain that this fellow is trying to sell you a flawed argument with a religious stamp on it. I think it would be more sinful in the eyes of God if you remained bound by an oath and got black-mailed. God is merciful not punitive.' I began to feel light, like a cloud floating in the sky.

'As you know Muslims all over the world are suffering,' I said. 'Omar wants to thwart this parliamentary vote. I agreed to join in this jihad to help the Muslim brotherhood, but perhaps I'm a very weak Muslim, I feel uneasy in my heart about it, so am I a coward, a feeble person or a hypocrite?

Mr Nazir smiled and looked at me and said. 'You are neither a weak Muslim nor a hypocrite. In fact, there is a cloud of good wishes and prayers over your head from someone who loves you dearly and this is what is preventing you from taking a wrong decision.' He paused briefly. 'Can you pass the glass of water for me please and I will try to clear a few cobwebs in your mind about jihad,' he said. 'Can I ask you what you understand by the word "Jihad"?'

I was not ready for this question. 'Jihad means a war against the enemies of Islam.'

'You have given me the western definition of jihad which is incorrect,' Mr Nazir said quietly.

'Really! Then what is the correct definition of jihad according to you?' I asked.

'Jihad is not equivalent to war. The word Jihad is derived from the word *Juhad* which means "to exert by utmost" or "to struggle hard." Jihad is not exclusively an Islamic concept, it is the biggest reality of life, and is a universal phenomenon. We are all involved in some kind of struggle for our existence so the whole of this world is full of *Jihadis*. What you are talking about is *Qitaal*, which is the 10th step on the ladder of jihad.' He stooped to take a sip of water. 'Would you like me to take you through all the nine rungs of the ladder leading up to Qitaal?'

'Yes please, I am listening.'

'The first step is to control yourself, your basic self. This is the most important and most difficult step of Jihad. Hunger and libido are the two most powerful feelings in this world. Both need to be satisfied by lawful means. Freud has described this as the "id".' He seemed energised by talking; the background music of the rattling keys re-appeared. 'Are you familiar with the Freudian structure model of psyche?' he asked me.

'Not really.'

'This is not the time and place to explain this theory to you. Briefly, id, ego and super-ego are the three parts of the psychic apparatus. Id contains the basic drives and impulses which need immediate satisfaction. We all are id-ridden but the mastery comes from becoming id-controller.' He stopped to drink water and continued his conversation.

'The second step is not to flow with the mob and the third step is to resist the crowd. I hope this is all making sense to you.'

'Yes, definitely, very much so. Please carry on.' Like last time, I began to enjoy his conversation.

'The fourth stage of the ladder is to confront the mob's views with a personal conviction. Socrates was charged with corrupting youth and failing to acknowledge the Greek gods in 399 BC. He was given the option of paying a fine for his views or drinking a cup of poison. Socrates did jihad for his views and opted to drink a cup of poison rather than to revoke his teachings.'

There was a knock at the door and I quickly put the mobile phone in the pocket of my jeans.

'Round time please,' a staff nurse said as she entered the room. The consultant whom I had met last time followed her.

'I think I'll wait outside.' I said, and got up.

The consultant shook hands with Mr Nazir. He looked in a sombre mood. He looked at me and said, 'I think we have met before. You are Ali?'

'Yes, I am,' I said. I was very impressed with his memory.

'Ali, you don't have to go out,' Mr Nazir said 'You carry on, Doc.'

'Mr Nazir, how are you feeling today?'

'OK but this swelling of my face and hands is gradually getting worse,' he said.

'Unfortunately your kidneys are packing up. Your blood potassium levels are rising, which could be serious. With your permission, we could start dialysis. I think we have reached a stage where we have to give it serious thought. With dialysis, your potassium level will come down, the swelling of your body should lessen and you would feel better. I think, initially, we'll see the response by doing dialysis twice every week.'

'I think, like my kidneys, I should be packing up as well.' he said with an effort full smile. 'Aren't we fighting a losing battle here? When the stability of elements in the body is disturbed, it can't be good.'

'We don't like to think in that way,' the consultant said. 'Ok, we'll start dialysis in a few hours, if you agree.'

'You don't like to give up, Doc,' Mr Nazir said.

'No, not that easily,' he said with a reassuring smile and both the consultant and the nurse left the room.

'If you wish, I could leave now,' I said to Mr Nazir.

'No, no, keep sitting,' he said. 'Where was I?'

'You were explaining to me the various stages of Jihad,' I said.

'Yes, I had reached the fourth stage.'

'That's right,' I said and became attentive again.

Mr Nazir started his conversation again.

'Broadly speaking, a society comprises of mainly three types of people. I mean mental types, the brains trust,and the intellectual elites of society. The first type, usually are in a minute minority but have wrestled with various philosophies like Marxism, Darwinism, positivisms and set the thought and tone of society. You can only penetrate them through logic. You cannot bring about any change in society without the help of these people. The second type is the common people, the herd mentality. They flow with whatever the crowd says. They can become looters and vandals one day and another day could play an important role in raising millions of pounds for a charitable cause. You can change them but as a preacher the only thing they expect of you is to appear clean; no earning of money by unfair means; no sex scandals. The third group of people are the salaried missionaries, who do a paid job. As a part of Jihad, one needs to tackle all three of these groups which complete the six steps of the ladder leading up to Qitaal.'

He stopped talking, his face became tense, and his cheeks appeared pulled upwards thus lengthening his lips. He looked to be in pain.

'Can I do something for you? Or should I call the doctor?' I said.

'No, no, there is no need to call the doctor. My feet are killing me. Can you put them on the stool,' he said weakly.

I lifted his feet, which were swollen, felt soft like fresh bread and gently placed them over the foot-stool.

'Are you feeling any better?' I asked him.

'Yeah, that's much better. This swelling is quite painful,' he said quietly.

He stopped to drink water again and continued.

'The seventh stage is to change the system and in fact this is also one of the most difficult parts of Jihad. Initially, one has to show passive resistance which means to face persecution without retribution. This requires courage of a high order, the courage to resist injustice without rancour, to unite against the utmost firmness with the utmost gentleness, to die but not to kill. There are numerous examples of this in history; the Prophet Mohammad, peace be upon him, and his followers faced opposition for thirteen years in Mecca without raising a finger in self-defence.'

'Was Ghandi's non-violence movement based on a similar approach?' I asked.

'Yes, non-violent resistance by Ghandi in the 1920's was a recent example of this. However, when your group consolidates and becomes bigger then you can practice active resistance. This is direct confrontation with the system. But there is no killing even at the eighth stage of jihad. You can take steps to weaken the opposition's economy, for example.'

He paused, closed his eyes firmly and massaged his forehead with the finger-tips of his right hand. The rattling of keys faded in the stillness of the room. He started again. 'The ninth step is to be fully physically ready for confrontation. In olden days, people participating in battles were mainly self-selected volunteers on both sides. This isn't the case anymore. Now, there are professional armies, equipped with state-of-the art stealth and visible weapons, which could annihilate the opposition by a tiny movement of a finger on a button, thousands of miles away from the battlefield.'

'That is so true. I never thought of this point before,' I said.

'The final, tenth stage of Jihad is Qitaal which means to physically fight with your opponents. One has to go through all the stages of Jihad before committing to Qitaal,' he said.

Mr Nazir looked at me again and said, 'I hope I have explained to you the mistakes Muslims often make in the difference between Jihad and Qitaal and unfortunately muddle up the process of Jihad leading to Qitaal.'

'Yes you have. Please correct me if I'd misunderstood you. The emphasis of Jihad is mainly on self-restraint and dialogue with your opposition. Do you think Qitaal has any place in the modern world?'

'I think you've understood it correctly. To enforce Qitaal, is the responsibility of a state not of individuals.'

'But if some individuals feel that Islamic states are not fulfilling the obligation of Jihad and Qitaal, can they take this into their own hands?'

'No, they can't. There're certain things which individuals or persons cannot implement and this is one of them. They can't just start doing Qitaal at their own discretion.'

Suddenly, it began to rain heavily outside and there was a splashing of rain water onto the floor of the room. Mr Nazir looked through the window. There was a smile of amazement in his eyes. I closed the window.

'So to add this bug to MPs food is not Jihad?' I said to clarify my point.

'No, this is not Jihad, absolutely not. This is deception, blatant murder and I do not want you or your friends to become involved in it,' Mr Nazir said. 'We should not let this happen. We need to inform the police to stop these people before it is too late. When are they going to mix this bug with the food?'

'I don't know the exact timing, but it will be communicated to us all in due course,' I said.

'Today, I think, possibly, I have understood the reason why I chose to come to England for my treatment,' Mr Nazir said, looking deeply immersed in his thoughts. He looked at his peculiar looking wrist watch and said, 'I think, Ali, you should be going now. You should ring and tell your friends to abandon this idea and seek repentance from God before it is too late. The one who kills a person is akin to one who kills the whole of humanity.'

As always, I didn't want to leave. I wanted to listen to more of him but at the same time I couldn't afford to annoy him, so I shook hands with him and came out of his room. I was thinking on my way why did I like Mr Nazir's explanations? Simply, because I wanted to hear that? Why was there such a huge difference of opinion between Mr Nazir and Omar? I should also resist the temptation of labelling my friends as id-ridden, id-laden people .....I should think of something else...the sight of sun set provided me an excellent distraction.

CHAPTER 16

I Said, 'Please meet Dr George,' as I introduced him to Mr Nazir. 'He is one of the close friends of Dad's. He works in the same hospital, and he is a baby specialist.'

'Many thanks for visiting me. It's very kind of you. In these busy times not many people would like to visit a sick old man like me,' Mr Nazir said. His nose and cheek bones appeared more prominent. His eyes were sinking in his face.

I think he looked frailer every day. He was sitting in the high-back chair, his jacket slung on the back of it. He was wearing a creaseless white shirt. The left sleeve was folded up above the elbow, and two plastic tubes were emerging underneath which were attached to a machine, which was making a soft humming noise. I presumed he was being dialysed. His blood was seen leaving his body through one tube and after spinning for a while in the machine was re-entering through the other. I found the whole sight of this circulation of blood somewhat gross but it appeared it was not causing any pain to Mr Nazir.

'The purpose of this visit is twofold,' George started in his usual style. 'First, to see you and to stand in place of Ali's Dad. Second, is to meet you, to talk to you, to ask you some questions, to seek answers to some queries. Ali is full of praise for you and for your understanding of things.'

'Ali has a gentle soul,' Mr Nazir said in a soft voice. 'Even if he tried to find fault in someone, he would not. He is from the category of people who always find the positive in other people.' I could feel my ears were beginning to glow, I felt flattered to hear these remarks: I felt honoured.

'You are absolutely right, Ali's dad is a very lucky person in all respects,' George said. He continued his conversation by asking. 'Are you satisfied with your treatment?'

'Yes, I think the doctors are doing their best. At this age and stage of my life, I'm bonded to a new partner,' he said with a smile and pointed towards the dialysis machine. 'I have to spend three hours on alternate days with my life's saver. The swelling of my feet has certainly got better with dialysis and now I'm able to walk.'

He pointed towards a large, silver fresh fruit platter and said, 'Please help yourselves, it has just arrived.' The platter was highly aesthetically decorated with big blocks of contrastingly coloured fruit: bite-size pieces of melons, black and green grapes, raspberries, strawberries, blueberries, fresh figs and dates. The whole platter looked so delightful that I and perhaps George also, thought it should be left untouched.

'I insist,' he said. 'Please have some. I'm sorry but I won't be able to join you, I hope you won't mind.'

I looked at George and handed over a plate lying next to the platter. George loaded his plate with strawberries and I took a fig which looked enchanting.

Mr Nazir looked carefully at George and said, 'What questions do you have on your mind?'

'Quite a lot,' George said laughingly, chewing on a strawberry. 'If it is ok by you, could I ask you some questions which have been bothering me and I'm unable to find answers to these puzzles from any internet search or from any books?'

'Yes, please go ahead. I'll try my best to answer,' Mr Nazir said and as usual he lowered his gaze to the floor.

'I would like to embark on the journey of finding the truth, the real, the true truth but I don't know how and whereto start this journey. I have made several attempts to start this voyage but either I end up in a cul-de-sac or even worse, sometime later I realise it was a false start, a complete pseudo-start.' George said.

'My dear,' Mr Nazir said with a mild smile on his face, 'to search for the truth, to go onto the path for truth is not easy. Why would you choose to trek on such a stony, thorny path?'

'I love challenges. Life would be very dull without challenges, and also I'm not afraid of difficulties as long as I know that I'm on the right track. This would be my personal choice,' George said unequivocally, looking at Mr Nazir.

I readied myself to hear an interesting conversation.

'Well, I must warn and congratulate you at the same time, warn you for choosing a very difficult path and congratulate you for your choice. The journey for the truth-seeker starts itself. You don't have to undergo electric cardio-version shocks on your chest to change the rhythm of your heart. Provided you are true to your search, the path will open up itself for you. A red carpet would unfold under your feet. Don't worry too much about blind ends or stop-starts; just carry on with your search.' He stopped to catch his breath and said, 'In fact the people who have traversed this path say that the joy of the search is far greater than reaching the final destination and some become so elated with their journey that they even pray that they may never reach the final goal. There is a world of difference between the voyages of Sinbad and the travels of the truth seekers.'

I looked at George, for the first time he seemed lost for words, his lips were parted in amazement, and his cheeks were glowing with excitement.

I was once again totally amazed by the way Mr Nazir was speaking. If I had closed my eyes and listened to him, I would not be able to guess that I was listening to a very unwell person. There was no sign of weakness in his voice.

Mr Nazir continued. 'The ego, the self, should attain a state of self-realization before it embarks on its journey towards truth. The clearer the mirror of the heart, the easier for it to receive the images of truth. The first thing therefore is self-reformation, enabling you to know what the radiance of truth means.'

The jingling music of his key chain continued to make a sound in the background.

'Thanks, I'm sorry, I'm still muddled-up. The question remains: how do I start self-reformation, do I have to convert to your religion?'

'The process of self-realisation, self-reformation starts by loving God's creations and giving up self-love. One has to get rid of negative forces within oneself. The low emotions such as hatred, backbiting, revenge, jealousy and gossiping have to be abandoned. To commence your journey by converting to our religion is entirely your choice, your selection. It is not an obligation, not a prerequisite. No matter how many thousand miles a river traverses in valleys and plains, eventually it meets the measureless oceans.'

The last sentence of Mr Nazir's brought a slanted smile to George's face and he said. 'I'm very sorry if what I'm going to say offends you. I do not believe in any God.'

I looked carefully at Mr Nazir's face to pick up any sign of annoyance but he looked quite composed as before and so George continued. 'I do not think that any such thing as God exists.' George said this with a side-to-side movement of his hand. 'God is the psychological need of weak people. We scientifically-minded people couldn't afford to dwell on such old-fashioned ideas. These sacred old books tend to limit the scope of human imagination, make one narrow-minded, and give one tunnel-vision.' George clenched his right hand in a fist as he said, 'I am a child cancer specialist and every day I see young kids suffering from incurable diseases, enduring pain and causing agony to their parents. Why does this happen? Why are the prayers of their parents not answered? These innocent children have not committed any sins so why this punishment? I am sorry to say, if there is a God he must be very, very sick, because he has no sense of justice.' George said this with an obvious disgust.

My blood was boiling to hear this blasphemy from George. I thought it was extremely rude of him to use such language about God. I was sure George's eloquence and huge vocabulary would have allowed him to choose his words a bit more carefully but he did not. Did he do this purposefully to provoke Mr Nazir? I had heard George's views so many times yet never got an impression that he was an atheist. Why was he doing this? It seemed it hadn't been a good idea to bring George to Mr Nazir. I resisted the urge to interject and just nodded. Sadness and frustration were mounting in equal measures as I continued to listen. I looked at Mr Nazir.

He looked cool, totally unperturbed as before and said, 'To believe or not to believe in a god is your choice. But I would only urge you to take this decision after careful thought and consideration. It isn't God's duty to descend-down from the heavens and to present Him in front of you to believe Him; this hasn't happened before and will never happen. He has gifted you with intelligence and it is your duty to 'search' for 'His signs' to reach Him, just like you do in medicines to look for symptoms, signs and perform investigations leading you to a diagnosis.' Mr Nazir stopped to take a breath and said, 'your decision of not believing in a God should not be clouded by the argument that you are born free, your ideology and your thought processes are free and that if you believe in God then your thoughts would be reined in and it is then much more easy for you to deny the existence of God. If you are following this argument of "ease" then you are making you, yourself a god, worthy of worship.'

The bunch of keys he was jingling slipped out of his hand onto the floor. I quickly leaned forward, picked up the keys and handed them to him; I didn't want any break in his argument.

'There are more scientists in this world who are believers in God than non-believers,' said Mr Nazir. 'A religion does not blinker the human being and prevent the scientific development. In fact; quite the contrary. In the Quran, the last testament for mankind, humans are encouraged in several places to ponder and not to become believers like a blind person who may have limited faculties to carry out any investigations. I would say that as believers in God, we are encouraged rather than discouraged to do scientific research.'

He stopped. With his eyes still shut, he scratched his forehead with his right hand and continued. 'In reply to your query about why an innocent child becomes sick, please remember that sickness is not a punishment but a trial, a test, to check your faith, your steadfastness. And you also asked why the prayers of some people are answered and of others not. The problem here is that we try to understand God before accepting Him. To understand the ultimate supreme power one has to traverse from the outer circle of acceptance to the inner circle of understanding. If you get this order wrong you will lose your path and the end result would be restlessness and confusion.'

Mr Nazir reached for the glass of water from the table close to him and quietly took long sips and said, 'What is due from us is submission, not investigation. Investigate the world and submit to the sublime. Let it not be the other way round that we submit to the world and begin to investigate our creator.'

He stopped and thought for a while and continued. 'I do not have hard scientific data to back my theory but it is my observation that non-believers in God have a high incidence of alcoholism, depression, heart disease, high blood pressure and kidney problems.' He smiled. 'Well, as it is clear from my own example, such diseases are not exclusive to atheists,' and he said, 'I do not have enough time on my hands to scientifically prove this but some budding doctor like Ali could take up this project to prove me wrong.'

I could see George appearing much more serious as he said, 'Are you saying that an atheist is more likely to develop depression than a believer?'

'It is quite possible. Because an atheist questions whereas a believer accepts fully and wholeheartedly whatever happens to him. I know it is not easy. We like to ask the question "why me"' but, perhaps it would be more appropriate to ask "why not me"?'

He paused and said, 'If you allow me, I could cite you a couple of examples to show you that believers in God do experience depression.'

'That would be good, please go ahead,' George said, looking very interested in what Mr Nazir was about to say.

'I'm sure you must have heard or read the story of the Prophet Jacob who went through an immense emotional turmoil when his beloved son Joseph was taken away from him. Due to his intense sorrow he lost his vision which is one of the symptoms of extreme depression. There is no doubt that Jacob was a true believer and although I may be wrong I think Jacob did suffer from depression.

I can give you another example of Mary, mother of Jesus Christ. After the miraculous birth of Jesus, she is quoted to say in the Quran, "I wish I was not born". Who says such things unless one is depressed? Was it a post-natal depression or a depression of some other kind? I leave you medics to decide but one thing is clear that a believer in God could suffer from depression.'

I could see George's lower lip was flapping like a fish's mouth and his eyes were bulging as if he would cry any minute. He said, 'Ali was absolutely right about you. I only wish I could have met you earlier. I really wish that you get well soon. My soul is very restless. Have you got any tried and tested recipe for a peaceful life?'

'It is very thoughtful of you to say such kind words,' Mr Nazir said jiggling his keys. 'In the great book of time in which the date and time of your birth and the day of departure from this world are written, it was also written that you would meet me today. The important thing is that we met, not that we did not meet earlier. As regards the recipe for peace, do not quarrel or argue with your Lord, your creator. First try to obey Him wholly and completely. Come within His sphere of work, then vision will descend on you and the whole paradox of life will be unveiled in front of you. Then there will be no complaints or quibbles only peace. I will pray that your journey towards Him is smooth and uneventful.'

Mr Nazir lifted his gaze up from the floor and looked at George whose eyes were red, with tears rolling down his cheeks.

'How do you know the answers to all these queries? You seem to have pondered upon these and every angle of life. This is amazing, absolutely incredible,' George said and his voice was shaking.

'It is incumbent upon me to pass on whatever knowledge I have. Yes, it is true that the person who has imparted to me all these thoughts had spent ages reaching the conclusions, which I am able to share with you in a matter of a few minutes or hours. The idea is to make your life easier, to avoid the inconveniences, difficulties of search and research.'

Mr Nazir reached for the glass of water again and took a small sip, moistened his lips with his tongue, while his eyes were still closed and he continued. 'In the language of science, this is called the vortex effect. Are you familiar with this phenomenon?' Mr Nazir asked.

'Not really,' George said and I also shook my head.

'I'm sure you have seen migratory birds flying in the skies in V shaped pattern. Scientists have determined that the "V" shaped formation that geese use serves two important purposes: One is to conserve energy by taking advantage of the upward vortex field created by the wings of the birds in front. The other is to facilitate orientation and communication among the birds. At this point in time I may be the goose in front facilitating your flight but at some time I'll be tired or maybe not in this world at all and then you'll have the responsibility of making other's lives easy. This cycle has to go on. This is the rule of nature.'

Mr Nazir suddenly looked tired. He paused for a little. He sluggishly opened his eyes and said, 'I'm grateful to you for taking time to see me to chat with me. I pray that God makes your life easy and gives you an opportunity to make others' lives easy as well. Best of luck.' Mr Nazir raised his hand to shake hands with George. 'I am sorry I cannot even get up to see you off. I feel very weak today. Please take care.'

George wiped tears from his cheeks and firmly shook hands with Mr Nazir and said, 'I'll pray for you to get well soon. I have learnt today more that I have learnt so far in my life. I need to meet you again soon.'

'God willing, we will,' Mr Nazir said and then he looked at me and said, 'Can you come tomorrow, Ali? I have not been able to go out for the last three days.'

'I'll be here tomorrow.' I was glad that I would be able to meet him again.

Both of us came out of his room quietly. George was slowly mumbling, 'At last the drought is broken. Heavy rain. A tiny rain drop meets the ocean, onto limitless, surging waves. A truly amazing day. I want to tear off my clothes, and run shouting on the streets calling *Eureka, Eureka.*'

I looked at George, he appeared completely different today. I didn't know what he was mumbling about. Very bizarre. I don't think he was gullible or easily influenced. Had Mr Nazir removed all the layers from George to reveal his true character or was he always like this and was keeping his identity concealed from us all? George's theory of four categories of people echoed in my mind: was he 'high octane' waiting for a flame to come near him? Or had he simply gone cuckoo.

George looked at me and said, 'those strawberries were really divine. So fresh, so crisp. Never had such ever before in my whole life.'

'Yeah, the figs were also garden-fresh, very nice,' I said.

As we walked in front of the nursing station, I saw the staff nurse who was re-directing the bouquets to the children's hospital.

I stopped and asked her, 'Hi, how is everything, what is the bouquet count so far?'

'All well, busy as usual. I can't remember the exact number of bouquets,' she replied, 'but it is in excess of three and a half thousand. He has broken the record of one of the princes from the middle-east who was admitted here last year and received thirty-two hundred.'

'Because he is a king,' I said smiling. 'I think he not only gets flowers, he gets fresh fruit as well. We just had the most amazing fresh fruit today.'

'But he did not get anything delivered today,' the nurse said by looking in a book. 'In-fact, he has not received anything in the past three days.'

'May be it was delivered when you were on your break,' George said. 'That fruit we had in his room was freshly picked not three days old.'

'No, I'm sure there was nothing for him this morning,' the nurse said quietly.

'Anyway, it's time to go. I'll come to see him tomorrow. Bye for now,' I said.

'Bye, see you tomorrow,' the nurse said pleasantly.

George was walking and his face was telling me that he was deeply immersed in his thoughts. I decided not to disturb him and walked silently along with him. As we came out of the hospital, George stopped and turned toward me and said, 'What do you think about where the fruit came from?'

I shrugged my shoulders and said, 'Dunno.'

George's face suddenly began to beam with joy. 'I can't believe our height of good luck, today. We had the fruit which is only given to the very special, selected, chosen people.'

'You mean ....' my mouth opened widely in amazement and I could not complete my sentence.

'Yes, that is exactly what I mean.' George began to laugh hysterically and this fit of laughter freaked me out.

Has he suddenly lost his marbles? He had never behaved like

this ever before. He was attracting the attention of passers-by. Oblivious to all this, George was walking away from me and I thought it was best not to follow or accompany him at that time.

George never went to his home after that day.

CHAPTER 17

'Ali, I would like to visit a cemetery. Is there one nearby?' Mr Nazir asked me and I was quite surprised to hear this.

'Why do you think like this?' I asked with surprise. 'Don't worry, you'll be fine and I'm sure you'll go back to your home country, soon, fully recovered and healthy.'

'One should not be afraid of death. Rather one should remember it every day. Anyway both statistically and health wise I am close to death so there is no harm in visiting my future resting place,' Mr Nazir said with a half-smile on his face.

My heart filled with sadness to hear this from him. I wanted him to live a very long and healthy life. I wanted to have a very lengthy, everlasting friendship with him.

'I fully appreciate that death is an inevitable fact but why live your life in the light of a tragic, bitter fact?' I wanted to tease out his views.

'It is far better to live in the light of a tragic fact, rather than to forget or deny it, and build everything on a fundamental lie.' He ran his finger into his thick eyebrows, wrinkles appeared on his forehead and he said, 'I think it was DH Lawrence who said:

"Oh build your ship of death, oh build it!

For you will need it

For the voyage of oblivion awaits you"

I was very impressed with his memory.

He closed his eyes and continued in his usual way. 'Death is one of the two great events of our lives. Beyond early childhood we must live with the certain knowledge of death. Death is a part of you and if you endeavour to evade it, you evade yourself. Without death every birth would be a tragedy as today the world is already overpopulated and polluted.'

He paused to drink water. His shaking hands caused a mild tremor in the water.

'Today the doctors are obsessed with the idea of prolonging life. A huge sum of money is spent in the intensive care units to prolong life for a few days when all that makes life valuable has gone. I have recently read in articles that only about a fifth of patients emerge alive from American intensive care units. There is also a misconception among the public that doctors can hold back death. They cannot. Doctors run these warehouses of death in the form of intensive care units because they regard death as their own failure, their own defeat. The medical schools need to incorporate this missing piece in their medical students' curriculum.'

As always I was very impressed with his knowledge and his views. Who might have told him about medical curriculum? I thought. But I wanted to hear his views about something else. 'I may have misunderstood you, are you in favour of assisted dying?'

I asked sheepishly.

'I apologise for my miscommunication, no I am not advocating assisted dying by any means. That would be suicide in my opinion. One has to go through various shades of light like a candle flame does before it extinguishes itself at dawn.' He said this waving his hand in the air.

I could see emotions were running high in his mind. I had to change the topic.

I was so embarrassed by the way George behaved in front of Mr Nazir the other day. 'I must apologise, George was contemptuous and blasphemous. In fact I never knew that he was an atheist. I myself was shell-shocked. I don't know why he behaved liked that in front of you. I've never seen that part of his personality before. I still think he is a nice person,' I said looking at Mr Nazir.

'There is no need to apologise and I didn't take any offence at what he said. Negation is a form of affirmation. I knew well that he was a firm believer. He was just trying to shrug the responsibility of taking the post,' he said.

'What post?' There was an obvious surprise in my tone.

'Sometimes, you ask too many questions,' he said gruffly. 'I'm not obliged to answer all of your questions.'

'I'm so sorry.' I felt embarrassed to have annoyed him and changed the topic of our conversation once again by saying. 'There is a cemetery nearby. If you want to see it, could I call a cab?' I did not think that he would be able to walk to the cemetery.

'If it is not too far, I would prefer to walk. I like to walk,' he said softly and got up. He wrapped a scarf around his neck which gave a glimpse of his prominent neck veins and muscles. He was wearing a crisp, starched *Shalwar Kamiz* and a jacket. He looked very weak and his clothes hung loosely on his body. He was stooping on his walking stick.

'Are you sure that you would like to walk?' I asked again.

'Absolutely positive,' he said quietly, 'if you don't mind carrying my water bottle, please.'

'Not a problem,' I said. I decided not to impose on him and let him walk.

As we passed by the nursing station, a nurse who had an air of authority in her manners got up and said in a questioning tone 'Alright, Mr Nazir?'

'Yes,' he replied briefly.

'What are we up to today?' she asked again.

'I'm just going downstairs to have a bit of sunshine, a bit of fresh air. It's a lovely day out there. Ali, is with me,' he said by clapping me on my shoulder. 'We'll be back soon.'

'That's ok, but please come in an hour, which will be your medicine time.'

'Oh, I nearly forgot,' he said with a twinkle of mischief in his eyes, 'We have to rush back in time.'

The nurse understood the joke and smiled.

He was tenaciously holding on to the railing of the stair-case and began to climb down step by step, stopping at each step by putting both feet on it. 'You will have to put up with this old man,' he said.

'That's not a problem. You take your time.'

Soon we were out of the hospital and we turned left. It was a really bright, sparkly day. The sun shone on our shoulders and gave pleasant warmth, which sank into the body giving a sense of well-being. As usual, people were walking hurriedly along the street with no time to enjoy the rare sunshine. Mr Nazir's face broke up into a kind smile when he saw a mother who was pushing a twin pram. He stopped and followed her with his gaze until she disappeared at the end of the street. A flashy car driver honked lengthily at a taxi that overtook before jumping through the orange traffic light. He stood to catch his breath by a fruit stall on the footpath, which was selling freshly pressed fruit juices. The seller was also exhibiting a pyramid of pulpless skins as a testament to his freshly squeezed juice. Mr Nazir walked for a few minutes and then stopped by a newsagent.

'Would you like to buy a paper?' I asked.

'No,' he replied, 'no news is new news for me anymore.' We crossed the road by the pelican lights and he looked clearly impressed that cars were stopping to give pedestrians right of way.

'We are not very far from this cemetery. It is just over there.' I pointed towards the black wrought iron gates of the cemetery.

'It is closer than I expected,' he said as if he was talking in his thoughts.

He stopped and looked with an interest at the road dividing into two. He raised his walking stick, pointing towards the junction and asked, 'what do you call this? A road bifurcating into two?'

'You mean a Y junction or a Y intersection?'

'Yes,' he shifted his weight from one leg to another, held my shoulder and looked at me and said. 'Nature tests us all. Throughout our lives, we are tested by Y junctions or cross-roads and we have to make a choice, a choice made with a God-given gift called intelligence. I'm referring here to the common people. The general public who have an IQ of somewhere between 90 and 110. The people gifted with superior intelligence are judged with harder tasks.'

'That's fair enough,' I said.

'Let me explain this to you with the help of a short story.' He took the water bottle from my hand and took a couple of sips.

'I like stories anyway,' I said with an interest.

'A village was about to be flooded and people were frantically fleeing to save their lives. A person who was about to make an escape in his four-wheel drive jeep, noted an aloof person sitting in an empty house, so he went to the person and said that he had room in his jeep and he could take him to the hill top to save him from the flood. The person looked at him and said that his God would save him. The jeep driver went away. The flood water entered the village and a rescue boat saw this person floating on his bed in his house. He declined to be rescued a second time and said that his God would save him. The water rose further and this person was now seen sitting on the roof top and a helicopter came to air lift him but he declined again by saying that God would save him. Eventually the person was engulfed by the rising, whirling tide of water and was drowned. This person demanded to see God straightaway after his death and said furiously to him that He did not save him and that He had betrayed his trust.'

Mr Nazir looked at me and asked, 'You know what God said to him?' He sounded a bit short of breath and took another swig from the bottle.

'No, I don't.' I was very curious to know the outcome of this story.

'God replied, "I tried to save you three times, I sent you a jeep, a boat and a helicopter. I gifted you with intelligence to make the right choice but you didn't, you never asked my help to help you to make a decision so don't blame me, blame yourself".'

'That's brilliant.' I said.

'It is the choice, the selection at the cross roads which makes us a dweller of heaven or hell. God is very fair, much unbiased. He has given all of us humans a free will, the ability to make a choice and now it is up to us what we choose. We must always pray to God to help us to make the right choice.'

'This topic of free will really confuses me, do we really have free will, and can we really do what we want to?' I asked.

'Yes, you are absolutely right. We are granted only a limited free will. The day we are born and the day we die is already decided. We can't choose our parents. When we are hungry we eat and when we are tired we sleep. The free will we have here is to choose to eat meat, vegetable or fruit, but nothing more. A person having perfect twenty-twenty vision can only look to a certain distance and not beyond. Within that sphere you are allowed to do whatever you want to do, but not outside that.'

'I think you are absolutely right.' As always his answer to my query was ready made.

As we entered the cemetery, acres of land were seen strewn with headstones on each side of the tarmac road. I found the whole atmosphere greatly oppressive and grim.

'As probably you could work out, the graves on the right side are of Christians and those on the left side of the cemetery are of Muslims,' I said like an experienced guide.

He strolled towards the Christian side, walking in the aisles. Headstones covered with green moss where nothing could be read and the granite headstones with gold engraving of dates of birth and death, porcelain statues of the Virgin Mary and angels with open arms and furled wings placed by family and friends were creating a sense of unease inside me. Was I afraid of death? Mr Nazir was silent and was walking in the aisles, between the graves, reading the headstones intently. Some graves had real flowers which were dead or dying and others had plastic ones.

'Artificial flowers look good but they cannot bring peace to the inhabitant of a grave. A stem of fresh, green leaves is better than a bunch of plastic flowers,' he said quietly.

'Ali, will you promise me, maybe once in a year, you would lay two green leaves on my grave. I do not want anything more from you,' he said. He looked very serious.

'Sure, that should not be a problem.' I was swept by a wave of sadness at losing him.

'This place looks very peaceful. Without a doubt, gentle souls are resting here. Would you promise me, Ali that I will be buried here?'

'I will.' My stomach lurched and my eyes swelled up with tears.

Oblivious of me, Mr Nazir was looking at the horizon and walking slowly. He stopped walking, placed his heavy hand on my shoulder, looked into my eyes and asked, 'Have you read the famous Punjabi, Sufi poet Baba Bullay Shah?'

'Not really. I can understand a bit of Punjabi but can't read it. Was he good?'

'He was very good. Baba Bullay Shah in a mystic verse says that after his death, the dead body lying in the grave is not his but of someone else as death is not his destiny.'

'Wow, that's wonderful. This is called steadfastness towards death, isn't it?' I asked Mr Nazir. 'Is it not part of certain cultures, especially Asian, to show indifference or steadfastness towards death or are they just methods of coping with or giving up to the inevitable, or is it a form of some sort of learned helplessness?'

'Facing death steadfastly and being indifferent to it is not the same thing. The first is not unusual but I do not think the second is ever genuine.' As usual, Mr Nazir appeared to know the answer to every question. 'Steadfastness and indifference towards death are different in their moral quality and mental motive. Steadfastness towards death can be based on a certain belief that death is not the end and that the dying person is fully satisfied that they have successfully played their part in the cycle of life.'

'Ok, Mr Bullay Shah's lack of fear for death was steadfastness and what does this indifference towards death mean?' I asked inquisitively.

'Most of us learn not to fight or fear the inevitable......... others perhaps blind their terror by wearing the mask of indifference.'

He stopped talking and said. 'Let's raise our hands and ask forgiveness for all buried here in this cemetery.' He steadied his walking stick against his body and raised his palms towards the sky. His face became very solemn and his lower lip was quivering. He read something for a few minutes and brushed his hands over his face.

'Time to go back,' he said.

I could see that he was walking slowly as if his legs had grown heavier and he had to make an effort to walk.

When we came out of the cemetery he said, 'I think it's time for a taxi ride back to the hospital'.

He did not speak a word all the way back and seemed absorbed deeply in his thoughts. As we reached the hospital entrance he said, 'Ali, could you please get a wheel chair for me from reception.' He looked paler than before and the wrinkles appeared more noticeable on his face.

'A porter has just taken a wheel chair patient to the ward. If you wait a couple of minutes he should be back, unless you want to help yourselves,' the receptionist said with a pleasant smile on her face as she pointed towards a wheelchair parking lot.

'No, I don't mind,' I quickly took a wheelchair to the front of the hospital where Mr Nazir was waiting.

A smile appeared on his face as he saw me bringing the wheelchair.

'I'm very sorry to give you this inconvenience. May God always keep you in peace,' he said as he slumped in the chair.

'It's my privilege,' I said with pleasure.

I pushed his chair onto the ramp and into the corridor. Two porters in theatre scrubs were pushing a stretcher and I stopped to give way to them. Both bobbed their heads and said, 'Thank you sir.'

Mr Nazir brought his hand in front of his chest and gently squeezed my hand. His hand was stone cold. My heart fluttered. He needed to be seen immediately by a doctor. I pushed his chair swiftly along the corridor. In the next five minutes nurses were helping him into his bed, his closed eyes were making me panic and I felt better when he said, 'Thanks, Ali, you may go back home and take rest. Bye for now.'

CHAPTER 18

My mobile rang. Who could it be ringing me at this time? I said to myself. I was barely coming out of my deep sleep.

'I am extremely sorry to bother you at this time. This is Staff Nurse Margaret from Bromwell hospital. Mr Nazir's condition has suddenly deteriorated. He would like you to come to the hospital, right now. I'm really sorry for this inconvenience at this time.'

'OK, what time is it?' I asked the Staff Nurse, my eyes were still shut.

'It is almost quarter past three. Should I tell him that you are on your way?'

'Yes please. I will be there as soon as I can.'

I turned the bedside lamp on and squinted at the light. As I got out of bed, I felt weakness in my legs which could hardly take my weight. My heart was racing very fast. I sat on a chair. I felt sick.

'I got to go to the hospital now. I can't be sitting here,' I said to myself and took a couple of deep breaths.

I changed quickly.

As I came out of my room, I saw both Mum and Bari Ammi standing on the landing. Bari Ammi was supporting herself by holding the bannister with both hands.

'Who was it, Ali?' Mum asked.

'It was Bromwell hospital. Mr Nazir's worse and he is asking for me.'

'God have mercy on Nazir.' Bari Ammi said.

'I will come with you Ali, jus' wait a minute.' A shadow of fear crossed Mum's face and she turned to her room.

'Mum, please, there is no need for you to come. I should be OK; hopefully I'll be back soon. I wouldn't like to leave Bari Ammi home alone at this time.'

'Don't you worry about me, Rose. I will be fine here, both of you can go.' Bari Ammi turned towards me and said, 'Keep me informed. You do not have to worry about me.'

'No, Mum, you stay at home please. I'll ring you from the hospital, and I should go now,' I said.

'Are you sure Ali? It's almost half-three in the morning, it is still dark outside.' Mum sounded worried.

'Don't worry Mum. I'll be just fine. It'll be morning soon.' I said.

'Ali, your dad's absence has made you a big, brave boy. God keep you in His *amman*. Drive carefully,' Mum said.

'Thanks Mum.' I said. This was not the time to relish compliments. As I walked towards the car, I was praying in my heart that this call from the hospital should prove to be a false alarm. I wished him health and longevity. I could feel a blooming spring of loving affiliation in my heart towards him, an affiliation you only develop for your loved one, someone very close, and someone you could trust. The mere thought of losing him unsettled my nerves. I felt my heart ripped out. I wiped the tears flowing down my cheeks as I drove off.

The roads which were buzzing with people and traffic during the daytime were deserted. Occasional taxis were moving swiftly. I was coming across one red light after another. Why do red lights seem to last so long when one is rushing? Should they not make the red traffic lights shorter may be after 2 AM? I thought.

At a pelican crossing, a drunken man was standing in the middle of road. He was holding an unfinished bottle in his left hand. He had frizzled hair and his face was hidden behind the conglomeration of his moustache and beard. His ragged long coat was open revealing his vest. I stopped well before the zebra lines to let him cross. He was swaying sidewise to chase his centre of gravity.

'Aoi, this is my road, I'm walking here,' He said by pointing his trembling index towards me. He spoke in such a manner that each word was embedded into the next. The way he was standing, I couldn't work out which way he would go. I slowly moved the car to the zebra line and stopped well before it. He had a sudden burst of energy, dashed towards the car and raised the bottle held in both hands, above his head like a lumberjack holding an axe before dropping it on the wood. I knew exactly what was going to happen. I closed my eyes. He smashed the bottle with such titanic power onto the bonnet of the car that I felt a forward jolt. A loud bang disrupted the peace and quietness of the night. The glass shrapnel flew everywhere and the drink splashed all over the windscreen, blurring my vision. The man howled deep from his throat and jumped into the darkness. The rain sensor windscreen wipers began to move automatically.

This was not the time to call the police or to assess the damage to the car. I raced towards the hospital.

I parked near the hospital reception and quickly climbed the stairs, two at a time, to reach Mr Nazir's room.

'Thanks for coming.' A staff nurse escorted me to his room. 'Dr Hammond is the Consultant on call. He's just arrived, and he would like to have a word with you before you go in.'

Dr Hammond appeared very cool. He was wearing a suit and necktie even at that time of the morning.

'Good morning,' Dr Hammond said in a pleasant voice. He showed no signs of being awoken from his sleep. He continued, 'you are aware that Mr Nazir has signed a "do not attempt to resuscitate" form which we call a "DNAR form", but he can still change his mind and if required we can resuscitate him. Of course, only if he agrees.'

'I'll ask him but I doubt very much he would change his mind,' I said.

'Could you please confirm this to us?' Dr Hammond looked very serious now. 'And also he is declining any pain relief.'

'Sure, l will.'

'Thanks.'

The nurse opened the door of his room and led me in. I could sense the tense situation. A nurse was leaning over him applying an oxygen facemask. It was getting misty with each breath. Mr Nazir was lying in bed with his eyes shut. Sweat was flowing from his forehead to the side of his face, rolling on to his glistening neck. His neck veins were tense like a tightrope. He was clenching his teeth to overpower the pain, which made his jaw muscles stand out. Another doctor was also present in the room.

'It's me, Ali.'

'Thanks,' Mr Nazir opened his bleary eyes slowly and said whilst removing his oxygen face mask, 'I'm very sorry to put you into trouble at this time of the night. I apologise profusely for this inconvenience.'

He raised his trembling hand and shook hands with me.

'Please don't say this,' I said.

'Please listen to me carefully. I am not left with much time and regard this as my last will.' He made an attempt to sit up and the nurse pushed the pillow under his neck. 'I've signed the DNAR form and would like this to be respected,' he said.

'Hi, Mr Nazir, I am Paul Hobson. I am the anaesthetist on call tonight,' the doctor in the room said extremely politely. 'If you agree, Mr Nazir, we could put you off to sleep and attach you to a machine for breathing.'

'What will you achieve by doing that?' Mr Nazir opened his eyes and asked the doctor.

'This will help us to buy some time to ....'

'You can't buy any time any longer, it's all spent.' Mr Nazir interrupted the doctor, who looked a bit embarrassed. 'My time is up. There is none left. It's time to packup.'

'Listen, Ali, I am sorry to put you under this responsibility, but perhaps that is how nature wanted it to be. Please inform my son in New York and my wife in Lahore. Their phone numbers are in my diary.' He stopped to catch his breath and pointed towards his bed side with his shaking finger. 'I would like to be buried as soon as conveniently possible and please do not delay my burial waiting for any of my relations or friends to arrive.' He stopped again and said. 'I don't want any headstone over my grave.'

'Please don't talk like this. You'll be OK. You'll be alright soon.' I said. I could hear my voice was trembling. I put a hand on his shoulder, which was damp with sweat.

'OK, Ali, thank you. You have been good company. As a souvenir I would like to give you my watch. Good bye. God bless you.'

His usual smile appeared on his face. He closed his eyes again. A sense of peace appeared over his face. His lower lip was quivering as if he was saying something, offering some last minute prayers. Then he bent his knees upwards, which made a little tent of the white bed sheet, which he was covering himself with. He straightened his legs again and his feet were visible now, his toes curled backwards and a gentle shiver went through his body before coming to a final stillness. His breathing was turning into gasps. His face gently moved to his right side; there was no sign of any pain on his face only a mild smile, peaceful and serene. The machine attached to his heart made some irregular beeps before it showed a straight line.

Dr Hobson leaned forward and carefully listened to his chest with a stethoscope. He took the stethoscope out of his ears and hung over it his shoulders, took out a torch from his pocket and shone light into his eyes.

Dr Hobson put his arm around my shoulder and walked me out of the room. A flood of tears was ready to come out of my eyes. I clenched my fist, brought it in front of my face; turned my lips inside and bit them to contain myself.

I looked behind and saw the staff nurse covering Mr Nazir's face with the bed sheet.

'Game over.' Mr Nazir's voice echoed in my ears.

'I'm very sorry, he was a great person, and I was greatly privileged to look after him,' Dr Hobson said.

'I know,' Was all I could say.

Dr Hammond was still present at the nursing station. Dr Hobson said quietly, 'He passed away.'

Dr Hammond got up from the chair and said, 'I'm very sorry, Ali, really very sorry. He was a great person.' He continued: 'We'll respect whatever he said as his will. First thing in the morning, I'll speak to the coroner and I'm sure there would be no need for a PM here. Hopefully, we'll release his body as soon as I've spoken to the coroner. Would you like us to contact the Muslim Chaplain to arrange for his funeral?'

'I think he has already made arrangements by himself. I just need to inform the chaplain.'

'Really,' Dr Hobson looked astonished, 'I knew he was ahead of us in the game but never knew that he was miles ahead.'

'He was a winner,' I said.

I slowly descended the stairway and reached the car. I sat inside, made sure all the windows were fully closed; I cried and cried so loud that I hiccupped.

CHAPTER 19

The bell rang and the bus stopped with a sharp jerk. As I got out of the bus, it was dusk, a velvety dusk — the bluish shadows after sunset were shifting into darker shades. Bari Ammi never liked that time of the day. A cloud of fear would eclipse her face at dusk and she used to say that she got palpitations at that time. I could never give her or myself an explanation of her phobia but I think subconsciously she had regarded day as life and the beginning of night as her end of life and perhaps this could be the underlying cause but who knows what the truth was.

Our home was a good ten-minute walk from the bus stop. I was in no hurry to reach home and gently ambled across the road. It was a relatively quiet, breezeless, muggy evening. There were unusually very few people walking on the footpath or waiting for the buses at the bus stop. I thought, once I reach home, I'd take a hot shower, have food and lie in front of the TV before dozing off to sleep.

Suddenly, three men jumped out of the darkness and stood in front of me, blocking my way. They were tall. Even if I was on the tip of my toes, I would have not reached their shoulders. They were wearing black face masks, only exposing their eyes. The whiteness of their eyes looked even more prominent against their masks. An intense wave of fear went across my body, which began to shake like a leaf. My mouth turned dry. I felt I was choking and was finding difficulty in catching my breath. My heart was pounding in my chest. My palms became wet. I knew I would be mugged and now I had to make it as painless as possible.

Unconsciously, my hand went into my trouser pocket and brought out my iPhone and raised it up in the air like an Olympic torch as I walked towards them and said without giving an impression in my voice that I was scared, 'You can take this.'

One of them snatched the phone from my hand, smashed it on the footpath and stamped on it with his heel and said, 'Do you think I'm a fucking fool? I know the police could track us if we take your phone.'

'What do you want?' I asked instinctively. 'I've only a tenner on me.'

'We don't want your fucking money,' the man who destroyed my mobile said. He sounded irritated and came close to me and held my chin in his firm grip. 'What we want is, your fucking lips to remain sealed, you fucking traitor. Do you hear?' He shook my head.

'I think you're mistaken. I'm Ali. I think you're looking for someone else,' I said.

'We know very well who the fuck you are,' he said and the other two men came behind me and each twisted an arm outwards. Their sweat had the spicy smell of pot-noodles. I was in a difficult situation: there was a man who was holding onto my chin and another two who were twisting my arms standing beside me. I had no chance to run away.

'What have I done?' I still thought they were mixing me up with someone else. The twisting of arms was becoming excruciatingly painful.

'Why did you record the meeting on your phone?' the person in front snarled at me.

'What meeting? I don't know what meeting you are talking about,' I said, and looked from the corners of my eyes if there was someone around to help me.

'You know very well which meeting I'm talking about. You won't understand like this,' the person holding my chin released it and without much warning punched my face. My glasses flew away off. I could feel the salty taste of blood in my mouth.

The same person grabbed hold of my face again and poked his thumb and fingers sharply into my cheeks. I was unable to speak. 'You think you can fool me?' he said in a voice of steel and shoved me into the wall, banging my head and crunching my ribs against the stone. He placed his heavy hand around my throat and said, 'You fucking liar, never mess about with Omar, do you understand? If you make any wrong move…' He got a knife out of his cargo trouser pocket, which flipped open with a loud click. The blade was the size of a dagger, with serrated edges and shone in the dim light. He waved it in front of my face and said, 'this will have your guts out in no time and nobody would ever be able to find your body. Do you understand?' he shouted again and jabbed his finger sharply into my chest and took his hand off my lower jaw.

'I do,' I said doubling over, rubbing my throat and taking gulps of air like a drowning man. I was coughing and a coarse thread of spit hung from my mouth to the ground.

The person in front of me made a V sign with his index and middle finger and first pointed towards his eyes and then onto me and said. 'I'll be watching you closely, very closely,' he jerked my head up with a rough thump under my chin and threw another punch in my stomach, with all his body weight behind it.

The other two people loosened their grip on my arms and one of them brought his face closer and said, 'We also know where your Mum does her shopping.'

I felt dizzy. My legs could not take my weight. My head was spinning; I was swept by a surge of nausea. I could hear noises, sounds that appeared to be now coming from a distance. Whistles were blowing in my ears. I was bending towards the ground in slow motion. I felt my right cheek resting against the cold flagstone and darkness reached out and overtook me. I don't know how long I remained there and then I felt the warmth of Mum's hand all over my face. I thought, this was life after death and I could feel Mum holding my head in her lap and both Dad and Bari Ammi who were present in the background had pleasant smiles on their faces.

'He isn't drunk,' said, a girl who was kneeling down. She sniffed over my face and asked, 'Were you mugged?'

'Am I alive?' I asked the girl. I was very surprised to be alive.

'Yes, you are,' she said. 'Strange, they didn't take your phone.' She bent down and picked up my shattered phone and handed it over to me. 'It's all broken…..Literally.'

'Can you help me to get up?' I asked the girl as I tried to get up. The girl was wearing a black jogging suit. There were signs of worry for me in her big brown eyes and alarm in her voice.

She bent and extended her right hand to me. Her hand was warm. In a kind of hand-shaking manner she helped me to lift myself off the ground. Her touch, a concoction of her perfume and sweat, surged a sudden raciness in me.

'Thanks,' I could only say.

'The police and ambulance are on the way,' she said. 'I've rung

999.'

'Oh, thanks. I think, I'll be OK,' I said. I didn't want the police to be involved at this stage. 'Could you please look for my glasses? They fell off.'

'Here, they are,' she handed me over my glasses, which miraculously appeared undamaged.

I was able to stand. I took a couple of careful steps like a toddler and looked back at her again. She was probably the same age as me. She was a tall, white, slender girl. She held her ponytail and parted her hair into two halves and pulled those forwards so that the rubber bands were close to her neck. The prominence of her neck muscles and collar bones gave her a heavenly elegance. I felt my heart rising to my throat. I swallowed spit and said, 'thank God, it doesn't feel like I have broken any bones.' I rubbed the side of my mouth and looked at my hand, which had a smearing of blood on it but not to an extent to cause alarm. I wiped my hand on my jeans and combed my hair with my fingers.

'Did you see anything?' I asked her.

'Yes, I saw three men. They were pinning you against the wall. I saw them from a distance. I shouted at them that I'm gonna call the police and they ran away in that direction.' She said by pointing her finger towards the dark area they had seemed to come from.

The wailing of sirens of an ambulance grew closer and it stopped just in front of me. Two paramedics energetically jumped out and walked towards me.

'Are you OK, Sir?' one of them asked me and wrapped a blanket around me.

'I think so. I was mugged. They banged my head against the wall. I did pass out for a while, don't know how long for, although I feel ok,' I said.

'Well,' one paramedic said, 'If they bashed your head against the wall and you went unconscious then you need to go to hospital to get checked out.' He said this whilst feeling my pulse and performing a quick general examination.

'Em... yeah, you look OK apart from this bruise on your cheek,' he said.

A police car pulled in at that time. The police officer in the driving seat wound the window down and said, 'You rang us about the mugging?'

'Yes, I did,' the girl stepped forward; her voice was filled with confidence.

'I assume you are going to the hospital now,' the police officer asked.

'Yes, he is,' the paramedic responded instead of me.

'Should I follow you to take your statement or you could come to the police station later to report it. Tell us, what you want us to do?' the policeman said.

'I'll come to you after the hospital,' I said.

'That's absolutely fine, see you soon.' And the police officers drove away.

I looked at the girl. There was something I liked about her.

'I could come with you to hospital if you want me to,' she said.

'That would be great,' I said, as this would provide me with an opportunity to be with her a little longer.

The paramedic opened the back door of the ambulance. I thought, if the paramedics come to know that this girl is not related to me, they might not allow her to come with me in the ambulance. I could see the paramedic's intention of helping me into the ambulance. I totally ignored him and asked the girl, 'Could you help me in please?'

She held my hand, which I held to climb in and the girl followed me. I was quite pleased with myself that I made the paramedic believe that she was related to me and also there was no time for the paramedic to ask any questions before we closed the door.

'Two weeks ago, I had never been inside an ambulance but in the past two weeks this is my second time,' I said looking at her.

'You mean,' she said smilingly, 'you are now getting mugged on a regular basis.'

'Of course yes,' I said and both of us laughed.

'You could let your family know about this.' She took her mobile from her pocket and passed it on to me. 'I could also give you my mobile number to act as a witness for you to the police.'

'That's very kind of you. You are a very brave person. Not many people would volunteer to be a witness. Yes, certainly I would like to take your number.' I said this concealing my excitement. She smiled and made a figure of seven of her index finger to clear tiny beads of sweat from her forehead.

I took the mobile phone from her and called Mum.

'Hi Mum, this is me. I'll be a bit late......., yeah, I'm fine, I thought I'd just let you know....I don't know where I lost my phone.....no this is my friend's phone....I don't think you could ring me on this number.....yeah, yeah, I'm OK.....I'll see you soon....bye.'

'Thanks.' I gave her phone back.

'By the way my name is Sophie.' She was still smiling. A faint but elegant semi-circular line appeared on her face beside her laugh lines, which would make anyone looking at her wish that she smiled all her life.

'Thanks, Sophie. I'm Ali.' I extended my hand to shake hands with her. Her hands had slim fingers, nails well-manicured. I was still holding my shattered iPhone in my left hand. Turning it over, I said, 'Hope, the insurance company will replace it soon.'

'Don't worry about the phone. Hope all goes well for you at the hospital. I can see you have got a very impressive bruise on your right cheek,' Sophie said.

'I think I can feel a bump on my head as well,' I said, running fingers over the back of my head.

At the hospital Accident and Emergency department, the first person I bumped into was Dad's radiologist friend, Dr Farooqi, who was very concerned to hear about the mugging incident and me losing consciousness. He asked one of his consultant colleagues, in Accident and Emergency to examine me.

After a very thorough examination he said, 'I think clinically you look ok but we need to do an urgent MRI to exclude any concealed internal bleeding.'

'But I feel ok. I don't have any headache or any other problem. I think I will be fine,' I said. I had vaguely heard before that claustrophobics do not tolerate MRI well, and I belonged to this group of people. However, I didn't want Sophie to know about my fear of closed spaces, especially on our very first meeting.

'Well, if a doctor thinks this test is necessary then you must have it,' Sophie said decisively.

'Absolutely,' Uncle Farooqi who had also joined us said. 'Well, I got to go. I have to go and do a procedure. Luckily MRI is empty and I'll ask a technician to do your MRI right away and if all is OK you could go home soon afterwards.'

'But I feel fine, I don't think I need an MRI,' I said looking at Uncle Farooqi.

Uncle Farooqi did not seem interested in what I said and continued to fill in the request form. 'It does not hurt to have an MRI, young man,' he said and led us to the MRI room. The radiographer greeted us with a smile.

'When you have done the MRI,' Uncle Farooqi said to him, 'Give me a ring and I'll review the images myself. I'll be in my office.'

'Will do, boss,' the radiographer said.

'Good luck Ali,' Uncle Farooqi said as he swiftly walked away.

'Thanks, Uncle.'

'He is a very nice person, is he your real uncle?' Sophie asked.

'No, my Dad works here in this hospital and Uncle Farooqi is also a close family friend,' I said.

'I see, now I know why you are getting all this preferential treatment: you are the son of a doctor,' Sophie said with a smile on her face.

'Well, these are the only few perks you get if your dad works for the NHS,' I said.

'Mr Ali,' the radiographer asked, 'you don't have any metal implants in your body?'

'No,' I said.

'That's great,' He said.

'You are aware that there would be a lot of buzzing and noisiness inside the machine?'

'Yes, I have no problem with that.'

'And lastly, you are not claustrophobic?'

This is the question I was dreading to hear. 'I am,' I said quietly, looking at the ground. I didn't wish to make eye contact with Sophie and was cursing Uncle Farooqi in my heart. Why had he asked for an MRI? What would Sophie think about me after this? Perhaps not a lot, I thought.

'I'm sorry, at present we don't have a wide bore MRI machine free,' he said, scratching his head. 'If your phobia is not too bad, your girlfriend could come inside the MRI room and could hold your feet while you are inside the machine, I think this is the best option I can offer now.'

I looked at Sophie. She looked blushed and said immediately, 'I'm not his girlfriend. We just met after the robbery.' She stopped and said, 'But I don't mind coming inside.'

'I'm sorry, Miss, I thought you were with him because .....' he left the sentence incomplete.

'Are you sure?' I asked Sophie. I was disappointed that I didn't have any other option except to be dependent on her to have the scan.

'Would this be OK by you Sophie,' I asked again.

'Yeah, yeah,' she said hurriedly. 'That's fine by me.' I think she was still thinking about the word 'girlfriend'.

'I'll give you these headphones.' The person doing the MRI handed me over large DJ style earphones, which would cover not only my ears but half of my face. 'You could listen to music as a distraction whilst having the scan and Miss, if you just keep your hands on his feet when he goes into the tunnel. Ali, there is a two way intercom system and I'll let you know when the scan starts and finishes. If at any stage you feel that you can't carry on, just talk to me and I'll terminate the scan, please stay very still during the scan.'

'Am I allowed to breathe during the scan?' I asked. I didn't want to show outwardly that I was experiencing a severe sense of humour crisis at that time.

'Of course you are,' he replied and laughed. I think my state of mind was obvious through my eyes.

The MRI machine was a long white tunnel, with a narrow slab extending from the centre. I could see,once ready, that the slab would be pushed inside the tunnel. My heart missed beats with the thought of being inside the narrow tunnel.

I had to bite the bullet and appear brave. I took a couple of deep breaths and lay flat on the cold slab. A curved cushion was placed under my head. I put the earphones on, and screwed my eyes shut. The slab slowly slid me into the machine. My heart was hammering, I wanted to tear off the earphones and run away. Then I felt the soft touch of Sophie's hands on my feet. She had moved my socks down to my ankles and she touched my feet, skin-to-skin. A sense of calm descended upon me, my nerves steadied. I took my mind off the scan by re-running the events of the evening in my mind. I hoped that CCTV surveillance on the road had recorded the whole event but it would be too difficult to identify the culprits. They were fully covered. How did Omar come to know that I had recorded the meeting? My jaw was hurting and instinctively I wanted to rub it but I had to stay still until the scan had finished.

'Your scan is done. Well done.' The voice was music to my ears. I felt normal. Had I overcome my phobia? Or was it the presence of Sophie? I felt elated.

The slab brought me out of the machine; I handed over the ear-phones to the technician and gave Sophie a huge big hug. She seemed taken by surprise by this bold move.

'Thanks Sophie, you made it easy for me.'

'Anytime,' I liked the shyness in her eyes.

'You may go now,' the person doing the scan said. 'Dr Farooqi should be able to look at these images on his computer.'

'Where is his office?' I asked.

He thought and wrinkles appeared on his forehead and then he said, 'It's very difficult to tell you the direction from here, I'll take you there.'

'Thanks,' both of us said.

After five to seven minutes of walking along the maze of corridors through various departments of the hospital, we were at his office.

Both of us thanked him again and he warmly shook hands with us. I knocked softly at the door and heard Uncle Farooqi's voice.

'Come in.'

He did not look up to see who had entered the room, but continued to look at the scan images on a tall computer monitor.

'I had my scan, Uncle.'

'I know, I'm just looking at these images,' he said, continuing to look at the screen. 'They look fine, no bleed, and no abnormality seen; now I can confidently send you home.'

'That's great news.'

'Yeah, when is Taj back?'

'Exactly two weeks from now.'

'Are your mother and grandmother ok? I'll drop in at the weekend to say hello to them. Please give them my regards.'

'I will. Thanks for your help.' And both of us came out of his room.

'What next?' Sophie said. 'Now to the police station?'

'No, no I won't bother you any more, we'll take a cab, and I'll drop you home first.'

She interrupted me and said with her eyes sparkling with mischief and a playful smile on her face,

'Well, well. Mr Ali, you need to slow down a bit. You are being over smart. In the last two hours you have acquired my phone number, that person in hospital thinks I'm your girlfriend, you came out of that freaking, buzzing machine and hugged meas if you had climbed Everest and now you want to see me home. What next, do you want to meet my parents or take me directly to the registry office?'

'Yeah, I would love to take you to the registry office but it might be closed now,' I said looking at my watch. 'Could I meet your parents now? Should we go?'

'No, you are not coming with me. I'll take a taxi home by myself.'

'I don't think that's a good idea, it's almost the middle of the night. I think I need to drop you home safely. OK, promise I won't look at your home. When we are about to reach it, you let me know and I'll close my eyes. I promise I won't look.' I said by gently leaning forward and by placing a hand on my heart.

'Ok, you better close your eyes.'

'I will. I promise.'

I waved to a taxi, which stopped just beside us. I opened the taxi door for Sophie who stepped inside and loudly told her address to the driver.

'I haven't heard it, just let me know when we reach your home and I'll shut my eyes'. The taxi zoomed off along the streets of inner London.

'What does your Dad do?' I asked her.

'He is a Professor of mathematics at Imperial.'

'Wow, maths is the most perfect science. And your Mum?' I asked.

'She....' Sophie interrupted her sentence and said, 'Mr Ali, you are so inquisitive, would you not like to know that I already have a boyfriend?'

I was saddened and went totally silent as if someone had pulled the plug and began to look outside through the window. I had not thought of this possibility. It was so stupid of me. She was such a pretty girl; she had every right to have a boyfriend or maybe more. The taxi slowed and stopped in front of a large gated house.

'Sophie, I am very thankful to you for all you did for me this evening,' I said shaking hands with her. 'I hope you will just ignore my silliness. I am not usually like this. I don't know what happened to me today, perhaps it was an adrenaline rush ......I'm so sorry.'

'It's ok.'

'Please don't worry about your phone number. I'll delete it from mum's phone when I reach home.'

'You are a good boy.'

'Good night.'

'Bye.'

* * * * *

On my way home, I was thinking of what to tell Mum and Bari Ammi. The situation had clearly become quite worrying. Omar's hit men were able to identify me and they knew my whereabouts. Today I had got away with only bruises. Next time it could be worse. I had to inform the police but wanted to keep this a secret from Mum and Bari Ammi until Dad had returned.

As expected, both Mum and Bari Ammi were waiting for me in the front room. Mum started crying when she looked at me and said, 'Who did this to you? Where have you been? Why were you not answering your phone?'

'I was mugged and they broke my phone,' I said quietly, looking at the floor. I did not want Mum to look into my eyes to catch any glimpse of the truth.

She was touching my face and hugging me, 'Are you ok?'

'Yes Mum, I am Ok. As a precaution I did go to hospital to get checked out and Uncle Farooqi did an MRI scan on me and all is ok,' I said.

'Thank God. I'll give *Sadaqat* for you tomorrow.' Mum was very reassured to know that I had been to the hospital. 'God bless Farooqi bahi, he is an angel.'

Bari Ammi had been quietly watching all this and her eyes appeared to me alive with questions. She walked towards me, erect like a sentry and said. 'Why did muggers break your phone and not take it?'

I wasn't expecting this question from Bari Ammi and immediately said without looking at her, 'Muggers have become quite clever these days. They don't take these smart phones as they know that they could be tracked down by the police.'

'So why did they break it if they did not want to take it?' Bari Ammi said.

'The phone.... was in my back pocket,' I stammered as I spoke. 'I fell on the ground and it broke,' I said by looking at her from the corners of my eyes. Bari Ammi did not look convinced and adjusted her hearing aid, perhaps to hear more from me.

'Bari Ammi,' Mum said in an angry tone, 'must you nit-pick at this time? Please stop your investigation and leave my son alone.

Already he has gone through a lot this evening,' Mum hugged me again. 'Did you inform the police?'

'I thought I'd come home and let you people know before going to the police.' I said.

'Yes, you did the right thing. I was getting a bad feeling about you.' Mum began to cry again.

The landline rang. The phone was on a small table near the staircase. Mum wiped tears and picked the phone up and said, 'Walakum Salam Sajid, how are you... how are your parents... yes you should come over sometime... yes, he is here.' And she handed the phone over to me. She was still wiping her eyes.

'Ali, what's wrong with your mobile? I've been trying to ring you for the past two hours and it kept going onto your answering machine,' Sajid said.

'It's broken,' I said briefly.

'I wanted to inform you, the dinner is served,' he said. 'Omar did not include you in the plan, and I don't have a good feeling about this. I think you should disappear from the scene for a couple of months. Perhaps, it would be best if you go to Pakistan.'

'Why should I go?' I asked.

'Just go, man, just go out of the country, anywhere. I don't want to alarm you but your life could be in danger. They aren't as nice people as I thought. Jus' do what I tell you, go somewhere.' And he hung up.

'What was he saying? Where did he want you to go?' Mum asked.

'I don't know what Sajid was on about. I'll ring back and speak to him,' I said.

I pressed the call-back button on the phone. The phone went

on ringing and someone eventually picked up the phone and said, 'This is a phone booth. Whom are you ringing you lonely person?' I put the phone down.

'What was Sajid saying?' mum asked. 'Is he OK?'

'Yeah, he is OK,' I said.

'Why has he hung up on you?' Mum asked again.

'He was in a rush,' I lied again.

'When will you go to the police?' Mum asked.

'I think going to the police now won't make any difference, I might go in the morning,' I said as I wanted to buy some time to think the situation through.

'OK, I'll get you some food,' Mum said affectionately.

'I don't feel like eating. Can I have a hot chocolate instead please?'

'I'll have one as well,' Bari Ammi said as she walked towards her room. She turned back and looked at me; she still appeared immersed in her thoughts. She opened her mouth to say something but shook her head and began to climb the stairs. I think Bari Ammi knew that I wasn't telling the truth.

I slumped on the sofa and put my feet up on the footstool. Both Mum and Bari Ammi had gone to their respective rooms. While taking sips of hot chocolate, I was thinking and trying to get events in order in my head to inform the police. The ringing of the landline again interrupted my thoughts. I picked the phone up quickly so as to avoid the disturbance to both Mum and Bari Ammi. Not surprisingly, it was Sajid again.

'Bruv, God is great. Have you seen the news?' Sajid said with exhilaration.

'No, I did not yet get a chance. Why, what's happening? Why

did you hang up on me?' I asked.

'The dinner is served and is very delicious. They are not saying it on TV but six MPs have already departed to the other world.' He was laughing loudly, from the back of his throat. I felt sick. 'Watch the news channel,' and his line dropped again. I didn't like the way Sajid was behaving. I didn't think he was ever like this. Had they brain-washed him?

My heart sank when I heard the breaking news on the TV. A total of twenty eight MPs had been admitted to the hospital as an emergency and out of them seven were reported to be in a critical condition in ITU's. A news report was showing the Prime Minister visiting the hospital. He looked in a sombre mood. He was shown to fulfil all the rituals of entering the hospital including rolled-up sleeves, tie tucked into his shirt, rubbing disinfectant gel on his hands. A male patient, whose face was blurred out and I presume was an MP, was shown in a glass cubicle with an opaque tube coming out of his mouth which was secured with a bandage around his mouth. His nightshirt was unbuttoned to his stomach, revealing his chest on which four circular white patches were attached and connected to the machines with wires. The machines in the background were showing numbers and graphs. A nurse was in attendance. She was wearing a visor over her eyes, a face mask, gloves and an apron which surgeons wear in the operating theatre. It all looked very grim.

The political editor of the BBC was reporting live from the House of Commons with Big Ben in the background. He was blaming the causes of infection on eggs or possibly on eating raw beef imported from Germany. Surprisingly, there was no speculation about any terrorist activity. Perhaps, the unseen hand of terrorism had been seen and reported in so many plots in the news recently that the news editor did not even bother to rule it out.

The phone rang again. 'Yes, Sajid, I have seen the news,' I said as soon as I picked the phone up.

'I have bad news now, very bad,' Sajid's voice was trembling. 'The cook, Hanif, himself is at the receiving end. He is seriously ill. He is unconscious. Omar, the bastard, didn't want him to go to the hospital; he wanted him to die at home. He only agreed to call an ambulance when Hanif slipped into a coma. I think he's been rushed to the same ITU which you saw on the news. Omar thinks that by mistake he contaminated himself.'

'How sad,' I said. 'Do you think he himself had the contaminated food?'

'That's the puzzling part, no one could be that stupid, but never forget this is a very deadly bacteria. Only a few on his hand could lead him into this situation. God only knows whether by mistake he splashed some bacteria onto his hands or in his mouth and it is also quite possible that he has been taken ill from something else, something entirely different, some other infection. I don't know, you jus' get out of the country. It's getting messy now. I'm ringing you from different phone booths every time. It is possible our phones could be tapped. Don't try to ring me back,' Sajid said.

'Are you OK, Sajid, where are you now?' I asked.

'Bruv, I'm sort of OK. After the news of the cook's illness everyone looked shit scared. Omar and his friends are worried that the cook might tell the plot to the police. They're hoping and praying for him to die. And this Omar guy is a *pukka harami*. Hanif also told me that *sala* sniffs coke. Yesterday, by mistake, I entered Omar's room as his door was semi-open. He was sitting on a chair facing the door, his trousers down to his knees and *bhanchud* was jerking himself off. I was so, so ashamed I can't tell you.'

'No way, was he? At such a stressful time!' I was shell shocked to hear this.

'Yes, actually, perhaps he was de-stressing himself,' he said laughing. 'I don't know whether he was distressing himself or making himself happy but worst of all, he wasn't embarrassed, not even for a second. When he saw me, he just pulled his trousers up and looked away as if nothing had happened. He didn't even get up to wash his hands.'

'Dirty, bastard.' I felt nauseous to imagine what Sajid had seen.

'Yes, they all are, they are keeping an eye on me like hawks. I can see mistrust in their eyes. No one is allowed to use mobile phones any longer. I feel frightened. I wish ......' and I could hear Sajid crying on the other side of the phone as his line dropped yet again.

It was late in the evening. I wished Dad was here, with me, right now, so that I could talk to him about all this. I felt very lonesome. I didn't want to run away to Pakistan like a coward. My eyes were swelling up with tears. I hadn't taken any part in this criminal plot. I hadn't done anything wrong. I felt very sorry for all the MP's who were taken ill and my heart cried out loud for all who were already dead. 'They are not very nice people. I don't have a good feeling about you,' Sajid's voice echoed. Perhaps, at this time, Omar's blood-thirsty hounds were sniffing for me, to silence one more witness. I thought if it was my time to die, then far better to look directly into the eyes of death and do something that I thought was right. No doubt, this time was very painful and testing for me but this was the only time I had. It was not the time for self-pity, or delay. I looked at my wrist watch, it was 11.40. I looked outside through the window, the street was very silent. I could see a man walking his dog. I had to go to the police now. I could not wait until morning, I thought.

CHAPTER 20

I wished Mr Nazir was still alive. I would have taken him with me to Scotland Yard. The thought of his death filled my heart with grief again. He came into my life and went away so abruptly like a dazzling firecracker, lighting the dark sky on a November night, so short lived. Why was all this happening to me when Dad was away? It could not be safe for me to go to Scotland Yard just driving by myself, I thought. I looked out of the window once again. The street was lifeless but there was no point in taking any chances with these people. It would be much safer to go by taxi. I ordered a taxi. I needed to let Mum know that I was going to the police station. I kept the broken iPhone in my pocket.

I noiselessly climbed upstairs to Mum's room. I didn't wish Bari Ammi to be disturbed and after softly knocking at Mum's door I entered.

Mum turned her bed side lamp on. She pulled the blinder off her eyes over her forehead, and said, 'Are you OK, Ali? I hope you aren't feeling scared.' There was fear in her voice.

'No, I'm OK, I'm fine,' I said gently squeezing her hand. 'I thought, there is not much point in delaying informing the cops, so I'm just going to the police station to report my mugging, so that the Police can be vigilant and this group does not attack others.'

'That's ok, Ali, but it is almost twelve. Is it not too late to go to the police now? I'll come with you,' she said and pulled the quilt off her to get off the bed.

'No, no, Mum. You please stay at home. I'll be back soon, and I'll take a cab,' I said assertively.

'Are you sure?' she said. There was uncertainty on her face over whether to let me go on my own.

'Yes, absolutely certain. I'll be fine, just fine. Just don't worry.'

'OK, you take care.' She opened the drawer of her bed-side table and handed me two twenty pound notes.

'I have my debit card,' I said and took the money off her. 'Thanks. Hopefully, I'll be back soon.'

'May God keep you safely,' she said.

'Good night Mum.'

I went downstairs without a sound and when I reached the door to look outside through the peephole, there was a man standing there. My heart jumped into my throat. Can I not go out of our home now?

'Taxi is here.' Perhaps the driver saw my shadow through the hazy glass of the door.

I gave a sigh of relief and fumbled with the door chain to have a look before opening the door.

The taxi was just parked outside. I unchained the door, went outside and pulled shut the door.

'To Scotland Yard. Please drive fast,' I said to the driver as I sat inside. I turned around to look behind but could not see anyone around. The taxi slowly moved out of our street, I was still trying to spot if anyone was trying to follow me. There was a cyclist behind the taxi. My heart was thudding. The chase was on. The cyclist was peddling fast to keep the race alive but was lagging behind as the taxi was increasing speed. I looked back again and there was a bus and a couple of cars but no cyclist. Could he be informing his other accomplices over the phone about my whereabouts and the taxi number I was in? It was quite possible. The taxi turned, extremely slowly as it reached Marylebone station.

'Please pull up here,' I shouted and threw a twenty pound note towards the driver. I jumped out of the moving taxi and slammed the door shut. The taxi driver took both of his hands off the steering wheel and raised them in the air in a sign of annoyance.

I had to appear calm, I said to myself and I looked at the people who were loitering at the ticket kiosk. At that time everyone seemed to me a gang member of Omar's network. I paced quickly to reach the taxi at the top of the queue. My heart jumped into my mouth as a pigeon, close to my feet, suddenly flew off the footpath, and brushed its wings against my face. I sharply moved backwards in a reflex action, was unable to keep my balance and fell flat on the ground. Luckily, I did not bang my head on the foot-path as I landed on my shoulders. Laughter emanated from the front of the station. This was twice in a day I had found myself lying, fallen on the footpath. Could things get any worse? There was no time for self-pity, I had to get up and go. 'Stupid pigeon,' I said loudly to lessen my embarrassment. I gathered myself up and walked briskly, without looking to see who was laughing at me, to the taxis. In the next minute, I was in another taxi. I was amazed at the speed with which I got off the ground and got into the taxi. I pressed both my shoulders, which were aching from the fall, against the back of the seat.

'Could you take me to Scotland Yard please,' I said to the driver.

'You mean New Scotland Yard, the Met police station, the one on Broadway?' The taxi driver asked.

'Yeah, yeah,' I said although I never knew the location and looked over my shoulder to see behind. It was difficult to know if anyone was following, but there was no cyclist.

'Is someone chasing you?' the driver asked me looking in the rear view mirror.

'Possibly,' I replied briefly.

'Don't worry. I'll keep an eye on the cars behind. I'll take you through the quickest route with no traffic lights.'

'Thanks,' I said and thought, 'oh, no, shit, could he be one of them? Now he could take me by some unknown route and safely deliver me to Omar.'

'No, no, you stay on the main roads. Anyway, it's not very far from here,' I lied to give him an impression that I knew the way to the police station.

I was relieved to see the rotating sign of Scotland Yard. I saw a car stopping behind and the driver was on his mobile. Was he following me or was I imaging everyone in the world to be a part of Omar's network? As the taxi stopped, I hurriedly got out and handed the driver the other twenty pound note and ran towards the building. I felt safe as I entered. I followed the sign to the reception. I was expecting the place to be bustling with people and long queues but it was deserted. A police officer was sitting behind the window, head down, writing something in a book.

'Excuse me,' I cleared my throat and said; 'I would like to speak to someone from the anti-terrorism team.'

The person behind the window stopped writing but did not

look at me. He was probably in his mid-forties, wearing a white short-sleeved shirt. The epaulettes were arched and to them were attached silver stars and four-digit numbers. His slanting nose appeared purpose-built for the reading glasses he was wearing.

'You mean you would like to report a terrorist activity?' he said quietly.

'Yes.'

'Could I know your name, date of birth, address and contact number please?'

He was taking down my details too slowly and I had the impression that he was not taking me seriously.

'Officer,' I said, 'it's a very serious matter. I know it must be very important for you to take down my details, but I need to speak with someone right now, this minute. It's a matter of national importance.'

He took his glasses off, scratched his bald head and twisted the tip of his nose with his forefinger and thumb and said calmly without looking at me, 'Listen, young man, I've been doing this job since well before you were born. I know what is important and what isn't and I also fully know the order in which things need doing. I hope you understand this. Yes, now could I have your mobile number, please?'

It was becoming very difficult to keep my composure but I knew that he wanted things done his own way and so without further explanation I gave him the number of the broken iPhone.

'Now tell me, where did you witness the terrorist activity?' he asked without looking at me.

'Please officer,' I said, 'could I speak to the anti-terrorist team. I can promise you, I'm not wasting your time.'

He looked at me for the first time and said, 'Do you know what time it is?' He looked at his wrist watch and pointed at it with his finger and said, 'twenty-five past midnight. They are all gone home, they'll be back here in another seven hours. I can take your statement and will pass it on to them in the morning.'

'Ring them at home, get them here now, right now.' Unintentionally, I shouted at him.

He looked at me in disbelief and as he opened his mouth to say something and before he could utter a single word, I shouted again.

'The blood of all those MP's will be on your neck,' I pointed a finger at him, which was shaking with anger.

'Control yourself, young man,' he said swallowing spit and his prominent Adam's apple moved up-and-down, 'What MPs are you talking about?'

'The ones who are fighting for their lives in the hospitals, poisoned, dying and dead, and God knows how many more will be gone if we don't stop it now.' I banged my fist so forcefully on the counter that the paper clips lying on it flew up in the air like a swarm of flies.

The officer hastily jumped off his chair as if he had been touched by a live electric wire and stumbled towards the door and said, 'I'll get the duty Inspector for you now.'

I instinctively turned around to look at the entrance door which was flapping, opening and closing as if someone had been there. Fear struck the back of my spine like a cold wave. Could they harm Mum and Bari Ammi while I am here? I didn't know how long it would take to give my statement here. First thing, I needed protection for my family.

I saw a police officer entering the reception area along with the officer who was behind the counter. I presumed he was the duty inspector. He was tall. He darted a glance at me, and his eyes were cold and clinical.

'Could we go and talk next door?' He pointed to the room next door to the reception, which he entered from reception and opened the door to let me in.

'It's not a formal interview or collecting a statement,' he said in his unsympathetic, hard voice. 'I just want to collect a few facts. I understand you would like to report something about some terrorism activity?'

'Yes, I do,' I said. 'But first I want some safety surveillance for my family. My Mum and my Grand Mum are alone at home. I think someone has been following me here. I have been already beaten up by this group of people this evening and they know where I live......' My voice trembled as thoughts ran through my mind that Mum or Bari Ammi could be in trouble because of me.

'Do you know who they are?' He was not moving his gaze off my face.

'Yeah, sort of,' I said. 'Omar is the mastermind behind the plot. He teaches history at the Metropolitan University. They planned to add E coli 157 to the MP's food so that they were taken ill and could not cast their vote in this forthcoming crucial parliamentary vote which gives the PM a right to attack any country in the world without any consultation with the cabinet.'

'How do you know Omar?' The lines on his face deepened.

'Through my friend.'

'Did you take part in the plan?'

'No, I just attended a couple of their meetings and apparently they didn't trust me and in the end excluded me from the plan.'

'Do you know it is a very serious offence to accuse any innocent person of terrorism? If you are proven wrong, you could rot in jail for years. Are you fully aware of the implications of what you are saying?'

'Are you trying to say that I'm making this up?' I felt frustrated that he did not believe me. I took the iPhone out of my pocket and placed it on the table.

'I sneakily recorded one of their meetings, it's all in here.'

He looked at the phone, sucked his teeth and said, 'You have said that someone beat you up this evening, did you report this attack to the police?'

'I didn't but one of the passers-by did. I also attended hospital after that and had an MRI,' I said.

He took down the details of the place where Omar's men had attacked me and the time I had attended the hospital.

'I need to make a few enquiries and I'll be right back.' He picked up my phone and left the room.

It was a small room with no windows and there was only sufficient space for three chairs and a small table. During this time, I dozed, slumped sideways and awoke with a jerk. I was making a concerted effort to keep my eyes open. My head felt so heavy that my neck was unable to hold it up. I crossed my arms over the table and placed my head on them and closed my eyes. My eyes were burning and my head was throbbing due to the adrenaline overload, which I had been experiencing all evening and it was well past my bed-time.

I must have drifted off to sleep for the best part of an hour. I heard the voice of the duty inspector clearing his throat to attract my attention. His eyes shone with preparedness. I felt sick and jet lagged.

'We have managed to listen to the recording, looked at a CCTV recording from the evening and also confirmed your hospital attendance. The chief-superintendent and counter-terrorism team are on their way and we need to take a formal statement from you.' He stopped and said, 'Do you want a cup of tea before the statement?'

'Yes I would. What about my family, can they be protected from Omar's hit-men?'

'I apologise,' the Inspector said in an embarrassed tone. 'I'm sorry that I did not inform you, two police officers are already deployed in ordinary clothes around your home. Don't worry, their presence won't create any panic among your neighbours, they won't even notice them.'

He opened the interview room door and said in a loud voice to the officer at reception. 'Get the medical director of the hospital on the phone for me please. The doctors need to be informed of this infection.'

'Medical director of which hospital, Sir?' he asked coolly.

'Perhaps,' the inspector said gruffly, 'you could find out where the MP's are admitted. This information is everywhere.'

'It is St Paul's Hospital,' I informed him.

As usual the Duty Officer spoke without looking at me and ignored the info I gave him. 'Not a problem, Sir, I shall find out first the hospital where the MP's are admitted and then get the medical director on the line for you. Anything else you would like me to do?'

'Can you just go away from here and do what you are told.'

'Not a problem, Sir. I shall go now.'

'Thank you so much,' the Duty Inspector said sarcastically and rolled his eyes up, giving a sigh of relief.

Suddenly the door was flung open and three people entered the room. One was dressed in a suit, maroon braces supporting his trousers and the other two wore jeans and jackets. The people had heavy voices. It seemed both had been dragged out of their beds in the middle of deep sleep. Their eye-lids appeared swollen, hanging over eyes which appeared red.

The person in a suit had a warm smile on his face and he had an air of authority in his appearance: a man used to being obeyed.

'Thanks, Ali, I'm Tom, Chief Superintendent. We are very grateful to you for your help.' He pointed towards the other two persons and said, 'Please meet Michael and Mark, who lead the counter-terrorism team. They will take you to the interview room and record your interview; you'll be a Crown witness in the case.'

'Dave,' he said to the Duty Inspector, 'have you informed the hospital about this infection?'

'I'm in the process, Sir,' Dave said looking at the floor.

'Gosh, we have been keeping an eye on these people for so long but could not get any lead. Thanks, Ali, for your help. This is the breakthrough I was waiting for,' Tom said. He looked at the Duty Constable and said, 'We'll have to raid them tonight. Close all the roads within a mile radius of the area where the ambulance picked the chef up. In my experience these people move houses every hour. We may not find anybody in the house now but check all parked cars and vans. Also ring the hospital to find out the chef's condition. If possible, we need to quiz him.'

'Ok, Sir,' Dave said obediently whilst taking notes.

'Also, I need to inform the Mayor and the PM now but we have to make sure the press doesn't get a sniff of this. I'll code name this project as...' He paused to think then said 'Ready, Steady,

Cook ……….. or any other ideas?'

There were smiles on everyone's faces and Michael said, 'that aptly describes our mission.'

Then he looked at me and said, 'Should we go to the interview room?'

'Sure,' I replied.

I followed Michael and Mark through long corridors. Outside, dawn was slowly washing away night's darkness. A set of double doors led us into the interview room. The top half of the second door was made of glass. The room was slightly bigger than the previous one but similarly had three chairs and a small desk on which a tape-recorder was placed. Michael inserted an old fashioned cassette tape into this triple tape-recorder and checked it was recording by saying 'Hello testing 1, 2, and 3' and pointing towards a black bumble bee type object on the ceiling.

'This is a miniature camera,' said Mark. 'We do covert recording to study the body language of our witnesses. We are doing this in your case just to fulfil the formality. We don't intend to carry-out any psychological review of your interview. Do you have any objection to this?'

'No, I don't mind,' I felt dizzy with the banging headache. I was hardly able to keep my eyes open and just wanted to get the whole process over and done with. Mark decanted black coffee into three polystyrene cups from a thermos and moved one each in front of us.

Michael pressed the recording button and gave the date, time and the names of all-present to commence the interview.

I was finding it hard to concentrate. I knew it was vitally important to be accurate. I took a big slurp of coffee to steady myself. I looked at the moving spools in the recorder and began to narrate the events from the day I met Omar to our last meeting. I spoke for more than an hour. Neither Mark nor Michael interrupted me during the statement.

Michael energetically ejected all three tapes from the recorder and handed over one to me and said, 'This one is for your own records; we might contact you in future if required.'

'I assume my iPhone will remain in your custody?' I asked.

'No, no,' Michael replied. 'We have copied what we wanted to. It's ready for your collection.'

'So, am I free to go home now?' I tried to be cheerful.

'Yes, you are from our point of view but let me speak to Tom,' Michael said, thinking.

At this point, Chief Superintendent Tom himself appeared behind the split glass door of the interview room. His eyes appeared baggy with tiredness but his face was glowing with excitement. He was not wearing his jacket; his braces were off his shoulders, arching beside and behind his hips.

He raised his right hand and punched the air, 'all rounded up, every single one of them.'

'Excellent,' Michael tried to emulate excitement in his reply. 'Caught in pyjamas in their homes, as usual?'

'Certainly caught in pyjamas but as I suspected no one was at home and they were found sleeping hidden in hay in a livestock van just a mile down the road.' Tom laughed hysterically. 'I've just seen the videos. It was so funny to see them coming out, cloaked in hay.' He laughed again violently and this time both Michael and Mark joined him.

Tom took out a handkerchief from his pocket and after wiping both his eyes said, 'Ali, your safety and that of your family is of paramount importance to us. I have thought of two options for you.' I leaned forward to hear his options carefully as he had a breathing voice.

'At the moment we don't know the size of their network or who is supporting them. Is there an outside hand? All these questions need answering and hopefully will be answered in due course. I think this should happen in a matter of days not weeks. In the meantime, we could either move you and your family to some safe place, another house or maybe a hotel. Once we are sure there is no threat to you or your family than you could be re-housed or alternately we could provide twenty-four seven police surveillance to you and your family,' he said and it was apparent from his face that he was weighing and balancing both the options. Then he said. 'I think option two would be the preferred one.'

'So that you could use us as a bait to catch Omar's hit men if they come back?' I said rather abruptly.

Tom reached out and placed his hand over my shoulder, clasped it and said, 'precisely, but not in the spirit you are implying. We all, including the Prime Minister, are eternally grateful to you for your help in this serious matter. I must admit, we all were at a complete loss to pin-point exactly what was happening to the MP's. We instructed the media strongly not to talk about terrorism. But we were finding no lead until you came. You have helped us, the whole British nation. We will protect you and your family, come what may.'

'Thanks, I trust you,' I said. I felt a bit embarrassed for what I had said. 'Could I go home now? I have to attend a funeral at 10 o'clock.'

'Yes, we will drop you off at home in a private car, and we will provide you with police surveillance for your safety and security,' Tom said and warmly shook hands with me.

It was a quarter past five in the morning and the day was breaking. My escort opened the back door of the car for me. I looked through the window as I sat inside. The dark clouds were swirling fast in the sky, making it look as if the day was being swallowed by the night again. A curvy, wavy bright lightning appeared splitting the sky, forcing me to close my eyes, followed by loud thunder. Soon, heavy rain droplets changed into a lashing deluge. The driver leaned forward, peering through the windscreen, as despite the swift movement of the wipers the visibility was poor. The street lights were on again. Regardless of this torrential rain, the streets of London were becoming alive with newspaper vans and milk trucks, moving slowly and splashing water.

I noiselessly opened the front door. The silence I met as I entered my home re-assured me that no untoward incidents had happened in my absence. I took off my dripping jacket and spread it over the radiator and tiptoed upstairs. I quietly opened the doors of Mum's and Bari Ammi's rooms. Both were sleeping soundly. I went to my room and fell on my bed. I had only four hours to catch up with my sleep before Mr Nazir's funeral at 10 o'clock.

CHAPTER 21

It was really nice to see Dad after six weeks. He looked tanned and a bit worn out. It seemed he had caught a cold soon after landing back in Britain. We sat together in the study and I was taking him through all the events in a chronological sequence. Although, he kept his composure I could feel an undercurrent of worry, suspicion and apprehension in his eyes. He had another spell of six sneezes and he put his hand at the back of his head and said, 'Oh that did hurt.'

He blew hard into a tissue, producing a noise which resembled a rocket flying into the air before exploding and said looking at me, 'I don't understand this Crown witness thing. I need to speak to Arif. He should be able to explain the full implications of this. He is a criminal lawyer.' He waited for a while and asked me, 'How long are the police going to provide us with surveillance? Three months? Six months? How will we know when we don't need any surveillance? It could be very tricky.'

'I did ask Tom, the Chief Superintendent, this question, and he said that there is no time limit. They would provide us with security as long as it is required, for years, tens of years,' I replied. 'He also said that he doesn't wish us to become home hostages, and I think I agree with him. It would be more harmful psychologically for us to shut ourselves inside and to start doing online shopping. I think we should live our lives as normally as possible and the hot number which I've entered on everybody's mobiles will get extra security, if required, within a few minutes and Tom, he'll periodically assess the levels of security required by us.' I looked at Dad, who was hiding his face behind a tissue in anticipation of another bout of sneezing.

Mum entered the study and handed over her mobile to me and said, 'I think, this is the same girl whose phone number you deleted.'

'Sophie?' I was pleasantly surprised as I held the phone and slowly walked out of the room. 'Hello Sophie, is that you?' I asked.

'Yeah, it's me. You never rang back.'

'You never told me to,' I could hear her giggling.

'How are you? And how are your bruises?'

'I'm fine. My bruises are showing all the colours of the rainbow. My face has a mottled appearance like an autumn leaf.' I could hear her laughing loudly.

'Well, I was thinking……. if you are free……..We could hang out for some time today or tomorrow or whenever you are free?'

My heart missed a beat, was I invited to go on a date? I had never been asked by any girl to go out with her. Had she broken up with her boyfriend? Was this a rebound friendship? But that would not be the most appropriate question to ask.

'You think beautifully, Sophie. I also think we must, we must go today. Honestly I was about to ring to ask you if you are free, then we could go out for a meal or something.'

'So, you didn't delete my phone number?'

'No, never. I'm not that stupid,' I looked at Mum who was smiling and shaking her head.

'I'm doing work experience at a solicitor's office near Marble Arch tube station. I'll finish work at six, quarter past six.'

'Should we meet just outside Marble Arch tube station at six thirty?'

'Ok, that's fine. I'll see you at six-thirtyish over there, bye.'

'Bye for now.' I felt as happy as if I had touched the moon.

'You told me about everything but not about this girl, you rascal!' said Dad, who was eavesdropping on my conversation.

'Sorry, Dad. Sophie took me to the hospital after the mugging event.'

'Oh, George's theory of falling in love during vulnerable times or is this an act of desperation,' Dad was enjoying the situation.

'I'm not too sure at the moment, but I'll keep you informed.' I said bending forward and placing a hand over my heart.

'If this is an act of desperation then I have to tell you this story of my one-time flatmate. This story is several years older than you.'

'Go on Dad.' I readied myself to face some humiliation.

'This chap showed such a degree of desperation to hook-up with girls that he resorted to spraying himself with some 'female alluring perfume'. He spent all night in a nightclub without much luck, however, while walking back home he seemed to have attracted all sorts of black, brown moths over his shirt. Not surprisingly, he was mortified to his bones when a big bat, about the size of a raven flapped its wings on his face. No one is sure whether the bat was attracted towards the moths or this perfume. Anyway, he took off his shirt, threw it at the bat and come back home running, half-naked.'

'Don't make fun of my son,' Mum said by placing her palms over my cheeks. She looked into my eyes. 'When the time is right, everything will fall in place for him. He is not going to do anything like your desperate friends. I have already made a short list of the most beautiful girls suitable for my son from our family and friends. He is not going to marry a *gori*. He will marry a girl of my choice.'

'Mum…..' I said, 'I can't believe I'm hearing this.'

'Rose,' Dad said firmly. 'It's our son who is going to get married not you. Let him make his own choices.' Dad looked at me and said, 'You could use my new after-shave, the one I bought from the duty free. I can assure you it doesn't contain any female alluring pheromones.'

'Thanks, Dad.' I was feeling a bit embarrassed now. 'You are very generous.'

'You are welcome, son,' he said and brought out his wallet from his back pocket and handed me two fifty pound notes. 'Keep it, don't spend it all. I want at least one note back and mainly use your own credit card.'

'Thanks, Dad, I'll try to return some of it.' I waved the notes in front of his eyes before putting them in my pocket.

'I want at least thirty pounds back if not more,' he said loudly.

'I'll see,' I said.

'I forgot to tell you,' Dad said. 'George has taken early retirement and he's vanished from the hospital as if he never existed. I'm told he is back in Scotland but I'm not sure what he will be doing there.'

'Really?' both Mum and I said in shock.

'It is totally unbelievable; so many things have changed in the past six weeks. Nazir, my dear friend passed away, George left, you are completely transformed from a boy to a dating adult, Bari Ammi has her dreams back, it's amazing, truly amazing.'

'*Allah raham karay,*' Mum said, spreading out her palms. 'May God keep us all in his peace and safety.'

I waited outside a souvenir shop near the Hyde Park exit of the tube station and texted Sophie. There were prints of the Union Jack and the members of the Royal Family on almost every single item sold: caps, key chains, calendars, pens, mugs, T-shirts, umbrellas, flip-flops, chocolates and even on the suitcases. It was an interesting sight of the commercialisation of British heritage. Tourists fully armed with still and movie cameras were coming in and out of the shop. Nearly everyone had bought some mementoes and post-cards.

A tall, slim white man,with bulging cargo trouser pockets was standing at the street corner. He was holding a box of cigarette lighters of various colours. His nervous looking eyes were on the lookout for the police and at the same time he produced a penetrating, repetitive, tape-recording like voice with a prominent nasal twang, 'Pound for four.' I found the salesperson and his method of sale highly amusing.

I could see the same person lurking about in my peripheral vision that I had now seen several occasions outside our house. He lit a cigarette and leaned against a lamp post. He appeared totally unaware of and unrelated to me, but I knew he was keeping a watchful eye on me from the corner of his eye. He came close to me and said without looking, 'Who are you meeting?'

'My friend,' I replied.

'Not a problem. I'll be around, just in case,' he said and walked towards the footpath. Well, I had waited for this moment for so long and that was my fate. I was about to have my first ever date in my whole life – under the shadow of police observation. The story of my life had to be unique, I thought.

'Hello, Ali,' I felt a hand on my shoulder, my heart leapt into my throat and I jumped up in the air with fear.

'I'm sorry, I didn't mean to scare you,' Sophie said. She looked a bit embarrassed. 'Are you OK now?'

'You freaked me out,' I said, gently thumping my chest with the flat of my hand and pointing towards my heart. 'You got to handle it with care – very fragile.' We both laughed.

She was wearing jeans and a light blue cardigan; she wore a pink shirt reflecting the gentle glow on her face. Apart from a mild touch of lipstick, I don't think she was wearing any make-up. I loved her dark brown eyes which sparkled with intelligence, alive with life. She had a well-proportioned body.

'Should we have a little walk in Hyde Park, it's a lovely evening?' I asked her.

'Yeah, good idea. I have been sitting indoors all day. So how are you?' she said, closely observing my face. 'Are you OK now?'

'Yes, yes I'm fine.'

'It was very strange the muggers didn't take your phone. It seems they just wanted to frighten you or was it a case of mistaken identity?'

'Yeah, very strange, but strange things do happen in life,' I said and noticed the policeman following us from a distance.

'I'm very sorry I could not ring you before, I was very pre-occupied with Mum's illness,' she said.

I held her hand as we crossed the pelican lights to enter the park.

'Is she ok now?'

'Yeah, she had been very poorly. She had to be admitted to ITU. She had this rare infection from a bug called E coli 157. Thank God she has survived but she has ended up with renal failure. She needs to have dialysis twice every week and doctors say that she will need a kidney transplant. She is on the waiting list for a donor.'

A wave of shuddering went down my spine. I stopped walking and looked at her and asked, 'Is your mother an MP?'

'Yes, she is. How did you come to know?' She looked straight into my eyes and looked extremely serious. Her eyes welled up and I thought she would cry any minute.

'I have been spying on you. I have done a full homework on you,' I said playfully. 'I think I read it in some newspaper that some MP's were taken ill because of this raw meat imported from Germany, is that right?'

'Yeah, that is right. Let's not talk about it.'

'Have you ever tried Lebanese food?' I asked her to change the topic.

'No, I don't think so, why?' she said wiping her eyes with the back of her hands.

'I love Lebanese food. Do you eat meat?'

'Yes, only if it is *halal*.'

'Really?' I thought it was a joke and said, 'Seems, Ma'am, you have also done your homework about me as well.'

'No, it's a fact,' she said quietly. 'We only eat halal or koshered meat at home. Dad was a maths teacher at the University of Jordan and in fact, I was born in Jordan. We moved back to London when I was four or five. When we moved back here, Dad, who is still very particular about food quality and flavour, didn't like the taste of un-halal meat. He thinks that halal meat is far superior in taste than un-halal but I can't tell you the difference because I have never tried un-halal meat.'

'That's very interesting. Tell me one more thing, do you always do power walking?' I said as I was lagging behind her and felt breathless.

She laughed loudly and the lines behind her laugh lines again became more prominent.

We passed by Speakers' Corner, where a black man with short, grey curly hair was standing on what appeared to be a step-ladder and was addressing two Chinese tourists, who had to look upwards and seemed a little bit bemused with the whole situation. We walked past them and turned left into Park Lane and continued towards the Joy of Life Fountain. The lush green grounds of Hyde Park were packed with people who were enjoying a sunny evening but a mildly chilly breeze was forcing people to put on their jackets and jumpers.

'So you want to become a solicitor?' I asked Sophie.

'Hope so. My Mum would like me to become a QC like her,' she replied. I could see she really loved her mother.

'And also an MP like her?' I asked.

'No, no, I don't think I'm half as good as her. I don't think I could ever address crowds of people as she does. People don't realise that to be an MP is not at all a cushy job. She really has to work hard, some days with only two to three hours of sleep.'

We went past the statue of Achilles before passing in front of the Rose Garden. I wanted to take Sophie inside the garden but a couple was lying at the entrance in an uncomfortably intimate posture, they were so engrossed in each other that they did not take any notice of us and I decided to walk straight past towards the Diana memorial fountain. The Serpentine Lake to the right reflected sunlight and appeared to contain molten gold. There was no water running at the Diana fountain.

We sat on a grass plot near the fountain. She was sitting, her knees drawn to her chin and her arms hooped around her legs.

I looked around and saw my bodyguard sitting and dangling his legs in the empty fountain. It was difficult to know which way he was looking as he wore dark sunglasses.

Sophie looked at me with a bright smile, plucked a blade of grass and looked at it carefully and said, 'So what inspired you to go into medicine?'

'Humanity, love for humanity of course,' I said in a made up voice. 'I always wished to serve an ailing mankind.'

'You know, Ali, you are a bit weird,' she said with a smile, a breeze stirred the collar of her shirt.

'So you are saying I'm weird? I am bizarre?'

'No, you are not weird in a bad sense, you are weird in a good way,' she said and threw the grass blade at me. 'I like your weirdness.'

She fixed me with her straight and intelligent stare. She was trying to assess the impact of her last sentence on me.

'I feel flattered, I feel honoured.' My excitement was making me speak quickly. 'So you like me but love someone else that is unfair, very, very unfair. I'm very possessive.' I wanted to ask her about her boyfriend and was trying to conjure up a suitable, inoffensive sentence in my mind but blurted this out of my mouth like a bullet.

She laughed while bending forward and said, looking at me, 'I never had a boyfriend; I was teasing you the other day.'

'Never had a boyfriend! Are you normal?' I asked. I knew my

eyes were sparkling with excitement.

'Never ever, I promise. I've known a couple of boys in the past but they were very shallow, very superficial. I was waiting for a weir do like you.' She slowly walked on her knees, came close and held my face with her hands, looked into my eyes and kissed me on my forehead. Her warm breath gently moved over my face. My heart was beating violently and it appeared it would come out of my chest any minute. She looked into my eyes again, took my glasses off, threw them on the ground and placed her moist lips over mine. My head was filled with the sound of beating blood. I felt light-headed, the blue sky suddenly went fuzzy and there were fireworks of every colour in the sky with loud crackles. My body felt light like a feather, floating in the air.

'That was awesome,' I said as I lay flat on the ground. The quick movements of clouds in the sky made me queasy so I closed my eyes. I could hear her laughing timidly.

'I think Sophie, you should call an ambulance, I feel faint,' I said in a serious voice, my eyes still shut.

'What should I tell them?' She was still laughing.

I raised my head up and looked at her. She was holding her phone, ready to make a call. 'Well, you should tell them that a nineteen year old boy has had his first ever kiss and the cruel, killer beauty stole his breath away.'

'Well, stealing comes more under the jurisdiction of the police rather than paramedics, should I not call them?'

'Absolutely.' I got up quickly and stood on my feet. 'This is robbery, daylight robbery.'

'I'm running away, I don't wish to get arrested,' she said as she began to run away from me. I picked my glasses up and ran to chase her.

I looked behind and saw the bodyguard getting up. He began to pace along behind us.

We ran in between the people lying in the park and reached the entrance gate in no time. I caught up with Sophie and opened the door of a waiting taxi and pulled her inside. 'Edgware Road, please,' I said, short of breath. Both of us laughed again. I looked back. The bodyguard was hailing a taxi too.

'This is turning out to be one of the best evenings of my life,' she said. Her breasts were moving up and down with each breath.

'The best is yet to come,' I said, meaningfully looking into her eyes.

'Don't raise your hopes,' she said by pushing me.

'You cruel killer.....' I left the sentence unfinished.

'Bad habit, you should always complete your sentences fully. Cruel killer beauty,' she said with an emphatic movement of her index finger. The pleasure of being in love was surging in my circulation, giving a sense of heightened confidence. I held Sophie's hand and intertwined my fingers with hers. She glanced at me and appeared even more beautiful. I was fully caught in the trap of nature, the trap which had been laid since the ancient times of Adam and Eve, but who wanted to escape? Not me.

'Please stop here,' I asked the taxi driver as we reached Edgware Road. As soon as we got out of the taxi, a woman who was wearing a flared skirt with big pink flowers quickly came close to us and stretched her hand towards me. A little boy of two or three years was clutching her leg and was also taking swigs of milk from his bottle. I fished out a pound coin from my pocket and pressed it on her palm. A glint of success appeared in the little boy's eyes which shone darkly like the shell of a black beetle. Both of them swiftly moved towards another taxi.

'Can I have my fare please,' the taxi driver said as he saw my eyes chasing the mother and child. 'Yes, of course, I'm so sorry.' I brought a tenner out of my pocket and handed it over to him.

I held back the restaurant's door for Sophie to pass through. A spicy aroma of food welcomed us. The place was buzzing with people. Soft Arab instrumental music was playing in the background, giving a feeling of transportation into a cool, starry desert night, near an oasis. My stomach juices were flowing, making me feel even hungrier. I looked at Sophie, running my tongue over my lips. She smiled, momentarily closed her eyes and shook her head.

A waitress approached us and before I could say anything, she said, 'A table for two?'

'Yes.'

'You are very lucky,' she said in her middle-eastern accent. 'We just had a cancellation. We are usually booked weeks in advance. Follow me please.'

The empty table was just beside the large window of the restaurant, giving a perfect view of passers-by on Edgware Road. As I sat down I looked outside. The guardian policeman was right there, outside the window, rolling up a cigarette. His cap was pulled downward over his eyes.

The waitress had a hi-top fade hairstyle. Her right eyebrow was pierced with a broad-head-like thumbtack. I felt my eyes widen as she brought out a pistol-like lighter from her pocket, stabilised the nozzle on her left wrist and lit the candles in front of us.

I looked at Sophie and said, 'I have heard that it is difficult to hide it when you are in love and also even harder to pretend when you are not, what do you think?'

She blushed and retracted in her chair and said, 'I don't know. Why do you ask such difficult questions?'

'I'm not afraid of hard questions.' My voice sounded very confident. 'Ask me anything,' I said with a flowing movement of my hand.

'Ok, my little philosopher, define love.'

'Well, love can be defined whichever way you want to look at it.' I paused and then said, looking into her eyes, 'From the point of view of the soul, mind or body?'

'Really, go on I'm listening.' Her eyes flared wide in amazement.

'For the soul, love is an attempt to overcome another person, for the mind it is an act of mutual understanding and for the body,' I paused for a moment and said, 'it is an act of fulfilling the physiological urges of both parties.'

'Wow, you seem to have read a lot of books.'

'Not only books, I like to read people as well which can be even more interesting.' I looked at her again and she looked very impressed.

'Sophie, another question which is more interesting is: why do people fall in love, which is the most common denominator for falling in love?'

'I don't know, why?'

'It's vulnerability, my dear. Vulnerability plunges you into love. It could be emotional, or it could be physical. We are most likely to fall in love when we are vulnerable.'

'You mean events like your beating-up,' she said laughingly.

'Absolutely.'

'But at that time, you were the victim of vulnerability not me.'

'True, it doesn't have to be a double whammy.' I stopped for a while and said 'Women usually like some sort of weakness in their men, not physical of course, something very subtle, something very special, they like to fall for. I don't know whether you have fallen for me or my claustrophobia?'

'I had forgotten about that.' She seemed to be enjoying the conversation. 'No, honestly, not your claustrophobia, maybe the weakness of your eyesight. Your glasses suit your face.'

'I'm so disappointed, I thought you liked me but it turned out to be my glasses.' I took my glasses off and placed them on the table in front of me.

She picked my glasses up and wore them and immediately took them off and shook her head. 'Oh my God, they are too strong.'

'I'm not going to wear them again,' I said putting my glasses aside. 'I'll book an appointment for correction surgery on my eyes tomorrow.'

'Don't take this too seriously.' A wave of fear appeared on her face, wiping her smile off. 'I was only joking, I don't want you to have any surgery because of me.'

I laughed at her grim facial expression.

The waitress came again and laid out the food. 'Enjoy your meal,' she said with a business type smile on her face.

'It all looks very nice,' Sophie said.

'Well, let's not only look at it, let's give a tickling to our taste buds, and please tuck in.'

To eat in the company of someone you like, someone you have fallen in love with was most definitely a unique experience, an experience which can only be felt and not acquired by reading any book. I knew my face was glowing. I felt drunk without drinking.

'Hope it's not too spicy for you,' I asked Sophie.

'No, it's, perfect. Do you come here often?'

'Not here, but I take away from their other branch across the road.' I pointed to a restaurant across the road.

I was glad she liked my taste in food: one more hurdle in long-term relations had been overcome.

We were waiting for milk shakes as afters when Sophie asked me, 'who is this person who has followed us all the evening. Is he your bodyguard?'

'Yes, he is.'

'You need him because of the mugging?' She looked at me, astounded. 'You have taken that mugging very seriously.'

'It was not a mugging.'

'So what was it?'

'It was a punishment for being a witness to a criminal plot,' I said quietly.

'What?' a cloud of fear eclipsed her face. 'Tell me what happened, I would like to know.'

'No, you don't, let's not spoil our evening.' I said looking outside.

'Ali, look at me,' she said with the determination of a solid rock on her face. She brought herself closer to me by leaning forward. 'I would like to know the reason and hear the truth. If there is such a grave risk to your life that you need to keep a bodyguard, I need to know this. Why don't you want to tell me, do you not trust me?'

'No, no that is not the reason. I trust you. It's not a nice story.'

'Whether it is a nice story or not, I demand to know it,' her determination was not fading.

'Well, I nearly got embroiled in some terrorist activity............'
I slowly told her the whole story. I could see tears were flowing down her cheeks and her lower lip was quavering.

'Why did you……. why did you not contact the police earlier, when you knew the plot, why not?' She wiped her tears with the back of her hand.

'It never occurred to me that it would happen so soon. Hindsight is the best science. It's easier for you to say that I should have contacted the police earlier. I didn't know that the plot had been executed until the day I was beaten up and that is the day I went to Scotland Yard.'

'You know you are a coward,' she said in the cutting voice of a chainsaw. 'I hold you responsible for my mother's kidney failure. She has suffered all that just because of you.' She pointed her trembling finger towards me. 'And, now I know why you wanted to hide this from me, because you yourself know that you are responsible for the death of twenty-eight MP's and the kidney failure of twelve more. You go and hide your arse in the books. Go and get lost,' she said angrily and chucked the milk shake all over my face and stormed out of the restaurant.

'Please wait for me,' I said but she left without looking at me.

The buzz in the restaurant quietened suddenly and the background music now appeared more prominent. I could feel the gaze of dozens of eyes which was making me nervous. I had to maintain my composure, I said to myself. I cleaned my face with the starched napkin and put on my glasses. I continued to look straight at my table. I had drawn imaginary curtains to the sides, I just wanted to clean my face, pay the bill and get out of this place as quickly as possible. I called the waitress to bring the bill, which I think she anticipated and brought it in no time. The bill was for £67. I tossed both fifty pound notes in the plate and said with a smile on my face, 'Please keep the change,' and rushed out to chase Sophie. As I came out of the restaurant, I noticed the bodyguard just standing outside. I think he was keeping too close an eye on me and had witnessed the whole conflict.

'Which way did she go?' I asked him.

'That way,' I looked in the direction he pointed. I saw Sophie jumping into a cab.

I called her mobile number, although I wasn't too sure at all that she would answer my call, but she did.

'Listen Sophie, I need to talk....'

She cut me and said, 'You listen to me, Ali, I don't want to talk to you, don't you ever try to ring me again. I hate you, I simply hate you, I don't want to see you ever again.' I could hear her hiccups during crying.

I was walking slowly with both hands inside the front pockets of my jeans, clasping on and rotating my mobile inside the pocket. An empty juice carton was lying on the footpath. I swung my right leg forcefully and kicked it hard to the wall; a last few drops of juice splashed over a middle aged man walking on the footpath,who darted towards me and said with revulsion, 'Arsehole.'

'You got it right, that is my name.' I said it loudly, pointing my finger up in the air like a cricket umpire. 'If you come close to me, I'll bust your balls into mincemeat.' The man retracted, there was fear on his face and he quickly moved away. The crowd sensed trouble and parted to make room for me to walk on the footpath.

I kicked again in the air, which made me a bit unbalanced. I turned around and said to the police protection man, 'You had enough fun for the evening. You can go now and fuck yourself. If I ever see you following me again, I'll smash your face.' Fear had suddenly evaporated from my body. I could not care less about being attacked or killed by Omar's men or by anyone else.

The thought of losing Sophie, not being able to contact her ever again, went like a dagger through my heart. I hadn't realised until today how precious and how fragile love could be.

CHAPTER 22

There was a knock at the door. I was sitting in the living room, browsing through *The Daily Telegraph*. Mum was sitting beside me, she was wearing her reading glasses, which she only used whilst reading and writing messages to some of her friends on her mobile. Dad had his afternoon free from the hospital and was going through his paperwork in his study.

'I'll get it,' Dad said as he walked towards the front door. I could hear him talking to someone for a couple of minutes and then the door closed. He entered the room holding the mobile to his ear. 'This is Taj, look Arif, could you ring me as soon as you get this message? It's kind of urgent.' His face looked solemn. 'I don't know why people keep mobiles when they never answer them,' he said and slumped heavily into the chair.

'Is everything Ok?' I asked Dad.

'No,' he said fixing his gaze on the floor. 'It was the police. They want to record your statements regarding the night of

11th July, today before five o'clock.'

'What happened on the night of 11th July?' I asked him whilst trying to jog my memory. 'This was the night Mr Nazir passed away, how can I forget?'

'That's right, I remember that too,' Mum said. 'What happened?'

'Did you drive too fast to the hospital that night?' Dad asked.

'No, I don't think so,' I replied, trying to re-play the events of that night in my mind.

'Anything else, which occurred that night?' Dad asked me impatiently. 'Can you remember anything else which happened that night?'

'Well, I drove from home at about half three in the morning. The roads were quiet. I can't recall that I was driving too fast or let's put it this way, I can't remember being flashed by any of the speed cameras.' I closed my eyes and spoke while squeezing my forehead between thumb and index finger, producing a fold of skin.

Mum had moved closer to me and held my hand.

'Yes, a drunken man did bang his bottle on the bonnet of our car. That was totally unprovoked and he simply ran away after that. I don't think there was anything else to remember after that except at the hospital.......'

'Yes, I do remember you telling me about the drunken man, as there was only a small dent. I told Ali not to bother with the insurance people. Did I do wrong?' She looked worried.

'Are you sure, you didn't provoke him and nothing happened to him as a result of what he did?' Dad asked me, ignoring what Mum had said.

'No, nothing happened to him, I'm absolutely certain,' I said confidently.

'What did the police say, did he come to any harm because of my driving?' I asked.

'Yes, they are applying the Road Traffic Act, clause 170 to you, according to which if a personal injury happens to anyone on the road due to your vehicle, it was your duty to stop and report it to the police. Failure to do so makes you guilty of an offence. I don't know why all this is happening to you.' Dad's face appeared pale due to worry. He came close to me, held me by my shoulders and looked straight into my eyes and said, 'I'll hire a good lawyer. We'll fight this case, but Ali, you need to tell me the truth, tell me exactly what happened. This is not a trivial matter. It can have far reaching consequences. God forbid you should get a criminal conviction ......' He left the sentence hanging.

Mum was sniffling and she said, 'I'll take you to Pakistan. Before now I was not happy for you to be this Crown witness, and now another case.' She looked at Dad and said, 'It's a conspiracy against my son. What they want is to take the immunity of a Crown witness away from him. Sooner or later they will charge him for taking part in this terrorist plot. This police protection, this Crown witness, this is all a drama. I'll not let this injustice happen to my son. I don't want my son to face the courts at his age. I'll take him to Pakistan. He'll be much safer there. He can study over there. I'll not let any harm come to him.' She wrapped her arms around me and hugged me tightly.

'Well, I never thought of it from that point of view. Rose, you could well be right, yeah, going to Pakistan could be an option but I need to confer with solicitors,' Dad said deeply immersed in his thoughts.

'Taj, please ring your travel agent and book seats for us, we'll leave tomorrow,' Mum said, wiping tears from her face. 'You can consult the solicitors but I'll take my son away from this country.'

I could see that both Mum and Dad had already declared me guilty.

'Dad and Mum, I haven't committed any offence. I'm not going to run away. I'll prove my innocence. I can promise you no one came to any harm that night because of my driving,' I said assertively. 'How did the police know that it was our car, have they had a look at the CCTV footage? What is their evidence against me?'

'They are bastards, even if the CCTV footage does not lay the blame on you; they will find something against you. It's best we leave the country.' Mum seemed to have reached a firm conclusion on what was best for me.

'Yes, they have reviewed the CCTV footage. They didn't tell me the details but perhaps we can ask to have a look at that?' Dad said.

'Yes, we must. I think we should not make any hasty decisions to leave the country, actually such a thing can backfire, and we need to establish the facts first,' I said emphatically.

'Yes, you are right Ali,' Dad said and answered his phone saying. 'Thanks, Arif, for getting back to me. We need to talk.......can you come over......yes, right now if possible.......yeah, we'll make a cup of coffee for you.....thanks......much appreciated...... see you soon.....bye.'

'Arif is on his way.' Dad appeared a bit calmer now.

'Great,' I said. 'I have nothing to hide. I'm ready to record my statement to the police, and they can't deny what is recorded on these cameras. It's powerful, unbiased evidence,' I said and looked at Mum. 'Don't worry Mum, I'll come clean out of it, *inshallah*, God willing.'

'*Inshallah,*' Mum said and kissed me on my forehead. 'You have become a big boy, bigger than what I imagined. May God keep you under His protection.' Her eyes bulged with tears again.

* * * * *

Uncle Arif listened to my story and made some notes while sipping his coffee. 'I think we are ready to go to the police station to record the statement. It's our legal right to request to look at the CCTV footage and it's very difficult to misconstrue this sort of evidence. I think this drunken person died of something else and the police just want to complete their paperwork. Let's go. That is the only way to end your parent's misery.'

'Are you sure, Arif Bahi, no harm will come to Ali. He won't be arrested or anything?' Mum asked.

'Well, *Bhabbi*, I don't do anything other than questioning or representing criminals. I can tell you Ali is a reliable witness, *Inshallah*, I'm almost certain he'll come to no harm and certainly they can't arrest him as yet,' he replied.

'Thanks Uncle Arif, thanks for trusting me. Both of my parents had already convicted me of something which I didn't do,' I said.

Uncle Arif chortled. 'Let's go and put all of you out of this misery.'

* * * * *

'We have come to see PC Holborn,' Uncle Arif said to the policewoman at the reception.

'In connection with what?' Her blonde ponytail bobbed with the movement of her head.

'He came to 7 Convent Road for a statement from Ali Taj,' Uncle Arif said pointing at me. 'I'm his legal representative.'

'Sure.' The policewoman at the reception picked the phone up and said, 'Mr Taj is here......Ok ...thanks.'

'Please take a seat.' She pointed towards a row of fixed plastic institutional chairs. 'Constable Holborn will be with you in two minutes.'

Constable Holborn actually arrived in less than two minutes accompanied by a man in plain clothes. Constable Holborn was totally bald, with both arms heavily tattooed. He seemed to have a permanently poised smile under his handlebar moustache. He appeared suave. He introduced himself and firmly shook hands and said, 'Please meet my colleague, Inspector Moore.' He asked us to follow them to a room, whose plaque read 'Interview Room'. Inspector Moore was short, pedantic looking and the sort of a person who was ready to see the reverse side of every coin. The interview room was much smaller than the interview room at Scotland Yard and no recording machine was present.

'Let me just get the file,' PC Holborn said and dashed out of the room.

'Sure,' Uncle Arif said pleasantly and began to casually read the notes he had made.

Inspector Moore took his mobile out of his pocket and began to play with its keys. It was quite evident that he didn't wish to converse or have eye-contact with us.

Dad's eyes showed the apprehension of a lost deer. He seemed to be carefully inspecting the room from corner to corner and was constantly running a tissue over his forehead to wipe away sweat.

It was useful talking to Uncle Arif before coming to the police station as it helped me to get things in order in my mind.

The door creaked open and PC Holborn was back with a bulging red folder held in both hands.

'Could we please know the allegation against Ali before we start?' Uncle Arif asked PC Holborn before he could sit in his chair.

'Yes,' PC Holborn replied briefly and said, 'let me first find a factual record of events for the night of 11ᵗʰ of July. In fact, it was morning, early morning, is that OK?'

'That's right,' Uncle Arif said looking at me and nodding his head.

I narrated the events of that morning in as much detail as I could remember and PC Holborn made short notes without any interruptions. He looked convinced by my statement.

'Did Mr Nazir die that morning,' Poker-faced Inspector Moore asked in the end.

'Yes, he passed away maybe thirty-forty minutes after my arrival at the hospital,' I said.

'Ok,' PC Holborn said looking at Inspector Moore. 'It's easy to confirm. We can check the date and time of his death from the death certificate.'

'What is the issue then?' Uncle Arif asked.

'That a drunken person was found dead the next morning, lying in his own pool of blood,' PC Holborn said.

I could feel a knot in my chest. I looked at Dad, and the colour on his face had faded. Uncle Arif also appeared to be in shock and it looked from his eyes that he was formulating a response in his mind.

'Why, what happened to him?' I asked 'Have you reviewed the CCTV footage?'

'The post-mortem has shown that glass shrapnel which most likely flew off his bottle severed his jugular and he died of a massive haemorrhage. His blood analysis has shown huge levels of alcohol, which goes with your statement. The CCTV footage has shown exactly what you have described. What we want to know from you is that you didn't see him bleeding, did you?'

I could feel the gaze of everyone in the room fixed on my face.

'Ali, you don't have to answer this question if you don't want to,' Uncle Arif said to me.

'No, I want to answer this question,' I said. 'I am truthfully telling you, I didn't see him bleeding at all. Soon after he had smashed his bottle over my car, he ran away from me, into the darkness.'

'Did you bother to come out of the car to see what was happening?' Inspector Moore said with asperity.

'No, I didn't. I have already told you that I had to reach the hospital without any delay as someone was dying there,' I said.

'And someone also was dying there on the road,' Inspector Moore said. I could see that he didn't like my audacity in outfacing him. 'You think the life of a person living on the road was less important; they are creepy-crawlies, not worthy of any attention?'

'I think my client has clearly answered your question,' Uncle Arif said. 'He has told you that he was not aware that any harm had come to this particular person from his action.'

'That's reasonable, you didn't see him bleeding and therefore it was not your duty of care to stop your car and report it to the police.' PC Holborn said without looking at Inspector Moore. 'We'll record your statement and I'll liaise with your legal representative to close this case. I'm very sorry to have provoked anxiety in your minds but as you know, a person has died unnaturally and we're obliged to investigate it and to complete this paperwork.'

'That was very unfortunate,' Dad said, appearing very sad and asked PC Holborn, 'Did they comment on his liver in the post mortem?'

PC Holborn opened the red file again and after flipping several pages he said, 'Yeah, it says, shrunken in size..........., yes in conclusion it says end stage cirrhosis.'

'Why did you ask this question? What's its relevance to the case?' Inspector Moore butted-in again.

'It is very relevant to this case. This makes more sense now, why he bled to death. In patients with end stage cirrhosis, the liver can't produce the factor which helps the blood to clot and that is most probably what happened in his case. Because of his high intake of alcohol at that time he didn't feel the pain of his jugular being cut and bled to death due to a lack of clotting factors in his circulation.' Dad appeared much calmer after getting the story right in his head.

'Gosh, that explains everything. It makes sense to a lay person like me. You must be a very good doctor.' PC Holborn looked very impressed with Dad.

Inspector Moore pushed his chair back, producing a screeching noise, gave me a hard look and said to PC Holborn. 'I'm off; you could finish the rest of the paperwork.'

'Not a problem. Thanks for coming,' PC Holborn said, raising his right hand.

'Well done Taj,' Uncle Arif said looking at us, 'you solved the mystery. Right chaps, you go home and relax. I'll see you later. I've to shoot from here to the office after doing some necessary paperwork here.'

'Thanks, Arif, I can't tell you how valuable your support has been today.' Dad's face was drenched in compliments for Uncle.

'Well, if you have a son like Ali, you need not worry about anything. He is maturing into a very confident, responsible adult. Of course, all credit goes to you for your excellent supervision and nurturing.'

'All credit goes to *Allah*,' Dad said raising his index finger towards the ceiling and gave me a tight hug. He looked at my face, which he held in his hands and said, 'The events of the past few weeks seemed to have taught you so much which I couldn't do in the past nineteen years. My son, you truly have shown me today what nerves of steel mean. You really make me proud.' I wiped the tears flowing on his cheeks, put my arm around his waist and walked out of the room.

CHAPTER 23

I was lazing around on the sofa in the living room, legs sprawled out, with a laptop resting on my belly. The room was brightened by the midmorning orange sunlight. Our ginger cat Piers was lying on his usual spot in the room, under which the heating pipes ran. Piers woke up from his cat-nap, stretched forward on his front legs, which were white as if he wore ankle socks with knee socks on his rear legs. He produced a camel-like hump on his back to further stretch his body, had a good old yawn to exhibit his mouth up to the throat, and glanced casually at me before walking out of the room.

I wanted to go and apologise to Sophie's mum. I didn't wish to use this meeting as a lever to ease the strain between Sophie and me. The objectives of the meeting were absolutely clear in my mind – give a sincere apology. Although twelve MP's had suffered from kidney failure as a result of the infection, should I go to all of them, one by one, and give an apology? I was deliberating. Maybe I should, I thought. I should start with the person I knew. Did I know her? I asked myself. Well, sort of. I knew she needed dialysis and was on the waiting list for a renal transplant. I didn't know about the other MP's; how many had suffered permanent kidney problems or were in need of dialysis. I was able to find her office address through an Internet search without any problem. I rang the number.

After a couple of rings, someone picked-up the phone and said in a clear English accent, 'Mrs Barlow's office. How can I help you?'

'I would like to meet Mrs Barlow, please.'

'Unfortunately, currently she is off sick and hence not able to meet her constituents.'

'It's very important that I meet her,' I said assertively.

'Could you tell me what this is about?'

'To offer an apology, a sincere apology. This would really lift a burden off my chest.' I changed from being assertive to cajoling.

'So this may be important to you but possibly not to her?' There was a prominent question mark in her reply.

'I think it's important to both of us.' I was slightly taken aback with her response.

'OK, can you come here at 1o'clock? I know it is very short notice.'

'Yes, I could be there within an hour,' I said.

'That's fine. I'm afraid she may not be able to see you for more than 10-15 minutes. She is coming here to pick some files up. Is that ok?'

'That's perfect. I'll be there,' I said and confirmed her office address which I transferred directly into my mobile phone diary.

I stretched myself by raising both arms in the air and moved my neck in a semi-circle. I peeped through the window. The air outside appeared still. I didn't realise but it had rained earlier and the grass was shimmering with rain droplets. Little robins were chirping, chasing and hopping in the tree branches marking their territories. The blue sky had a floating patchwork of fluffy white clouds. I looked at my wristwatch. I had to go now, and I had less than an hour to reach her office.

I took a cab, which dropped me a couple of blocks from her office due to some on-going road works. A flock of pigeons were energetically bobbing their heads up-and-down, picking up bread pieces from the footpath. Their neck movement gave these dull grey pigeons a marvel of shimmering pink and green iridescent throats. They all flew upwards in a flurry, fanning me, as they saw me approaching them.

The office had a front garden with a small wrought iron gate. It looked like a posh office in a posh area. I'd driven past some of the MP's surgeries before and the majority of them were in high streets, crowded with shops. The stones scrunched underneath my feet as I walked on the gravel footpath. There was a smell of recently cut grass in the air, flowerbeds were neatly manicured. A climbing rose bush with golden yellow flowers covered the front of the red brick building. The entrance door was two steps high, flowerpots framing the steps, the door knocker was as shiny as a brass button. Before I dropped the knocker on the door, I looked at myself. I had turned up here without any preparation, in jeans, a blue T-shirt and dark brown deck shoes. My heartbeat became a little faster. Well, who cares, I consoled myself, and I'm here to apologise and nothing else. I knocked at the door.

'May I help you?' A voice came through the intercom.

'Yes, I'm Ali. I have come to see Mrs Barlow.'

'Ok, come in please,' and a buzzing sound unlocked the door.

A receptionist was sitting behind a large mahogany reception-desk; a slim crystal vase which had freshly cut flowers in it was casting a rainbow shadow near its base. The lady had grey hair which curled upwards as it reached her shoulders, reading glasses were swinging over her chest on a dainty gold chain. She wore a generous coating of foundation on her face to camouflage her wrinkles. Her eyebrows were pencil drawn, and her eyes appeared smaller on her face probably due to the heavy load of mascara on the eyelashes.

'Please take a seat,' she said pointing towards a single seat sofa. 'Mrs Barlow will be with you shortly.' She paused and said, 'Can I get you tea or coffee?'

'Thanks, I'm fine,' I said as I sat on the edge of the sofa.

'Yes Ma'am, Mr Ali is here,' I heard the receptionist talking over the phone.

Instinctively, I ran a hand from my jaw angle to my chin and realised that I hadn't even shaved before coming. The indoor plants in the room looked fresh; the plant's soil appeared darker, hinting that they had been watered recently. In the corner, there was a large poster-sized picture of Sophie's mum with the prime minister.

The door beside the reception opened and a woman appeared whom I could have recognised among hundreds of women as Sophie's mum without anyone telling me.

'Hello, Ali, how're you?' she said with a pleasant smile on her face. 'Please come through,' she said as she advanced her hand to shake hands with me, her hand was cold.

Sophie's mum's office, unlike other barristers' offices did not have floor to ceiling shelves of books. It was more like a living room with a couple of sofas and a centre table on which some magazines were placed. A small door on the right had the sign of a toilet and there was also a prominent 'no smoking' sticker on the wall. She appeared very pale and there was a bruise on the back of her right hand as if an ink droplet had exploded there.

'So what can I do for you, Ali?' she said and gestured to me to take a seat on the sofa.

'First of all I'm thankful to you for seeing me at such short notice.' I paused and looked at her.

'That's ok.'

'I'm really sorry and wished to apologise to you personally that you had to undergo this illness and now the inconvenience of dialysis. I don't know whether Sophie told you or not that I knew about the plot. What I was totally unaware of was when it would take place.' I paused again and looked at her.

She looked very serious and was looking not only at me but also at my soul with a piercing gaze, trying to establish the credibility of what I was saying and what I was about to say.

'I blame myself for this happening. I think I was childish. I was burying my head in the sand, hoping that nothing would happen, and it was an act of supreme folly, idiocy. They executed the plot without my involvement. I only came to know about the plot the evening I was beaten up to keep my mouth shut. In fact, Sophie took me to the hospital that evening.'

'Yes, Sophie has told me everything, every single detail.' I could see a sense of ease in her eyes, a trust for me for what I had said. She paused for a moment and said, 'I think you were put in a very awkward situation. I don't know whether any teenager would have acted any differently, especially when you could not confer with anyone as your dad was away. I think it was incredibly brave of you and you should feel proud of yourself that you went to Scotland Yard on your own that night despite being beaten and chased by that person's men. What was his name?'

'Omar.'

'Yes, Omar's men. I don't think you should blame yourself for whatever happened to me.' She stopped to take a breath and asked, 'Do you believe in fate?'

'Yes, I do,' I said unequivocally.

'I do as well,' she said rotating the golden bracelet on her left wrist with her index finger and thumb. 'There was only a maximum 25% chance of renal failure due to this infection, which means a minimum of 75% chance that no harm would come to my kidneys but it did. I think this was my fate. I could have had the kidney failure anyway, due to any other reason. I'm not going to fight with this fact but will just accept it.'

'That's very philosophical and if I may say, a very mystic approach to life, a life of contentment and happiness,' I said.

'Whatever you call it, mystic or pragmatic, I don't care, I don't mind. What I don't want to be is a victim of chronic anger syndrome, to be perpetually unhappy. And also I don't want anyone to feel guilty because of me so please don't blame yourself.' She had a faint blue vein on her right temple which became conspicuous as she spoke. Dark circles under her eyes looked more prominent on her pale face.

'But whatever is going on between you and Sophie, you have to sort it out between yourselves. I'm not going to act as a mediator between you two,' she said with a smile and it was not hard to notice where Sophie had inherited her laugh lines from.

'I didn't come to you for this reason,' I said. 'And could you please not tell Sophie that I came to see you.'

'I wasn't going to tell her anyway,' she said.

There was a faint knock at the door and Sophie's mum said, 'Come in please.'

A tall, slim man entered the room. He looked straight at Sophie's mum and said, 'I have mowed both the front and the back gardens, done all the flowerbeds, and watered all your indoor plants. I think I have earned a nice evening meal today.'

Sophie's mum smiled and looked at me and said, 'Ali, meet my husband. Our gardener has had an operation and today I successfully managed to persuade my husband to do the gardening for my office.'

'I'm so sorry, I didn't see you.' He came close, raised his eyebrows as with pleasure and firmly shook hands with me. He was at least six to eight inches taller than his wife and wore a well-kept, grey French beard, which gave him an aura of authority. He looked well organised. His hands were soft, the hands of a pure academic professor not of a manual labourer. I didn't think that he did gardening even as a hobby. There was grass staining around the white part of his joggers.

'I think you have done a good job. I was admiring your garden as I came in. It's very impressive,' I said and felt a bit embarrassed as it appeared to me that I might be trying to patronise him.

'Thanks,' he said with a loud laugh. I was a bit lost as to why he laughed. Was it funny, what I said or maybe that is how he is.

'You remember,' she said pointing at me, 'Sophie was telling us that she hurled a milk shake over her friend.'

'Yes, I do,' he said seriously.

'Ali was the recipient of that glass,' Sophie's mum informed him.

'Oh, I'm so sorry, poor you. She is generally not like that at all, tossing things at other people. In fact she is very embarrassed by that entire event,' her father said. I noticed wrinkles on the side of his neck.

'I don't think the milk shake was that bad,' I said with a smile.

There was loud laughter from both her parents and Sophie's dad said. 'A good sense of humour is exactly what you need to survive in this world.' He sat beside me on the sofa.

I asked him, 'Do you know the background of all that has happened?'

'Of course, I do, I know it well,' he replied.

I said, 'She got angry with me over why I hadn't informed the police earlier. She feels that if I had told them earlier, no harm would have come to you.' I looked at Sophie's mum and said, 'She loves you. She loves you dearly. To be in love or to be angry is like saddling a wild horse; it takes you to the places you never meant to go.'

'Very well said, Ali, well done.' Her eyes lit up in excitement. 'Yes, Sophie did tell me that both you and your father are avid readers so who wrote that?'

'No, I have not read that anywhere,' I said timidly, 'but sometimes ideas do come to my mind like finished products, like this one. I wish it happened to me more often, but unfortunately it is very rare. I'm not a thinker by any means. You don't have to be scared of me.'

'Wow, that's brilliant. No, we are not scared of you at all. We would love to meet you again,' Sophie's dad said, looking at his wife.

'Thanks, please don't tell Sophie that I was here today,' I said to Sophie's dad.

'No, I won't,' he said reassuringly.

I noticed Sophie's mum glance at the clock.

'I think I should be going now,' I said.

'I have an appointment at the hospital,' Sophie's mum said. 'It was nice to meet you, Ali, and don't hold yourself responsible for what happened to me.' She got up and the cracking of her knee joints was audible like dried tree branches breaking in autumn. 'I think I'm falling apart,' she said and bent down and massaged her knee.

'Would you like Linda to order a taxi for you?' she asked me.

'No, I'll be fine. Doing a bit of walking won't harm me. Thanks for seeing me at such short notice.'

'That's absolutely fine.' Both of them shook hands with me and Sophie's dad opened the door for me. I could see Sophie's mum turn back to her desk and pull open a drawer and begin to look for some files.

I came out of the room with Sophie's dad, who closed the door behind him.

He handed over a card to the receptionist and said, 'Linda, keep this chap's phone number. I think he did a good job in the garden. I can't understand why Becky would not allow any other gardener to come in. I was in no mood to argue with her on such a trivial matter today. I think we can call on him again until our old fellow is fully recuperated from his surgery.'

'Certainly, Sir,' the receptionist said, 'I think he was very careful. He did not spill a drop of water on the window sill while watering the plants.'

'Good. And I have earned a nice meal for the evening. It has been a win-win situation for all of us,' he said with a playful smile on his face.

'You deserve it, Sir, you supervised him very closely,' she said respectfully. 'You did follow him on the lawns like a shadow.'

'Bye, Sir,' I shook hands with him. 'Thanks for your help, Linda,' I said and came out of the office. I wanted to ring Sophie. I was cursing myself for being such an impulsive person. I had deleted her phone number yet again. I had to fish out her number from Mum's mobile.

CHAPTER 24

I admired my new cricket bat as I oiled it with linseed oil. 'It's harrow size,' I said. 'What size?' Dad asked from behind the newspaper. He was home; it was his half-day off from work.

'It's heavier and thicker than ordinary bats, it's good for slogging in T20 matches,' I said to Dad, who did not reply and remained deeply absorbed in reading the newspaper.

'Can't you just do this in another room? I can't stand the smell,' Mum said as she entered the living room, sounding annoyed. She handed a cup of tea to Dad, 'I'm also bringing some *samosas*.'

'That would be nice,' said Dad and continued reading.

'Great, I'll have some as well,' I said and hid the bat behind the sofa in the living-room.

The doorbell rang. I opened the door and was greeted by a totally unfamiliar face.

'Hello, Ali,' he said with a smile. I was hugely surprised as to how he knew my name.

'I'm DI Bill Davies, from Scotland Yard.' He brought his identification badge out of his pocket and flashed it in front of my eyes. I didn't get a chance to see his card properly. 'Our Chief would like to update you on certain matters and he would like to meet you now. Should we go then?'

'Now?' There was an obvious sharpness in my query. Why now? I said to myself, this sounds ominous. Why would the Chief like to meet us now?

'Do we have to go now?' I asked again.

'Yes please. He's only got half an hour so you must be quick. I'll give you a lift and I'll bring you back too. It shouldn't take more than an hour,' he said.

'Would you like to come in?' I asked reluctantly, opening the door to let him in. I wasn't certain whether I should have gone with him. I led him through to the study and sat him down.

'You cops work in pairs, don't you?' I asked. 'Where is your buddy?'

'Yeah, we do, he is outside in the car.' He said with a catch in his voice.

I went to fetch Dad from the living room. I felt something wasn't right in my heart about this person. I accessed the number for the surveillance team through my speed dial and was connected to them instantly.

'Hello, this is Ali,' I said in a rushed tone.

'Yes, we recognise your name and number from the priority list. What can we do for you?'

'A DI named Bill Davies has come to my home in order to take me to meet the Chief Superintendent now. Could you please confirm that this meeting has been arranged?'

'Have you checked his ID?' he inquired.

'Sort of, he flashed it in front of my eyes.'

'Ok, don't let him in until I can confirm...'

'He's already in the study,' I said.

'OK, I'll ring the Chief's office and find out if anyone's been sent to you. I'll ring you back in a second.'

'No, don't ring me,' I insisted. 'I'm gonna go and sit with him. Don't ring me, just text, I'll try and keep him busy. If he's not real you'd better send someone here quickly.'

'Alright, no problem, just wait for my text.'

Dad was reading a newspaper and sipping tea at the same time whilst sitting in his favourite chair.

'Dad there's a policeman who's come to take us to meet the Chief Superintendent now,' I said in a very innocent but loud voice, which Bill could hear, and winked at Dad.

'What? What is going on,' he said and I was quick to place my index finger on my lips as a signal to shush him without arousing suspicion. 'Just come with me,' I said as I took the tea cup out of his hands and placed it gently on the table by his side.

I walked Dad to the study and said, 'Dad this is DI Bill Davies who has kindly agreed to give us a lift to and from Scotland Yard.'

He shook hands with Dad and I could see a fine tremor in Bill's hand which was not there when he had met me before. Bill was probably in his late thirties. He had a prominent nose like a light bulb under which he had kept a neat looking moustache.

'We should go now,' Bill said. 'As I told Ali earlier, the Chief Superintendent has only a 20-30 minute slot free and if we miss that, God only knows how many days or weeks we might have to wait to get a meeting with him.'

'I'm extremely sorry, Inspector,' I said in an embarrassed tone. 'I was about to go to the toilet when you came. I have a condition and I have to go when I have to, otherwise I could ruin your car. Just give me five minutes, please,' I said and was impressed with my own acting.

Dad's face was wide open and he also said, 'Go and be quick.' Dad looked at the Inspector. 'I'm very sorry that he is wasting your precious time,' and he pointed at me with a finger and said, 'Just go now, sometimes he can be messy.'

'Really,' Bill said in disgust and sat down again.

The text I was waiting for arrived. 'No policeman sent. Keep him busy. Will be there in five minutes.'

'Dad, look at the texts my girlfriend has been sending me,' I passed the mobile to Dad, who moved his glasses onto his forehead to read the message. 'You still think I should sort things out with her?' I asked.

'You go and do whatever you were about to do. I'm sorry, Inspector, for wasting your time.' Dad said and handed me back the phone. 'Inspector, I'm expecting a delivery any minute now and I'd like to receive it before we go.'

'What?' Bill had lost his patience and looked angry now. 'Why can't you understand we have an appointment with the Chief. Waiting for a delivery is not important. Ok, I understand your son has to take a shit,' he mumbled and the rest was inaudible as he spoke under his breath with obvious repulsion on his face.

I came out of the room and went straight into the kitchen, where Mum was making *samosas*. I turned the burner off underneath the frying pan, put a finger of silence over my lips and whispered her to remain calm and to go to Bari Ammi's room and securely lock it from inside.

'Why, what's happening? I'm in no mood for any pranks,' Mum said angrily.

'Shush, we have an unwelcome visitor in the study, I'll tell you the details later. Just go upstairs and keep your mobile with you. Please don't tell Bari Ammi anything. Maybe you could ask her to take her hearing aids off for a little while. Everything will be fine soon.'

Mum tip-toed quietly upstairs to Bari Ammi's room and I could hear her bolting the door from inside. I hid myself behind the sofa and curtain in the living room, holding my cricket bat. I positioned myself in such a way that anyone entering the room would have their back towards me and I could see the whole view of the study in the wall-sized hallway mirror. Inspector Davies was sitting casually on a sofa with his right leg resting upon his left knee. My pulse was racing and my palms were becoming sweaty.

There was a knock at the front door. I could hear Dad saying, 'That could be the delivery, I'll get it.' The clunking of unlatching the door was audible, and then there was a silence for a few moments. I think a sign language conversation was taking place.

'Oh, yes come in please,' I could hear the creaking and clattering of floor boards below the feet of the new entrant to our house.

'Hello Inspector, I'm Commander Adam Seyes from Special Branch.' Commander Adam was tall and broad. He wore jeans and a black waterproof jacket. He extended his arm towards Bill to shake hands with him.

Bill jumped off the sofa in a flash, pulled a pistol out of his jacket and hurriedly screwed a metal tube onto the muzzle with the other hand. He leapt forward and grabbed Dad by the collar. It all happened so quickly that I think even the Commander was taken by surprise.

'Back off, Commander, hands over your head,' Bill yelled. 'Any wrong move and I'll kill him. There is a silencer on my gun, no one will hear the shot and he will be dead. Don't try to be over smart with me. No tricks, jus' follow what I say.' My heart was pounding. Tears bulged into my eyes as I saw Dad's face appear swollen due to Bill's tight grip on his collar, which he was twisting.

I could see the Commander's back with his hands over his head, revealing behind his back, his brown pistol holster. A wave of fear was making my body numb, this could get very messy here, I thought.

Commander Adam said in a composed tone, 'You should not carry out any foolish move like that. The house is surrounded by thirty commandos. You stand a better chance in a court of law rather than by stepping outside. These commandos will turn your skull into a sieve in no time. Just drop your gun and give yourself up.'

'No… no I'm not gonna surrender. Drop your gun and tell your men to get lost,' he said and pushed Dad out of the study, still pointing the gun at him. Commander Adam removed the gun from his holster, bent on one knee and placed it on the floor.

'A Taser gun!' Bill said and laughed loudly. 'You call yourself British police; you aren't allowed to carry real guns.'

Bill kicked Adam's gun away from him. I could see all three walking towards the living room.

'Open this window and tell your dogs to go away,' Bill glowered at Adam, who kept his face totally expressionless. His eyes were assessing the situation.

Adam entered the room, followed by Dad. Bill, whose back was towards me, was jabbing his gun into Dad's back to keep him moving. I had to stop myself from roaring out in anger by gritting my teeth and firmly clenching the handle of the cricket bat. I forced myself to remain still, waiting and watching for the right moment. I knew I had only one chance to strike and strike hard but at the right time. Any wrong move could put Dad's life in danger. My heart was hammering away.

When Bill was within my reach, I took a deep breath, and under the adrenaline overload, I sprinted out like a flash of lightning from behind the sofa and hit his head with the bat.

He said, 'Oh, no,' and groaned with pain as he collapsed on the ground like a fallen tree. The injury appeared bloodless. I looked at my bat, it was undamaged.

Adam was quick to respond as well but looked in pain; he was clasping his right shoulder but still got hold of Bill's gun. There was a smell of gunpowder in the air but I didn't hear any shot fired. I noticed Adam's shirt turning red, he was bleeding from the shoulder. It looked like Bill had shot him. Adam sat on the floor, gripping his shoulder with his left hand.

'Call 999, Ali,' Dad shouted as he sat on the floor with Bill. 'He is in pain shock. He needs to go to hospital urgently.'

'Adam's been shot in his shoulder,' I informed Dad.

'Oh, no. Call for two ambulances then,' he shouted. He brought Bill into the recovery position and checked his airway, breathing and pulse. Bill's fake moustache was peeling off. 'He needs to be seen by the neuro-surgical team,' Dad said and turned towards Adam.

'I think the bullet just brushed my shoulder,' Adam said, and pointed toward an irregular hole, freshly made in the wall behind him.

Dad pulled a curtain off the pole and ripped a broad strip out of it and, using it as a bandage; he tightly tied it over Adam's shoulder. 'Hopefully, that will stop any bleeding,' he said.

'Thanks, Doc,' Adam said. 'That should do for the time being.'

Adam sat down on the floor close to Bill. He was keeping his right arm very still and close to his body. He pulled the loosely attached moustache off Bill's face. Adam found Bill's ID badge in his pocket and compared him with a picture which he brought out of his jacket and said. 'Bingo, we have hit the jackpot. He's from Omar's group, and we have been frantically looking for him for the past two weeks. He must have stolen this ID badge. We need to investigate that as well.' He turned around to me and said, 'That was a good, clean stroke, young man. Good presence of mind. Today, you have helped us to catch a major player in this group, well done.'

Adam took a small mobile-phone-like gadget out of his pocket and spoke into it 'Suspect captured, we need to make a video of the scene, ambulances already on the way.'

'Where are the commandos?' Dad asked peering through the window.

'I don't think any came,' I said.

'Yes,' Adam said laughing. 'I was playing a bluff with him and he easily fell into the trap. Who would bring commandos to catch an imposter?'

'And within seven minutes,' I added.

'That's true.' Adam laughed, despite being in some pain.

'Impressive,' Dad said.

'I have to make arrangements for his car to be towed away. I asked my colleague to cut its electrics before coming inside, in case he tried to make an escape. Also, forensics will have to do some tests on the car,' Adam said.

A white van arrived and Adam said. 'This is my camera crew. I hope you won't mind if they make a video of the entrance to your house, the study and the area where he is lying.'

'No, we don't mind if it helps the police,' Dad said.

As the filming was being completed, ambulance sirens were blaring outside. Two paramedics brought in a stretcher and took the fake detective to the hospital.

Within minutes, another ambulance appeared. The paramedic cut open Adam's shirt to look at the wound. 'There is no active bleeding going on now but you still need an X-ray to make sure there aren't any bits of the bullet inside and you will require some sewing up afterwards, Sir,' the paramedic said.

'It's a professional hazard, I suppose,' Adam said.

'That's absolutely right,' the paramedic said. 'We'll wait outside for you, whenever you are ready, we'll take you to hospital.'

'Thanks, just give me a couple of minutes,' Adam said.

The deepening of furrows on Dad's forehead told me that he was wrestling with some thoughts in his mind. 'Adam, I think it is time for us to meet the Chief Superintendent. We are not safe in our own home now. My wife and my mother upstairs are totally unaware how closely we have dodged death today. It is difficult to live life with constant fear, and we need to talk about some better solutions.'

'You're absolutely right,' Adam said. 'As I said earlier, he was the last one we were chasing from the gang. I'm not allowed to disclose any further details, which the Chief might discuss with you. I'm confident, from now onwards, you and your family are pretty safe. But I take your point and I can arrange a meeting with the Chief. When would you like it to happen?'

'As soon as possible,' Dad said.

'Why do you think he was the only one left in the gang to be caught?' I asked Adam.

'We draw up a list of people, as we go through the interviews with the detainees. We call them "common factors" as they are known to everyone in the group. We feel we have landed every single common factor in this group now,' Adam said.

'Could you please arrange a meeting with the Chief and in the meantime I have to do a lot of explaining about the events of this afternoon to two very special women in my life,' Dad said with a grin on his face.

'Lucky you,' Adam said, looking surprised.

'Yes, one is my mother, who is a hundred times more sceptical of things than Ali.'

'Oh dear, God help you.'

'Yes, I could certainly do with some divine help at this stage in my life,' Dad said.

'As soon as I'm done with the hospital, I'll report back to the Chief and will be in touch with you,' Adam said, looking at me. 'Ali, you should feel very proud of yourself. You saved the day.' Adam waved at us with his blood-stained left hand as he walked down the driveway.

I hugged Dad tightly and he reciprocated as if he wanted to leave his body's impression on me.

'We have to clean this blood off the floor before your Mum and Bari Ammi come down,' Dad said as he rushed to the kitchen to fetch wet towels to clean the area. We scrubbed the wooden floor hard, which did become clean but left a dark, wet patch. Dad pulled a rug over it and said. 'It will do for the time-being.'

'What about the bullet mark and the curtain you pulled down,' I said, looking at the wall.

'We can't do anything about it. Let's hope they won't notice it immediately,' Dad said.

'Come down, both my darlings, I desperately need a good, hot cup of tea now,' Dad shouted up the staircase.

I heard Bari Ammi coming down the stairs, holding the bannister carefully. 'Nobody, tells me anymore what is happening in this house. Nobody cares for me anymore.'

'No, no, we all care for you.' Dad held her hand as she stepped off the last step. 'Should we have a chat over a cup of tea?'

'That's like my boy.' She kissed Dad on his forehead. 'I haven't had a cup of tea since this morning and why did you upset my *Bahu*. She was in tears upstairs. Now you go and fetch her and make a pot of tea for us all.' Bari Ammi looked around and said, 'I can smell a fire-cracker, is it *Diwali* today?'

'I'll go and get Rose. Ali will tell you about this smell,' Dad said looking at me and quickly climbing upstairs.

'It's cigarette smoke. The person who came to see us was smoking.' I said.

'Do you really think I am that stupid?' Bari Ammi said so forcefully that I took a step back, 'I know the difference between cigarette smoke and a cracker. I am going deaf but that does not mean that I cannot smell.'

Bari Ammi made herself comfortable in the chair and fixed her gaze on me.

'I have not seen your face since yesterday evening. What have I done to deserve it? I know how to set boys like you right. I am going to find a very pretty girl to marry you soon.'

'Well if you marry me to a beautiful girl,' I was in a mood to tease Bari Ammi, 'you may have to wait longer to see me as I'll be with her all the time.'

'I know you would be even worse than your dad, but I still want you to get married and unlike your dad, have lots of children, running and playing around me. That is my dream, to play with your children.'

I could hear Dad talking to Mum upstairs. I thought it would be best to keep Bari Ammi busy in her dreams

'But Bari Ammi, I am still a child. I want to complete my education. I want to travel around the world. I want to enjoy my life which won't be possible if I get married and have children.'

I think I blew Bari Ammi's fuse by saying this as her face grew red hot and her hands were shaking with anger. 'I can't understand young people like you. Why can't you enjoy life being married? Why can't you study and travel whilst being married? The ideal age to get married is eighteen so you are already late.'

'Late?' I said with obvious surprise. 'I'm going to have some juice and I think you need some as well.' I started walking towards the kitchen.

'Yes, I do but do not try to change the topic, I want your decision today.'

Decision? Today? I thought I'd sit for a while in the kitchen until she forgets and I poured myself a large glass of orange juice.

Both Mum and Dad entered the kitchen and were surprised to see me sitting on my own and sipping orange juice.

'Who are you hiding from? They are gone, no need to worry, man,' Dad said by putting his arm round my neck.

'I was hiding from Bari Ammi. She wants my decision...

today... now!'

'About what?' both of them asked in surprise.

'Getting married, as I am already rather late at the age of nineteen and have to have lots of children that she can play with.'

'I think both of us are with her in this matter,' Mum said with a big smile, putting her arm around Dad's waist.

'Dad, I asked you to fit wider windows in the kitchen but you didn't listen,' I said.

'But... what? Why are you asking now?' Dad looked surprised.

'It would have been a lot easier for me to slip out through the kitchen windows to avoid Bari Ammi rather than going out from the front door,' I said seriously.

They both laughed loudly. I was pleased that I was able to instil some routine family life into the home, sweet home again.

* * * * *

It seemed that Adam had briefed and delegated the case to one of his colleagues, Officer Hill, who told us that an x-ray at the hospital revealed a piece of a bullet in Adam's shoulder for which he had to undergo emergency surgery. Officer Hill fixed an appointment for us to see the Chief Superintendent at six o'clock, which was exactly three hours later. We were very impressed that he could understand our anxieties in the light of today's events and kindly volunteered to give us a lift to and from Scotland Yard. He also resurrected the police surveillance outside our house and also mentioned that "some other" possibilities might be discussed during the meeting. In all honesty, we could not have asked anything more of him.

Dad was thinking of taking Uncle Arif with us as our legal representative but unfortunately he was not available. Dad was torn between going and cancelling the meeting until Uncle Arif would be available. I thought and suggested to Dad that the purpose of the meeting was not to give or take any statements but to ensure our security and to learn the progress of the case, so we could go to the meeting without Uncle Arif. Once back we could write-up the minutes of the meeting whilst fresh in our minds to show Uncle Arif and for future reference. Dad liked the idea.

Our journey into the corridors of Scotland Yard could not have been easier. Officer Hill winked into security cameras and a quick swipe of his security card opened the doors. He had an energetic, upright posture and walked briskly with an air of authority. He appeared very easy-going and almost everyone seemed to know him. He had a tanned skin, suggesting he had recently been on holidays somewhere sunny. He asked us to wait outside the Chief Superintendent's office and pointed towards a hot drink-dispensing machine, which was making gurgling noises.

'Please help yourself; I'll just make sure that the Chief is free.'

'Tea for me, please,' Dad said. I made two teas.

'Yes, the boss is free to meet you,' Officer Hill said. 'Yes, you may take your drinks inside.'

The Chief Superintendent was sitting behind a large table with a green leather top on which dozens of files were open. There was a large picture of the Queen in a golden frame on the wall. He got up from his chair to greet us. 'You are Ali's dad?'

'Yes, I am.'

'Well, you must be very proud of him. He saved the day again. Adam told me that he very cleverly positioned himself to take the imposter. We are so pleased that this person has been caught. We searched for him everywhere, but could not find him. Thank you, Ali. In fact, I was at Downing Street at lunch-time and the PM is very impressed with your bravery.' I felt elated.

'Thanks,' Dad could only say. He seemed overwhelmed by emotion.

'I think we have now rounded up every active member of the group. They have all recorded their statements, which are identical in almost all cases and that will make our lives easier at the court. Hanif, the chef, unfortunately passed away as a result of E Coli 157 infection in ITU, but we did find petri dishes with his DNA on them at his home, confirming his involvement and contribution to the plot. We all feel that Hanif's laziness killed him, he wore no gloves to grow these bugs and we were able to detect his DNA from the dishes. We think that he accidentally self-infected himself,' Tom said as he looked at Officer Hill, who nodded his head.

'How can you be sure that every single member of the group has been rounded-up?' Dad asked seriously. 'Ali's security is my biggest concern after what has happened today. It's clear Omar's gang want to get hold of Ali. I don't know what plans they had on their minds but God forbid if they wanted to kill him today, they could've done it quite easily,' Dad said and his eyes bulged with tears.

'I can understand your concerns,' Tom said in a sympathetic tone. 'I think the safety issue of Ali, you and your family is important to us. I have discussed this issue with the PM and he has agreed to provide you with state funded 24/7 security at your present accommodation or if you wish we could relocate your accommodation in London or to any other city if you wish. I know you work in a hospital and Ali is about to go to Imperial Medical School. We can make arrangements for moving your job or his medical school place elsewhere. I know to move is not an easy solution but you can go home, discuss it with your family and friends and let us know what you want us to do and we will act accordingly.'

'Yeah, to move places is not an easy option,' Dad said, thinking.

'You don't have to make a decision now. We have already deployed some guards to keep a watch on your home. Ali, don't worry. They won't shadow you as closely as happened last time. My apologies, it must have been very inconvenient for you.'

'What happened?' Dad was surprised to hear of this.

'Nothing, Dad. I'll explain to you when we get home,' I said and felt a bit embarrassed.

'What does this Crown witness mean? Will Ali have to come to court every time a hearing takes place?' Dad asked Tom.

'A crown witness means that he would act as a witness in the case and as a result of this will be given immunity from imprisonment. We'll make sure that there is minimum disruption to his studies and he is only called in when absolutely necessary. This shouldn't put any blot on his future career. Today, the PM has told me that Ali might receive his nomination for a bravery medal from the Queen. But this is off the record. Please don't quote me on this.'

'Thanks for clarifying it. I was slightly concerned with this case going on about his future career as a doctor.'

'If you wish, our lawyers could contact the General Medical Council regarding this query of yours,' Tom said and looked at Officer Hill.

'I think this sounds like a good idea. If you agree we can make this clear from the GMC on your behalf.' Officer Hill said.

'That would be absolutely perfect, if you could find this out for us,' said Dad, who appeared a bit more satisfied with the discussion.

'Doc, let us know what you think of the security arrangements we have discussed this afternoon. There is no rush to reach a decision and I can assure you, your family's security has been our top priority. If there are no more questions, we could conclude this

meeting. Thank you for coming at such short notice to meet me.'
He looked at me and said, 'You deserve a special pat on the back
for your bravery and the courage you have shown today. Well done.'

Dad's face looked red with emotion. As promised Officer Hill
drove us back home. I already knew the outcome of the discussion
about moving house before it had even started between Dad, Mum
and Bari Ammi and therefore decided not to participate in it and
quietly went upstairs to my room. I had a strong craving to meet
Sophie but this was not the time to ask Mum for her phone number.

CHAPTER 25

The day was sunny and sparkling like a cotton field in full blossom. The shadows under the trees appeared darker. Our car made an unusual noise when I braked. I parked it in our drive under the leafy shade of a Chinese red birch tree. I opened the bonnet like an experienced mechanic and peered at the engine to see if there was an obvious problem. The cooling engine was making crackling sounds. There wasn't anything clearly wrong and I slammed the bonnet shut in despair as I hated taking the car to a garage. I was looking at the car as if my magical vision would solve the problem and I felt someone putting his hand on my shoulder. My stomach lurched and I turned to see who it was. I saw a familiar face hidden behind a profuse, milky white beard which was reaching to his chest. His moustache was shaven and he was wearing dark sunglasses to obscure his eyes. The creases on his face deepened as a faint smile appeared on his face.

Oh, my God, that is George, I said to myself. 'George,' I said in excitement 'Uncle George, is that you?'

'Yes, it's me.' He opened his arms and embraced me. George was wearing an off-white *Jellaba* with a brown woollen jacket on top, which appeared rather large on him. His head was clean shaven and he was wearing a white, round *toppi* with delicate golden embroidery. He had brown summer sandals with socks on his big feet.

'Oh, Uncle George, where did you disappear to? We all missed you, every day. Dad will be delighted to see you.' I stopped for a moment and said, 'I just remembered, he is on call today. He may not come until late, I know Mum has gone out shopping but please do come in and I'll make a cup of tea for you.'

'That would be good. I didn't disappear anywhere. You see, I'm here now,' he said calmly. He was exuding the *attar* of mild jasmine. 'How is everyone, you, your dad, your Bari Ammi?'

'They're all good,' I said. 'I really missed you when Dad was away. I wanted to talk to someone like you.' I opened the front door.

'But you had Mr Nazir to talk to. Did you not speak to him?' he asked me.

I was amazed how he knew that and wanted to explore this with him. 'How did you come to know that I spoke with Mr Nazir?'

'It hardly matters now,' he answered briefly and I could see a glimpse of Mr Nazir in his manners, the way he spoke, his careful, economic choice of words.

'I'll make tea,' I said. 'Would you like to wait in the living room?'

'I think I'll come with you to the kitchen. I don't have much time on my hands. I have to go soon.' He followed me to the kitchen.

I turned the electric kettle on and looked carefully at him. 'You look a bit different. What made you do this?'

'A quest for the truth. I don't know whether you remember or not but once I said to you that those who seek truth rather than follow the tradition of their forefathers should change their religion at least once in their lives.'

'Yes, I do remember you saying it, so you have done that?'

'Yes, but I feel I haven't done anything extraordinary. It's not too difficult to give up your views, to give up your faith. My family had the tradition of giving up their lives for the sake of other people, and that is true bravery, real valour.'

'I suppose what you've done is very brave, now, when people wearing *Jellabas* and long beards are looked down upon by the society,' I said and placed the tea mug before him.

'It does not bother me much now what people think of my outward appearance, it's the inner thing which matters most to me.' He slurped tea and said, 'well, what I have done is taken a place as the front goose in a flock in a V formation flying in the skies. When I'm not there someone else has to step in. It's a continuing selection process. One is selected to do the job. Who knows next time it could be you.'

'I can assure you it won't be me,' my heart fluttered as I said it. 'I don't think I could even reach your dust. Anyway, what job is this?' I asked George. I remembered asking Mr Nazir the same question but he did not answer.

'Don't be so sure Ali, when you're chosen, you're chosen. There is no escape. As far as your question about the job, I'm afraid I'm not obliged to answer all your questions. Certain things in life one has to wait patiently for before they reveal themselves in front of you, like a closed bud, enveloped with green, blossoming into a colourful flower.' I was amazed at the striking similarity of his reply to Mr Nazir's.

'Should I ring Dad and tell him about you?'

'I'll give him a ring myself. Can I ask a favour of you?'

'George, don't ask me. You can just order me. Please don't do this to me,' I said.

'Could you take me to the grave of Mr Nazir? I couldn't come to his funeral but I would like to go there and pay my homage to him.'

'Yes, certainly I'll do that for you. This'll also give me an opportunity to visit his grave which I've been planning to do for the past so many days.'

My mobile rang and a number appeared which had not been among my contacts.

'Hello,' I said.

'Hello, Ali, is it OK to talk?' A wave of pleasure went through my whole body to hear Sophie after more than two weeks.

'Yes, it is absolutely Ok to talk…. No, no you don't have to be sorry. Don't be silly, it happens sometimes, it can happen…No, I'm not… I can't possibly be annoyed with you…Yes that would be good. I'm free tomorrow as well…..Yes, our house number is 27….. SW1 7BL…..See you tomorrow at three…Bye.'

Uncle George looked at me with an affectionate glance and said with a smile on his face. 'Wow, looks like our Ali is in love. That's absolutely brilliant. Come on give us a hug.'

I blushed and felt embarrassed as if I had been caught stealing red handed and said, 'Maybe, maybe not. How can you say it with such confidence?'

George laughed loudly, from the back of his throat like he used to do in the company of Dad.

'When you are in love, your eyes become tongues and tell the whole story.' He took another swig and said. 'Those who fall in love are blessed. In the journey of this world, the one and only thing which is divine is love.' He spoke exactly like Mr Nazir.

'George,' I said. 'I don't believe in reincarnation but it looks like you have become very similar in your thoughts to Mr Nazir.'

'No, no, it's not that. I wish I was. Just think of me like a convertible car, I can change according to the needs of the season,' he said and stopped. I think he wanted to add something but he kept it to himself.

I was greatly amazed at his quick metamorphosis. There were no long bullet pointed discussions, just nuggets of wisdom, to the point. What makes people change so quickly? What 'job' was he talking about? Had he replaced Mr Nazir in that group of four thousand friends?

Before stepping into the car George said to me, 'Could we stop at a florist to buy some flowers?' and after that he remained silent, immersed in his thoughts throughout the whole journey to the cemetery.

Mr Nazir's grave looked prominent from a distance despite no headstone. The mound of soil was covered with freshly plucked red rose petals from the top to the bottom. A gentle breeze was blowing the petals to neighbouring graves.

I could not resist asking George, 'Who could have laid flowers on his grave? He never told me that he had friends living in London.'

George growled, looked at me and said curtly, 'Does it matter?'

He placed the bouquet at the head of Mr Nazir's grave and stood very respectfully near the foot. His breathing was getting laboured. He raised his hands to say *dua* exactly like Mr Nazir. There was a fine tremor in his hands. His eyes closed and he started mumbling something that I could not understand but I think he was offering his *duas* in Arabic. His eyes welled up with tears, which formed several streams before tracking into his beard. I think he continued his prayers for a good part of an hour and I continued to look curiously at his face, which changed colour from bright red to pale yellow. George spread his palms over his face then he brought a handkerchief out of his pocket to wipe his face clean.

'Thank you, Ali, for this huge favour to me.' His voice was still deep and it cracked with distress. 'God bless you. Give my regards to your family. *Inshallah* we shall meet some other time but I have got to go now.' He started walking towards the main gate.

'Uncle George,' I said loudly to stop him. 'Please let me know and I'll drop you at whichever stop you want me to.'

He turned round, the usual smile on his face. 'Thanks for the offer but my transport is already arranged. No worries.' He said and continued to walk.

I stood and watched him until he disappeared out of the cemetery.

Mr Nazir's voice echoed in my head. 'The gravitational pull remains functional because of these people: the soft caress of a summer breeze, the serenity of moonlight; the changing seasons; vegetation springing from barren soil.'

CHAPTER 26

I looked at my watch yet again, still there was half an hour before Sophie would come. I was sitting in the conservatory, uninterestedly browsing through the newspaper. Mum had just left for her yoga class and Dad had gone to the hospital before I had even got up. Bari Ammi had come down from her room and was habitually knitting something. As usual, she appeared well kept, wearing a light pistachio colour, creaseless *Shalwar Kameez* and brown shawl spread over her shoulders.

'Turn off the thing,' she said by pointing at the ceiling fan with her knitting needle, looking over the top of her half-moon glasses and watching me closely and saying, 'Time does not go fast if you look at your watch repeatedly.' She paused, closed her eyes, scratched her head with the knitting needle and said again. 'With whom are you going out?'

'With a friend,' I said with a stammer. I wasn't expecting that she would be able to assess from my demeanour that I was waiting for someone or was about to go out.

'Do I know this friend,' she said as she looked at me without taking her glance off my face.

'No, no, I don't think so,' I was slightly surprised and intrigued at her sudden level of interest in my friends.

'I would like to meet your friend.' There was a notion of instruction in her tone.

'Ok, ok,' I said and thought it is best to change the topic. 'Bari Ammi, how is your dream world? Did you dream last night?'

'Yes, I did.'

'Was it good?'

'Very good.'

'Would you like to tell me about your dream?' I said with a smile on my face and feeling happy inside that I had been successful in my tactics.

'I saw a wedding taking place, lots of activities, flowers, loads of colourful dresses, sweet smelling, bright red, crimson roses, girls singing and dancing, everyone was happy, very happy. The bride was very pretty, just like a partially open bud of a scented rose.'

'Great, I'm glad you seemed to have enjoyed your dream but are you sure it was a dream not some Bollywood film song which you had seen on TV?' I said while looking at my mobile.

She ignored my question and asked taking her glasses off her face, 'Would you not like to know who was getting married?'

'I would certainly like to know, so who was getting married in Bollywood style?' I said, still reading recent texts on the mobile.

'It was your wedding, Ali, yours,' she said and I could see her eyes bulging with emotion.

Oh no, not again. I just remained silent. I didn't wish to get her started on this topic. She was clearly getting obsessed. I wish she didn't have her dream back. That is very mean of you, Ali, I said to myself.

Sophie's name appeared on my mobile and her text read: 'I'm outside.'

'Ok, Bari Ammi, I'll be going now,' I said getting up off the sofa. 'I'm sure some day your dream will come true.'

'Has your friend arrived?'

'Yes.' I really didn't think that Sophie would want to come in at her very first visit to our house.

'Bring your friend in,' Bari Ammi said commandingly.

'Is it really necessary?' I asked her.

'Yes,' she appeared absolutely resolute.

'Ok,' I said nervously, 'I'll ask her, if she agrees, I'll bring her in.'

Sophie was waiting in her shiny, silver convertible Mercedes Benz sports car. When I saw her, the stress of the past two weeks seemed to melt away. I waved at her and went around and opened the passenger door and sat inside this two-seater which had the smell of a new car.

'I never knew that you're into topless cars.'

'No, I'm not,' she said, looking at me. 'Is everything OK?'

'Yeah, yeah, everything is fine.' I paused. 'The thing is that the only person at home is my grandmother and she wants to meet you.' I looked at her face. 'She is a very nice person and you can say no and I'll go and tell her. I don't like to tell lies to her, I'm sure she won't mind if you say no.'

'Let me get this right in my head,' Sophie said as she switched the car engine off. 'You have told your grandmother that I'm coming to meet you today and she wants to see me, is that right?'

'No, that's not right,' I said. 'I only told her that my friend is coming to see me. She doesn't even know whether the friend who is coming to see me is a boy or a girl. You can say no Sophie, and there is no compulsion.' I was expecting that she would say "no".

'Ok, no problem. Let's see her for a couple of minutes. I'm in no rush, are you, Ali?' she said and pressed a button on the side of the dash-board and the canvas began to stretch over the car as a roof, making a purring noise.

'Are you sure?' I asked her.

'Yes, why not?' she said as she opened the door to get out.

With a clunk, the central locking system remotely locked the car.

'Nice machine, Sophie.'

'You know, I just picked it up from the garage and I have come straight to you.'

'Wicked! Is this your birthday present or something?'

'No, not really. Dad said that I've been through a lot due to Mum's recent illness and bought me this, perhaps, to cheer me up a bit.'

'That's wonderful, how nice of him,' I said and opened the front door, I was praying and hoping in my heart that Bari Ammi did not start the topic of my wedding in front of Sophie. That would be hugely embarrassing.

I directed Sophie to the conservatory.

'Bari Ammi, meet Sophie,' I said shyly.

Bari Ammi took her glasses off her face, adjusted her hearing aid and said with a warm smile on her face, 'Welcome Sophie. The crows have been cawing all morning in the back garden. I knew some nice guest will visit us today.'

'Thanks,' Sophie said extending her hand to shake hands with her. Bari Ammi shook hands with her and gestured her to sit beside her. She was continuously looking at her face.

'You are pretty like a little gold ringlet.' She paused and said, 'If I remember correctly, you took Ali to hospital.'

'Yes, I did,' Sophie was blushing.

'I think you are the prettiest of all the list of girls his Mum is carrying in her bag. I hope you infuse some wisdom into this reckless person,' she said pointing at me.

'I don't think that needs doing,' Sophie's face was glowing red. 'He is already quite wise.'

'Wise?' Bari Ammi said stroking her palm on her forehead. 'Only two years ago, he loved hearing fairy tales, placing his head in my lap.'

I think by this time, I had had enough of Bari Ammi. She had told Sophie about Mum carrying a list of girls and now about the fairy tales. I had to cut this meeting short to prevent any further damage. I said, 'Ok, Bari Ammi, you wanted to meet her, and now you have met her. Can we leave now?'

'Have you completely gone mad?' Bari Ammi said. 'She has come for the very first time to our house, are you not going to offer her any tea or fruit juice?' She looked at Sophie and said, 'You call him wise?'

'Sorry, Bari Ammi,' I said. 'Sophie, please tell me, what can I get you?'

'No, no I'm just fine.'

'Ok,' Bari Ammi said, 'how much does it cost these days to have a nice cup of tea in a very nice restaurant?' she asked Sophie.

'Ten quid perhaps,' I replied instead of Sophie.

'I didn't ask you this question,' Bari Ammi said to me harshly. 'Sophie, you tell me.' I could already see the focus of her attention switching from me to Sophie.

'The same, ten twelve pounds,' Sophie said coyly.

Bari Ammi opened her handbag and got out some twenty pound notes. She licked her fingers and thumbs and counted up to five.

'Could you count these for me, please?' she asked Sophie.

'A hundred pounds,' Sophie said.

Bari Ammi said to Sophie, 'Go and have some tea with him. He still needs a lot of training.'

'I'm not a dog, Bari Ammi' I said. 'And you never gave me any money to spend.'

'That's lots of money for tea,' Sophie said. 'I'll just take twenty pounds of it.'

'No, you won't. I don't go out anymore and I'll be pleased if you spend them for me.'

Bari Ammi asked Sophie to help her to get up, held her face in both her hands and I closed my eyes as I knew that she was going to plant a moist kiss on her forehead, which she did.

'Thank you,' Sophie said to Bari Ammi. 'See you soon.'

'Yes, do come and see me from time to time'

'I will.'

'Will she get money every time she comes?' I asked Bari Ammi

'Yes, she will, but you are not going to get any. I told you, he needs a lot of training,' Bari Ammi said to Sophie and we all chuckled.

****

As usual it was not easy to find a parking space at Piccadilly. We were circling around one car park after another. I told Sophie, all the woman-driver parking jokes I had heard to pass the time and also to keep her smiling. I must admit that despite the frustration of driving through so many full car parks, she remained composed and proved herself to be a very skilled driver.

'Do you drive a taxi in your spare time?'

'Why? Do you have any objection?' she said understanding my joke.

'No, I just wanted to have the number of your car company, to ask for you all the time.'

'You already have.'

'Oh, yes, I nearly forgot.' Both of us laughed and Sophie spotted a space into which she skilfully reversed the car.

In spite of me dropping several hints to Sophie to go to any coffee place for tea, she looked absolutely determined to go to a posh place. She had performed an internet search for a Tea Guild award winner for 2012 and excitedly said, 'I want to have a high afternoon tea here.'

The place was at Piccadilly, overlooking Green Park and herds of tourists could be seen walking towards Buckingham Palace. I said to Sophie, 'I don't want to see you disappointed but such places are often booked weeks and months in advance.'

'I like to take my chances.' Her enthusiasm remained

undiminished.

The doorman opened the main door for us and we proceeded to the restaurant for afternoon tea.

'What time is your booking for, Sir?' said the maitre'd who was wearing a black suit and white shirt with a bow tie.

Before I could say anything Sophie said, 'Two o'clock, I'm sorry we're a bit late. We had difficulty in finding a car parking space.'

'Not a problem, Ma'am.'

'What name is your booking under?'

'Sophie Barlow.'

'Yes, we have a booking for you,' he said by looking at his list.' Would you like to follow me please?'

He led us to a secluded table in the garden. The table was covered with a spotless white table-cloth and exquisite freshly cut flowers were placed in a flower pot.

'That was a nice surprise. When did you book this table?' I asked Sophie.

'Weeks ago.' She laughed a hollow laughter. She appeared very tense. 'I liked your gran, she is a lovely person.'

'Yeah, I'm glad you liked her. She is a bit hard of hearing and uses hearing aids. She uses this disability to her advantage most of the time. She hears what she likes to hear.'

'Don't we all do this?'

'Maybe.'

Tears welled up in her eyes and she said, 'I thought this would be the beginning chapter of our friendship but it seems it's the final one. I think it is in the best interests of both of us to stop at this stage.'

'Don't say it like that.'

'Your mum is carrying a list of names of girls in her handbag for you to pick one, is that right?' she said.

'She can carry whatever she wishes to carry in her handbag but I have already made my choice and I don't think she could deter me from that,' I said assertively.

'Really, who is that, if I may ask?'

'Don't ask me this question. Just ask your heart. I like you. I like your company, you make me feel proud, you make me stand tall, and I would like to spend the rest of my life with you. Would you let me do that? Please, Sophie, tell me, and please tell me now.'

'So you're going to go against the wishes of your parents; it's never a good idea to start a new relation by breaking old ones.'

'I'm not breaking any relations, this is my life and I have every right to take this decision.'

'Yes, you have every right but have you given it any thoughts as to how your family and friends will react when they come to know that you are going out with me? How many people will you fight with? How many tongues will you stop? You are such a nice person; just don't make your life a misery.'

'Sorry, Sophie you're assuming a lot. We are in 2013 and nobody gives a damn anymore who anyone goes out with, obviously within reason though. I can assure you, my family and friends are broad-minded enough to accept you as a person, what you are, not because of the colour of your skin. Please don't think like that. Now you've asked this question, tell me, would your family accept me, an Asian, Pakistani as your future life partner?'

'I don't think there should be any problem,' she looked at me to assess my thoughts from my facial expressions.

I got up from the chair and hugged her tightly and kissed her on the forehead. 'With true love we'll overcome all the problems. Just have faith in your love.'

Her lower lip was quivering, 'I have faith but at the same time I'm afraid that I may not be as strong as you.' She was still in my arms.

I laughed, 'I wasn't strong before I had met you.' I stopped for a moment and said, 'You are the source of my strength. Don't underestimate your powers. Your magnetism is more powerful than anyone else's.'

Sophie kissed me repeatedly on my lips: her lips were smeared with the saltish taste of tears.

'I'm afraid. You'll find some other girl in your medical school…..' she pushed me back and said sitting on the chair.

'I promise, I won't even look at any girl in the school but you also have to promise me that you won't ditch me for some handsome solicitor.'

'No, I can't promise that,' she laughed and her prominence of laugh lines added elegance to her beauty.

'I think it would be best if we take a step back,' Sophie said, 'You have to go to your med school for five years and I've to go to this law school for four to six years, depending on how hard Mum pushes me. We should remain as good friends, close friends. We're in the same city, we can see each other. There is no need to rush things. What do you think?'

'Ok….I'll agree for your sake. Honestly, I'll miss you when we don't meet for weeks. We should meet more regularly. I myself don't want to rush into a relationship and I'm sure neither of my parents would like me to do so. Please don't take any notice of what Bari Ammi said this morning. Bless her; she is still living in the forties when people used to get married at the age of eighteen.'

'She is cute.'

I was about to say where is this tea coming from when I saw a waiter pushing a tea trolley towards us. The bone china cups had golden edges and the teapot was covered by a woollen, knitted tea cosy. The scones appeared to come out of the oven. I can't decide whether it was the effect of the company or the tea itself. I never had such a cup of tea in my life ever before. I tried my best to pay the bill but Sophie had already made the payment at the booking over the internet.

'As a matter of interest, when did you book this place?' I asked by looking into her eyes.

'The next day, after we went to the restaurant,' she said shyly.

'Let me get this clear in my head,' I said thinking. 'You wanted to meet me at this posh place to clear your conscience of the embarrassment of chucking a dessert over me, not for any other reason?'

'No, no, Ali, don't get me wrong. I thought about you and asked my heart, over and over again. What happened to Mum was an accident. I'm sorry I got carried away with emotions. I like you Ali, really I love you. I just want to be with you, please don't get me wrong.' Her big eyes welled up with tears spilling over her cheeks.

'Could you say it a couple of times more that you love me? I really like to hear that from your mouth.' I said and hugged her tightly. 'Did your parents tell you that I went to see them last week?'

She pulled herself out of my arms and said with obvious shock, 'You didn't, you did not meet Mum and Dad? Tell me you're joking.'

'No I'm not joking. I did meet your parents at your Mum's

surgery. I also met your Mum's secretary Linda.'

'I'll ask Linda. I met her yesterday, she didn't tell me anything.' Sophie was blushing.

I looked at my mobile as a reminder ring went off. 'Sophie, could you take me to Bromwell Hospital, please. I have an appointment there to pick up a watch. Dad's friend Mr Nazir, I don't think I told you about him, was admitted there. I sort of gave him company during his illness and he left his watch as a gift for me after his death.'

'Oh, I'm so sorry to hear this. Was he very ill?' Sophie said.

'Yes, he was. He was an extraordinary person. I'll tell you about him some other time. Should we make a move?'

'OK, boss, your personal chauffeur is at your service,' she bowed and said. 'I don't think this hospital is very far from here. What time is your appointment?'

'In fifteen minutes, but it doesn't matter if we are a few minutes late.'

Sophie shook her head in disbelief when she heard that I wasn't bothered about being late for an appointment.

We reached the hospital just in time. We climbed up the stairs to reach the ward office where Mr Nazir had stayed. Nurse Margaret greeted us with a smile. She was holding a register in her hand. She passed on the watch to me and asked me to sign in the register. It was quite a peculiar watch: it would tell time for all the six continents of the world.

'How many bouquets were received in the end?' I asked Margaret.

'I knew you were going to ask me,' she said browsing through various pages in the register. 'Let me first tell you how much money they generated. It was eight thousand five hundred and seventy eight pounds and the total numbers of bouquets were three-thousand nine hundred and ninety nine.'

'One short of four thousand,' Sophie said and her eyes widened in amazement. 'Was he a celebrity or something?'

'He was more than a celebrity,' Margaret said and I couldn't say anything as I found myself catapulted into grief again. I knew I wouldn't be able to stifle my tears for very long and said thank you to Margaret in sniffles.

Both Sophie and I were sitting quietly in her car which was crawling along slowly in London's evening traffic. I was holding Mr Nazir's watch in my hand. Sophie had seen tears rolling down my cheeks but she remained silent. Mr Nazir's voiced echoed in my mind, "The gravitational pull remains functional because of these people: the soft caress of a summer breeze, the serenity of moonlight; the changing seasons; vegetation springing from barren soil. Life exists on this planet only because of the presence of these four thousand people. Some living people are a burden on this earth and some people carry the weight of this world, not only during their lives but even after their death." I closed my eyes and could see a flock of birds flying in a V shaped pattern in the background of the azure sky.

Acknowledgments

I would like to thank all the members of the Cannon Hill Writers' group. The group meets every Thursday evening at the Hall Green Library in Birmingham and I have read almost every chapter of 'Four Thousand friends' on a regular basis whilst attending. I'm especially thankful to Pauline Morgan, Chris Morgan and Lynn Edwards for providing their useful comments and suggestions.

I'm greatly indebted to my friend, Peter Morris, who meticulously scrutinised every single sentence of 'Four Thousand friends' and offered valuable editorial support and guidance in bringing out this novel. Thank you very much Peter! Sumbal, my niece also helped in the final proof-reading.

'Novel writing' could be a lonely business. I have been extremely lucky to have the company and support of my work colleague, Alexander Pirie. He was always available to lend his ears to meet, to give advice and to support me during the 'trough periods' of the novel writing.

Finally, I'm thankful to my wife and children for their steadfast enthusiasm and faith. Ayesha, my wife, never doubted over the protracted years that I would finish the novel. Her love, support and understanding, like always has made the difference.